MW01241922

Finding Hope

Dear family,

I quit. Effective immediately, I am no longer the cook, laundress, shopper, housekeeper, chauffeur, landscaper or resident problem-solver. Oh, I'm also not the banker or the ATM. I am, however, the instructor. Classes will begin tomorrow and seating is limited, so you should sign up early.

A cooking class will be conducted at five-thirty sharp. Bring your inquiring mind and appetite. A cook book will be available. On Saturday, I will offer two sessions—general housekeeping and laundry. Supplies will be provided. However, if you are attending the laundry session, please separate clothing into lights and darks and bring those with you. This class begins at nine a.m. in the basement.

Housekeeping will commence at ten, once you have mastered washing machine settings and drying times. Rubber gloves are recommended for those who have delicate skin or have had expensive manicures recently.

Other workshops, such as money-management, will be scheduled as needed and announcements will be posted. Don't be late and get left out in the cold.

Janet R. DeMarco,

Wife, Mother, Person
(not necessarily in that order)

What They Are Saying About
Finding Hope

Finding Hope is told with light-hearted humor that will bring countless chuckles. The sparkling dialogue will keep you entertained page after page, and you will find yourself *hoping,* as does her ever-loving husband, that Janet never loses touch with Hope. An excellent read by the fireside and one that will send readers in search of more of Linda Rettstatt's novels.

—Carol McPhee
http://www.geocities.com/carolmcphee2003/

A book is usually read for review only once, but *Finding Hope* drew, no, compelled me to read it again. How Ms. Rettstatt compressed the total secret of life in a single book is nothing short of miraculous. A young woman who is not truly unhappy searches for her inner fulfillment. The process she chooses is elemental, but highly effective. The author cuts through psycho-babble crap and gets to the core of life. She learns fulfillment comes with the giving of oneself. Ms. Rettstatt has written an insightful book with humor, pathos and inspiration. I highly recommend *Finding Hope.* The reader will find, as I did, a fragment of their own life can be improved with this delightful book.

—A. Dee Carey-The Fox Lady
Foxpaw Reviews
http://careyfoxlady.googlepages.com/

Finding Hope is a moving, touching account of a woman's journey. Her brave search to uncover what is missing in her life will warm your hearts. I found myself racing to finish the story to find out what happened and to see how Janet ends up. I began rooting for all women who have the courage to reach out like Janet, to stand up and demand that they be treated with the utmost respect and be allowed to explore and become all that they desire. I highly recommend this book. Grab a nice cup of tea, curl up on a comfy chair, and dream along with Janet as you witness her journey, her search for hope. You, too, will be *Finding Hope* right along with her. I look forward to further novels by Ms. Rettstatt. Trust me, you don't want to miss out in reading her inspiring books. They will make a difference in your life.

—Suzanne M. Hurley
http://www.suzannemhurley.com/

Linda Rettstatt has tapped into a universal yearning many middle-aged women discover in themselves, and again delivers an emotionally strong story interlaced with humor and poignancy. *Finding Hope* is a story every woman who has ever wondered what she is missing from life should read.

—Kimberley Dehn
Southern Exposure
www.kimberley-dehn.com

Wings

Finding Hope

by

Linda Rettstatt

A Wings ePress, Inc.

Women's Fiction Novel

Wings ePress, Inc.

Edited by: Anita York
Copy Edited by: Jeanne Smith
Senior Editor: Anita York
Executive Editor: Lorraine Stephens
Cover Artist: Pat Evans

All rights reserved

Wings ePress Books
http://www.wings-press.com

Copyright © 2008 by Linda Rettstatt
ISBN 978-1-59705-681-6

Published In the United States Of America

December 2008

Wings ePress Inc.
403 Wallace Court
Richmond, KY 40475

Dedication

This book is dedicated to women everywhere who have the courage to stand on tiptoe and peer over the edge of their lives, seeking that which will make them complete. You are hope.

Acknowledgements

I have been privileged to walk through my life, to this point, with so many incredible women. And every one of them contributed to this book in some way. Those life questions that pop up and make us examine life can either stop us in our tracks or propel us forward. I want to acknowledge women who face their own questions with amazing courage, some trepidation, but always with hope: my spiritual mothers, Sr. Mary Morgan, CSJ and Sr. Rosella Lacovitch, CSJ; Sue Ann, Rosie, Rita, and Carmela—my fearless first readers; the women of the Women's Fiction Writer's Exchange—Carol, Judi, Priscille, Deborah, Verna, Angela, Meg, Laurie, Jen, and Sherry who, though you didn't critique this book, give me the courage to keep writing. As always, I thank the staff of Wings ePress, Inc.: Lorraine Stephens, President and Executive Editor, Anita York, Editor, Jeanne R. Smith, Copy Editor, and Pat Evans for the cover art design.

One

I held up my left hand to the construction crew boss approaching my desk while I shouted into the phone. "Teddy? Can you hear me? Where are you?"

"I'm right here. Talk fast, I'm busy. Jan?"

"Don't pull that 'you're breaking up and I can't hear you' stuff, Teddy. You've had three calls from Mr. Dunbar about the permits for the work on his guest house. You have contracts waiting to be signed and two that have to be delivered. Where *are* you?"

"Yeah, Jan. Uh, can you deliver those two contracts and call Dunbar back? Tell him I'm in a meeting, and I'll call him first thing in the morning. Leave the other stuff with the mail on my desk. I'll pick it up on my way home."

"Look, I was hired as the bookkeeper, and I have the payroll to get ready. I'm not your secretary or your gofer."

In the background and before he could respond, I heard, "And they're off!"

"Oh, for... You're at the track? I'm going nuts here running your business, and you're at the track? For the love of..."

"Relax, Jan. You're starting to sound like my wife. I'll come in later and sign whatever needs signing. Just leave it all on my desk. I gotta go."

The dial tone hummed. I slammed down the receiver and narrowed my eyes on the crew boss leaning over the counter. "What do you need?"

"I'm goin' home. Been feelin' lousy all day. I think it's the flu."

"Great. Who's running the crew on the Phillips job?"

"I left Mack in charge." He turned and sneezed loudly, then looked back at me through glazed eyes. "I probably won't be in for a few days. I'll have my wife come by to get my check on Friday."

He grabbed tissues from the box on my desk and left the office. I glanced at the clock—two-thirty. I still hadn't had lunch, and I had a bank deposit to make. I found the signed contracts and looked at the addresses. One stop was on the way to the bank, the other across town. I got the deposit ready and set it aside with both contracts. I fielded two more complaint calls, tempted to forward them to Teddy's cell phone at the track.

I've worked for DeMarco Construction for the past ten years. Teodoro 'Teddy' DeMarco is my husband Anthony's cousin. With an associate degree in business, I agreed to work for Teddy three days a week as a bookkeeper. Somehow this grew into full-time and then some, as I became secretary, receptionist, file clerk, delivery person and barista. If I choose to use the bathroom, I'm also the cleaning lady. I'd like to say this day was unusual, but it's pretty much this way all the time.

I pulled up the contracts on my computer and filled in the blanks. The door opened and our delivery driver walked in. He stood over my desk, slack-jawed, his dull gray eyes fixed on my chest. If I weren't sadly flattered by this attention, I'd have been pissed.

"What can I do for you, Bobby?"

"I can't work tomorrow. Court date," he said matter-of-factly.

I remembered. He was arrested during a domestic dispute. A chill slithered down my back. "Did you tell Teddy so he can get a replacement?"

"I'm telling you so you can tell him." His nubby fingers toyed with the name plate on the counter that defined this space as belonging to me, Janet DeMarco. The monogrammed gold on dark wood had been a conciliatory gift from Teddy for one of the many things he'd done to piss me off. I made a mental note to disinfect it later. "I'll be back on Friday. Ain't no way they're gonna bust me. Just a slap on the fingers."

I fixed my gaze on the computer monitor. "Fine. I'll let Teddy know."

He continued to leer down at me.

I stood and pulled myself up to my full five foot six, staring him in the eye. "Is there something else I need to tell Teddy?"

"Nah. That's all." He winked at me before he turned and sauntered out of the office. My stomach twisted.

I looked back at the computer. *I've had it. I'm sick of working with men. I'm tired of being taken advantage of; tired of running Teddy's company while he plays at the track and meets his girlfriend for nooners. I'm through with chasing him down to get his signature and deliver paperwork.*

My mind disengaged as my hands took over. My fingers flew across the keyboard and I watched the words form on the monitor.

> *Dear Teddy,*
>
> *I resign. No, I quit. I've resigned myself to too much already. I quit keeping your business afloat while you play the horses and... well, you know where you are most of the time. I'm done. This job*

has become much more than I ever wanted. I'll do this week's payroll, and then you'll need to find someone else.

Yours truly,

Janet

P.S. I'm giving myself one month's severance.

The phone rang. Mack asked me to dispatch Bobby with a load of drywall. "I'll try to catch him, but I'm not making any promises."

I hung up, hit the print button on the computer, and then paged Bobby. After giving him the order, I grabbed the contracts and Teddy's mail, put them on his desk and shut down the computer. If I left right away, I could get to the bank and still drop off the signed contracts before five o'clock. *I'm turning forty in a few months. I don't need this crap.*

From the car, I called home and my daughter, Gabriella, answered. "Gabby, would you turn on the oven to three-fifty and when the light goes out, put the pan of lasagna inside? I'll be home by six."

"Sure, Mom. You remember that I need a ride to school for play practice at six-thirty, right?"

"Ask your brother if he can take you. And turn the oven to four hundred so you can eat before you leave."

"Michael isn't home. He said he wouldn't be here for dinner. So, you'll take me, right Mom?"

I heaved a loud sigh and slammed on the brakes to avoid the driver to my right who decided he wanted my lane too. "Uh, okay. Forget the lasagna. I'll pick up something on the way home. Bye, honey."

I delivered the contracts and deposited the receipts in the bank. I spied a Chinese restaurant and swung into the lot. With four meals in two bags, I raced through the back door and dropped my purse on a chair, pulled plates from the cupboard and yelled, "Dinner's ready."

Anthony wrinkled his nose when he entered the kitchen. "I thought we were having lasagna. What's that smell?"

"Change of menu. Tonight's Chinese; tomorrow's lasagna," I said, dumping rice into a bowl and unwrapping egg rolls.

Gabby bounded into the kitchen and filled her plate. "Mom, can we leave a few minutes early and pick Megan up on the way? I told her we'd give her a ride."

"I wish you wouldn't make promises like that without asking me first," I said more sharply than I intended.

Gabby frowned at me. "Gee, Mom. What's the big deal? It's practically on the way." She hurriedly wolfed down her dinner.

I pushed my plate away, intending to heat up something when I got back. I needed time to breathe.

As I stood, Anthony asked, "What's wrong?"

"I'll eat when I get back. I don't want to swallow dinner whole."

He narrowed his eyes at Gabby, pointing with his fork. "You shouldn't expect your mother to run you around everywhere when she's worked all day."

"It's okay, Anthony. It's play practice, and I promised I'd take her. I thought I'd be home earlier, but your cousin..." I stopped, not wanting to put my frustrations on my husband. It wasn't his fault. He never wanted me to go to work in the first place. "Gabby, I'm ready when you are."

"Just have to brush my teeth. I'll be right back," she said, running from the kitchen.

"You spoil the kids, Jan. You shouldn't be expected to haul them around everywhere. Where's Michael, anyway?" Anthony asked as he pushed rice onto his fork with an egg roll.

"He's out with friends." I bit my tongue to avoid asking why *he* didn't offer to take Gabby to her practice.

Gabby—her nickname was no accident—kept up a running monologue about her day at school and about the play while I drove the six blocks to pick up Megan and then back across town to the high school. Gabby's a good kid. She keeps up her grades and belongs to the drama club. This is a small sacrifice to support her efforts.

"What time will you be finished?" I asked as the girls jumped out of the car.

"Around nine. Should I call when we're done?"

"Yes, and don't go anywhere else. I'll pick you both up right here. If I don't hear from you by nine-fifteen, know that I'll come looking."

Gabby rolled her eyes. "Okay, okay. I'll call. Thanks, Mom."

I chose the long route home, taking advantage of the quiet. As I came through the back door, I heard Anthony laughing in the living room. I walked into the room in time to hear him say, "Oh, come on, Teddy. Of course it's a joke." He waved me over. "She just came in. Here, she'll tell you herself." He handed me the phone. "It's Teddy. He says you quit your job, and he read me the letter." He gasped for breath. "I gotta hand it to you, Jan. And you gave yourself severance pay? That was a great joke. Here, tell him yourself."

I held the phone limply, my mouth hanging open as I stared at my husband. Then I realized I must have printed out the letter and left it on Teddy's desk with the contracts.

I raised the receiver to my ear. "Teddy?"

He was laughing just as heartily as my husband. "Jan, you got me good, especially with the severance pay. For a minute there, I thought I'd have to learn to brew coffee and type."

"Excuse me?" Rage swelled within me. "Why do you think it's so funny?"

My husband's grin faded, and he picked up the newspaper, avoiding my eyes.

"Come on, Jan," Teddy said. "You can't be serious. Look, we'll talk about a raise tomorrow. How's that?"

I didn't respond at first. Heat crept up my neck and across my face. *How dare they laugh at the idea that I would quit. How dare Teddy offer me more money and think that'll fix everything.*

"We'll talk tomorrow, all right." I disconnected the call and plopped the phone back into the cradle.

Anthony lowered the newspaper. "You...you were kidding, right?"

"What if I'm not? What if I do quit?"

"Hey, I never wanted you to work in the first place. It's fine by me. You've got enough to keep you busy around here." His gaze fixed back on the newspaper.

I hesitated, disbelieving what I'd just heard. "Are you suggesting I've neglected my duties around here?"

"No, of course not." He looked at me with a smile in his eyes, and I could see he was entertained by this whole thing.

"You don't take me seriously, do you?"

He lowered the paper again, still smiling. "I take you seriously. Come here, sit down." He patted the sofa beside him.

I sat down, and he put an arm across my shoulders. "What's this all about?"

"What happened to my life?" I asked.

"What do you mean?"

"I'm turning forty in a few months. I spend my days running Teddy's business while he's off playing around. I take the abuse from disgruntled clients, make sure he signs everything, get the payroll checks out and...well, I run the office. Then I come home, cook dinner and shuttle kids around all evening.

And what thanks do I get?" I dropped my head onto Anthony's shoulder.

Anthony rested his head against mine. "I tried to tell you years ago, but you wouldn't listen. There is no reason you have to work. And let the kids get rides with their friends once in a while."

I lifted my head and stared at him. "I don't work because I feel I have to. I like to work. I always wanted a career of my own."

He laughed. "A career? Working for Teddy?"

The laugh ripped through me like a knife. I pulled loose from him and shot to my feet.

"Jan?" He reached for my hand. "Come on, I'm teasing."

I jerked my hand away. "See. You don't take me seriously. Just because I'm not your mother; just because I don't find caring for husband and home the ultimate fulfillment…"

Tears stung my eyes and my throat clenched. I stomped to the kitchen, grabbing my purse and car keys. "I'm going out. Gabby will call around nine, and you'll have to pick her up at school."

"Jan? Where are you going? Jan?" he called after me as I rushed out the back door and slammed it behind me.

I jumped into my car, swung out of the drive and headed down our street. Two blocks from the house, I pulled to the curb, holding the steering wheel tightly to steady my trembling hands. Once the shaking subsided, I drove to the book store where I got a latte and picked up the latest Elizabeth Berg novel. I settled at a small table in the corner of the café and opened the book. My eyes focused on the words, but my mind was still locked in the exchange with my husband.

What the hell was that about? I breathed in the calm, tuning in to the soft murmurs of shoppers discussing books, giggles wafting from the children's section, and the aroma of muffins emanating from the café oven. I felt my body relax, followed by my spirit. I loved the atmosphere of the place. I sipped my drink and read until I heard the announcement that the store would be closing in ten minutes. I rose, dropped the empty cup into the trash basket and carried the book to the cash register.

When I arrived home, I pulled into the drive and cut the engine, then sat in the car for a few minutes. I looked toward the kitchen window to see Anthony peer out, look back at me, then disappear again. I didn't know how to get out of the car and go back inside. I didn't know if I wanted to go inside and make things *right,* or if I wanted to go inside and make things *different.*

I walked into the kitchen and Anthony called from the living room, "I put your plate in the microwave. Just hit the button."

"Thanks," I called back as I started the oven. I washed my hands and poured a glass of wine. I was sitting at the table when Anthony came in and stood staring at me.

"You okay?" he asked.

I looked up at him, my mouth filled with rice, and nodded.

"So, um…" He sat across from me. "Where'd you go?"

"I went to the book store."

"Reading emergency?"

I put down my fork and looked at him. "Don't be glib."

"Okay, seriously, what happened today, Jan?"

"I've just hit my limit. I'm sick and tired of being taken advantage of."

His eyes widened. "You mean at work, don't you?"

I walked to the sink and scraped my plate into the disposal, then turned to face him. "At work and here, too. I'm going in tomorrow to do the payroll, then I quit. Maybe I'll quit all my jobs."

"All your jobs?"

"Yes. I'm not feeling much like being a housekeeper anymore, either."

"You can't just quit being a wife and a mother. It doesn't work that way. We're in this together."

"Together? That's a good one. I go to work, come home and make dinner, shuttle Gabby around, do the laundry and cleaning. What do we do together, Anthony? Tell me that." My voice rose steadily as I spoke.

He stood and looked hard at me, then raised his hands, palms facing me. "Nothing I say is right, so I'm done talking. I can't talk to you when you're like this."

I whirled at him. "When I'm *like this*? I've never been *like this*. Maybe that's the problem—I need to be more *like this*. Ah, shit." Tears filled my eyes and my chin quivered. I turned away, leaning against the sink.

His hand approached my shoulder, giving off warmth. He stopped short of resting it there. "I don't know what you want from me, Jan."

I wiped my face with the back of my hand. "Never mind. Just go on to bed. I'll be up soon."

He turned and walked from the room, a deep sigh breaking the silence. I picked up my glass of wine, wiped my face and sat once again at the table. I heard the rumble of feet descending the stairs, and Michael, our seventeen-year-old son, trotted into the kitchen.

"Hey, Mom." He opened the refrigerator and peered inside. "Any leftovers?"

"There's Chinese in the containers. The lasagna is for tomorrow."

He opened a carton, sniffed it, and then removed several containers from the fridge. I watched as he dumped a mound of rice onto a plate and covered it with a variety of Chinese dishes. I took in his form—boy becoming man—the shadow of a beard spread across his face, his bicep muscles rippling. I was transported back fifteen years. My heart lurched as I remembered the little boy who'd clung to the counter by his fingertips and raised on his toes in an effort to reach the cookie jar.

"Mom? Hey, Mom. Why're you lookin' at me like that?"

I blinked and smiled at him. "Just remembering. Where were you tonight?"

"I had a study group at the library. Gotta keep my grades up if I'm going to get into Harvard." The microwave beeped and he grabbed a dish towel, removed the plate and headed toward the stairs. "Later, Mom. I've still got some reading to finish."

Michael had his life all planned out. He'd applied to colleges and planned to attend Harvard for graduate school. He wanted to pursue a law degree and become a defense attorney. Gabriella, at fifteen, had her sights set on a career in the theatre. I sighed as I realized my children had their lives more together than I did.

I settled in front of the TV and watched the late news. I waited long enough for Anthony to fall asleep before I climbed the stairs. It's not that I didn't want to talk to him. I just didn't know what to say.

Later, as I lay in the dark and listened to Anthony's even breathing, I thought about my day and my melt-down. I knew that, if I acted tomorrow as though nothing happened, everyone else would let it go, and things would return to normal. I also knew I couldn't do that. I couldn't back-peddle. I couldn't return to my life as I knew it. I also couldn't sleep.

Slipping out of the bed, I tiptoed from the room and returned to the kitchen where I sat at the counter and wrote another *I quit* letter. This one I wrote with care, with intention, and I posted it on the front of the refrigerator.

Two

A clatter from the kitchen jarred me awake. Anthony's side of the bed was empty. I looked across to the red numbers on the alarm clock—seven-fifteen.

"Oh, shit. I slept in."

I tossed the blankets aside and swung my legs over the edge of the bed. Then I remembered the note I'd left on the fridge last night. Sliding into my worn slippers and pulling on my robe, I stopped at the bathroom and then headed downstairs to face the music.

When I walked into the kitchen, all activity halted and heads turned. I stopped as well and stared back at the three faces turned toward me. "Good morning."

Several beats went by in silence before Anthony mumbled, "G'morning," and went back to his coffee-making. My first instinct was to take the measuring spoon from his hand and make coffee. But I couldn't. I didn't.

Gabriella spoke. "Nice note, Mom. Is this, like, a test or something?"

I stood and read the note I'd hung on the fridge:

Dear family,

I quit. Effective immediately, I am no longer the cook, laundress, shopper, housekeeper, chauffeur, landscaper or resident problem-solver. Oh, I'm also not the banker or the ATM. I am, however, the instructor. Classes will begin tomorrow and seating is limited, so you should sign up early.

A cooking class will be conducted at five-thirty sharp. Bring your inquiring mind and appetite. A cook book will be available. On Saturday, I will offer two sessions—general housekeeping and laundry. Supplies will be provided. However, if you are attending the laundry session, please separate clothing into lights and darks and bring those with you. This class begins at nine a.m. in the basement.

Housekeeping will commence at ten, once you have mastered washing machine settings and drying times. Rubber gloves are recommended for those who have delicate skin or have had expensive manicures recently.

Other workshops, such as money-management, will be scheduled as needed and announcements will be posted. Don't be late and get left out in the cold.

Janet R. DeMarco,

Wife, Mother, Person
(not necessarily in that order)

I opened the door and pulled the orange juice from the fridge, turned to face my stunned family and, to add to their confusion, took a swig directly from the carton—something I'd constantly told Michael not to do.

Gabby shook her head, Michael suppressed a smile, and Anthony glared at me.

"Mom, um, I need…" Gabby began.

Anthony caught her eye and, with a dark, warning look, shook his head 'no.' She swallowed the rest of her request with a gulp of juice.

I put two slices of bread into the toaster and set the butter and jelly on the table. Anthony, who'd succeeded in brewing a pot of coffee, poured a mug and extended it to me. "Coffee?"

"Thank you. I'd love some," I said, taking the cup of steaming liquid.

"Are you going to work today?" Michael asked.

"Yes, I am. It's my last week and I want to help Uncle Teddy find a replacement."

"You're quitting that, too?" Gabby asked, her eyes wide.

"Yes," was all I said in reply.

Anthony carried his coffee to the table as I rose to get my toast. We brushed past one another and I felt the chill. He was not happy. He was confused and trying to figure out what was going on with me. I smiled slightly, enjoying his dilemma.

Michael grabbed his backpack. "You need to move it, Gabs, if you want me to take you to school."

"I need a few minutes. And don't call me Gabs." She looked at me, her mouth worked into a pout, then yelled for Michael to wait.

Typically, I would drop her off on my way to the office. Apparently, they were all thrown off kilter by my resignation.

Anthony put his cereal bowl and cup into the sink and turned. "So, um, are we having the lasagna for dinner tonight or what?"

"Oh, I forgot about that. Well, I guess we can reschedule our cooking class for tomorrow night. I'll leave instructions for the garlic bread and salad, and the baking time for the lasagna. That should be simple enough, don't you think?"

His jaw hung half-way to his knees, and the confusion in his eyes made him adorable. I wanted to tell him I was just kidding, but I wasn't.

I put my plate and cup into the dishwasher and said, "Have a good day. I'll see you tonight." I hurried upstairs to get dressed so I could go and deal with Teddy.

~ * ~

The song I hummed as I drove the few miles to DeMarco Construction wasn't even registering in my brain. It was just a catchy, cheerful tune. I felt a strange power surge as I parked, slung my purse over my shoulder and entered the office. As soon as I stepped behind my desk, I was met with a barrage of requests and demands by two of the foremen and Teddy.

I held up both hands, palms out—the universal signal to STOP. I don't think it was my outstretched palms, but probably the cold stare and pursed lips that silenced all three.

"Teddy, you and I need to talk before I do anything else."

"But..." Mack said, leaning across the counter toward me.

I turned and locked eyes with him; he got the message, as did the other man. The two shook their heads and walked out of the office. Mack called over his shoulder, "I'll come back when you're not so busy."

Teddy ushered me into his office, where I chose to stand. "This won't take long. I quit."

"But, Jan... Look, how much will it take? I know you've gone above and beyond most of the time, and I owe you."

"Oh, you owe me plenty. Mostly for covering your sorry ass with Stella when she couldn't find you."

"So, an extra hundred a week? Shorter hours? What?"

Teddy and I stood eye to eye. Teddy, unfortunately, took after his mother's side of the family. He stood five foot seven. His mousy brown hair gave his hazel eyes a pale, foggy appearance. He looked nothing like his male cousins for whom the phrase 'Italian stallion' could have been coined.

"You're not listening, Teddy. I quit. I will do this week's payroll, mainly because I want my check and the very generous severance pay you're giving me. I will call the newspaper and place an ad for a replacement, if you like."

Teddy dropped into the plush leather desk chair and ran his fingers through his limp hair. "You're killing me, Jan."

I was not taken in by his drama. Teddy should have at least five Oscars on the shelf behind his desk for past performances.

"I want a life, and this isn't it."

"What does Anthony think about all this?" he asked, as if the question was logical.

My jaw tensed, and warmth spread across my chest. "What difference does that make? I'm a big girl, Teddy, and I can make these decisions for myself. Anthony has nothing to say about it."

"This place won't be the same without you, Jan."

"Yeah. It'll be chaos without caffeine, swimming in dust bunnies."

"If this is about cleaning, I can hire a cleaning lady."

I let out an exasperated sigh. "It's not about cleaning. It's about me realizing I want more than this, and deciding I'm not willing to compromise any further. Now, if you want the payroll done for this week, I have to get to work. Do you want me to put an ad in the paper?"

"Yeah, fine. Whatever. You know, I expected more from you, Jan. After all, we're family."

"And I could say the same," I replied before returning to my desk.

I nearly laughed when I looked up to see two pairs of eyes beneath yellow construction helmets peering through the window into my office, waiting to be invited back inside. I waved and, when the door opened, stated loudly, "One at a time."

~ * ~

When I called the newspaper, I had to fight the temptation to fill in all the unspoken duties of the job. I resisted, though, realizing that if I did that, no one in their right mind would apply. I ran to the bank to make a deposit into the payroll account, then returned to the office and cut the paychecks.

Teddy, who was usually gone by lunchtime, was still in his office, casting furtive glances at me every time I passed his open door.

At four o'clock, I took the checks in for his signature, handing him my paycheck and my severance check first. "These need your signature. If you feel this amount is unfair, we can talk about it."

"No, Jan, what? Unfair? I trust you. I just wish I could do something to get you to stay. I'll miss you, you know."

I grinned. "Yeah, like you miss a toothache once the tooth's been extracted? You'll miss me the first time Stella calls here looking for you and the new girl doesn't know enough to cover your ass."

"I can train her. After all, I trained you, didn't I?" He rolled his eyes up and glanced at me.

I was too hurt to get angry. He'd nudged a spot that was raw and tender. Teddy had unwittingly hit the nail on the head. I felt like a trained seal. I moved through my days, from task to task, responding to commands and hoping for a spare sardine to be thrown my way. My vision blurred as tears brimmed in my eyes.

"Ah, jeez. I'm sorry. I didn't mean that to sound the way it did," Teddy said, his face flushed.

"Forget it. It's not your fault. You can't help being an ass. Thank you for giving me this job when I wanted one. If the new girl has any questions, I'll answer what I can." I took the checks from his hand. "I'll see you around."

I gathered my purse, my coffee mug that said 'World's Greatest Mom,' and my spare umbrella and drove to the bank to deposit my checks.

I arrived home at five-fifteen to find Anthony standing in the kitchen reading my heating instructions for the lasagna. Gabby hunched over the sink and whined about not knowing how to make a salad.

"How can you not know how to make a salad?" Anthony grumbled. "You put vegetables in a bowl. Wait. You have to wash them first."

They looked up as I entered the kitchen. "You're home early," I said to Anthony.

"Yeah, a little. So, um, how was your day?"

"You mean, did I quit? Yes, I did. Your cousin's a real piece of work, you know."

"Did he say something he shouldn't have? Did he insult you?" he asked in his best macho voice.

"No, at least not intentionally. You know Teddy wouldn't do that. He tried to buy me out. I did get a nice little severance check. I think I'll treat myself to something special, a day at the spa or some new clothes."

Gabby heard 'spa' and 'clothes' and jumped right in. "Ooh, Mom. They have a mother-daughter special running at the spa on Penrose. It's two-for-one. I'd go with you. Then we can go shopping."

"I'm sure you would and we could, but I was thinking of a day just for myself."

Her face clouded and she scowled. She has her Uncle Teddy's flair for drama. I'd decided this was a genetic imperfection in the DeMarco family that had no bias as to gender.

"What time is dinner?" I asked.

Anthony looked at my hand-scrawled instructions for the lasagna and the baking time for garlic bread. "Another half hour, I think."

"Good, I can't wait to change out of these clothes and get comfortable." I headed through the living room to the stairs. "Oh," I called back, "I'll set the table when I come back."

When I returned to the kitchen, the overly browned loaf of garlic bread sat atop the stove. The pan of lasagna steamed in the center of the table, and a salad had been placed to one side. Michael was putting the last of the silverware at each place.

"Dinner's ready," Anthony said, sending bits of burned crust flying as he sliced the garlic bread.

I sat in my usual seat and filled my salad bowl. "Well, this is lovely. I'll conduct the cooking class tomorrow evening, same time, same station. Salad?" I asked, passing the larger bowl to Gabby.

"Grrr-eat," she growled, taking the bowl. "I can hardly wait."

Anthony flashed his 'that'll be enough' look, and she silenced, grabbing a large spoon and digging into the lasagna.

"Mom, I got an invitation today from West Virginia University. It says I should have a parent come with me to tour the campus. Can you go?" Michael asked.

"When is it?"

"It's a week from Tuesday."

"Sure. I'd love to. I won't have anything else to do that day," I responded, smiling. "Is that okay with you, Anthony, or did you want to go?"

Anthony filled his plate. "No, I'll have to work."

"Okay. It should be fun. A little mother-son time."

Gabby looked up at me. "Oh, sure. You can go with Michael for a day, but you can't take me to the spa with you."

"This is different and you know it. Pass me the bread, please." I refused to play into Gabby's hand. Anthony smiled as he chewed.

I offered to load the dishwasher and clean up. "I didn't resign from life. I'm willing to do my share."

No one argued.

I finished in the kitchen, then joined Anthony in front of the TV and watched three different episodes of "Law and Order."

When the news came on, I stood and stretched. "I'm going to take a nice hot bath."

The tub in our master bath is huge, and I can stretch my full length. After filling the tub and adding lavender bath salts, I eased into the steaming water. I felt my body silently voice an 'aaahhh' as I lay back and rested my head on a rolled towel.

Okay, Jan, I thought to myself, *let's talk. What's happening?*

Closing my eyes, I revisited the events of the past two days. I concluded that I felt underestimated, unappreciated and unfulfilled …too many 'uns' in my life.

I breathed in the scent of lavender and slid lower into the warm water, entering a semi-sleep state. I imagined what my life might have been like had I made different choices. I would've had a career, of that I was certain. I concluded it would have been something in the helping professions. I'm a good hand-holder and problem-solver. Just ask everyone in my family. They all look to me to solve their problems.

Marriage would have been in the picture. I like being married, having an 'other' to balance me out. Anthony does that, usually. He's the hot blooded, quick to anger and quick to react, stereotypically Italian husband. I've always been the mild-mannered, thoughtful, peace-loving and forgiving one. Some would say it's my English heritage. Some would say I have no backbone. I have had to learn to accommodate to fit into the DeMarco family—Italian on both sides for hundreds of years.

I would still have chosen to have children. I love the kids, miniatures of Anthony and me. I see much of myself in Michael's personality, though he looks exactly like his father— curly, dark hair, bronze skin, a straight nose with the tiniest bump and perfectly straight teeth. Well, the teeth he got from Dr. Stewart, the orthodontist.

Gabriella has my ash brown hair, full mouth and slender build, but her father's dark eyes and his flash of temper. She's loud and boisterous, a DeMarco through and through, whereas Michael is soft-spoken and reserved.

I could have been a good teacher or a nurse, perhaps. I enrolled in accounting classes at the community college because my mother insisted I go to college, and I didn't have a clue then what I wanted to be when I grew up. Maybe I still don't.

Growing up happened quickly when my mother died, leaving me orphaned at eighteen. My father had died in an accident at the steel mill where he worked when I was a toddler. My great aunt and uncle took me in, and I lived with them while I finished my two-year degree program.

Then I met Anthony and my destiny was determined. I worked for Breckman Insurance, and Anthony came in to purchase car insurance for his new Camaro. I can still feel the way my heart slammed against my chest wall when he smiled. We had dinner the next night and, within a year, were planning our wedding.

I shuddered as I remembered meeting Mama DeMarco for the first time. I had a few strikes against me: I wasn't Catholic, I wasn't Italian and I was looking to take her son away from her. By the time our wedding date rolled around, I'd converted to Catholicism and learned to make my own spaghetti sauce. And I learned that you never take an Italian mother's son away, even when you marry him. Angela DeMarco continues to make that clear at every turn.

I opened the drain with one toe and let some of the lukewarm water seep out, then closed it and turned on the hot water tap, refilling the tub. *Okay, Jan, so if today is the first day of the rest of your life, what are you going to do?*

Three

I stepped out of the tub, and goose bumps pebbled my flesh. I slathered on body lotion and let my silk nightgown slide down my body. *How long has it been since I pampered myself like this? Since I really felt like a woman?*

Anthony was already in bed as I eased into my side, trying not to disturb him. He rolled onto his back and looked at me. "You smell great. All relaxed now?"

"Yes. It was just what I needed."

His hand slid across my belly. "Want to know what I need? Or have you resigned from that, too?"

I thought about the question for a nanosecond, then turned toward him, feeling a rush of heat. The smirk on his face deflated any desire I had. "You really aren't taking this seriously, are you?"

His hand caressed my hip. "Sweetheart, I always take *this* seriously."

As he stretched to kiss me, I put both hands on his broad chest and shoved. "I don't mean *this*; I mean me. This whole thing about quitting and wanting something more is a joke to you. Well, buster, I have a news flash. I can quit *this*, too." I turned and rolled as far to my edge of the king-sized bed as I possibly could.

Anthony flopped back onto his pillow, exhaling loudly. "Okay, I'm sorry. I'm sorry if it seemed I was laughing at you. I wasn't. Jan?"

I bit my lip, refusing to answer.

"Are you going to stop talking to me, too?"

"Until you take what I have to say seriously, yes, I am."

His rhythmic snoring soon told me he'd fallen asleep. I, on the other hand, lay staring into the dark. *Maybe you've gone too far, Jan.*

Unable to sleep, I took my journal from the drawer in the nightstand, pulled on my robe, and tiptoed from the room. I settled on the sofa and began to write my list of wants.

I want to feel valued; I want to do something worthwhile with my time; I want to feel...I want to feel...significant. I want to be the person I'd once dreamed of becoming. Well, I'm not sure what that is. *I want hope.*

Hope. I rolled the word around in my head, then felt the way my mouth curved into an 'O' as I said it. "Hope."

If this was the first day of the rest of my life, I needed a new name befitting the journey. "My name is Hope," I said aloud to the empty living room. I spent the next few hours, energized and wide awake, sketching out the life Hope would live.

I returned to bed an hour before Anthony's alarm clock sounded. I remained still, feeling the bed shift as he rose, listening as he showered and dressed. He leaned over and planted a kiss on my cheek, then headed downstairs. I could hear footsteps and grumbling in the hallway as Michael and Gabby argued over who got the bathroom first.

"Go ahead," Gabby said. "I'll use Mom and Dad's shower."

"You will not disturb your mother," Anthony said firmly.

I smiled, realizing he was trying to give me time and space, and to understand what was happening. *Good luck. Even I don't understand it.*

Soon the house grew quiet and I dozed. I wakened at eleven and went to the kitchen to make coffee. Standing at the window and gazing out into the back yard, I let my mind drift to my journal notes. I'd decided my new name would be Hope, and I'd let everyone know that this evening. *Jan, they're going to have you committed.*

The phone rang, jolting me from my thoughts. "Hello."

"Janet? This is Angela. I called you at the office, but Teddy answered and said you quit."

"That's right. Yesterday was my last day."

"It's about time. I always told Anthony he should be ashamed to have his wife go off to work every day."

"Working was my idea. We've been through this before." My mother-in-law is, shall we say, 'old school.'

"Yeah, well. Still, I think it's a good decision."

"Is there something I can do for you?"

"Oh, yes. I was calling to remind you about Carmela's birthday party next Sunday. Make sure Michael and Gabriella come, too. We hardly see them anymore."

"I know. Since they've gotten older, they're so busy with school and friends."

"In my day, family was the most important thing. Sunday was a time for dinner together. Kids today have no respect for family."

I rolled my eyes. "I'll tell them they're expected. Can I bring anything?"

"No, no. I'll take care of dinner. Just make sure you, Anthony and the kids are here on time. Three o'clock."

I heard what wasn't said, *'You cook Italian food for the family? I don't think so.'*

"Thanks, Angela. We'll be there." I hung up the phone and thought, *now, there's a woman who needs a fantasy.*

Carmela is Angela's mother, Anthony's grandmother, and I love her. She's about as different from Angela as a mother and daughter could be. Carmela stands all of four eleven in her orthopedic shoes. Her hazel eyes sparkle and crinkle when she smiles, which is often. White curls cap her head, and she peers over glasses that should have been replaced two years ago. But she refuses, saying she won't live long enough to make it worthwhile. So far, it looks as though Carmela might outlive all of us. She's eighty going on eighteen.

I took my coffee with me and ran upstairs to dress. My closet bore hanger after hanger of work clothes—slacks, skirts and blouses in a variety of lights and darks for every season. I found two pair of jeans, one of which still almost fit. I tugged those on and lay across the bed to zip, then rolled around a bit, struggling to sit upright. *No more lasagna for you.* I snatched a tee shirt from Anthony's drawer and pulled it on, then slipped into my sneakers. In the bathroom, I looked at myself in the mirror and drew my hair into a pony tail, a style I hadn't worn since high school. I was shocked at how much younger I looked.

On my way to the stairs, I went to Gabby's room and borrowed her personal CD player that had been recently replaced by an MP3. I didn't have a clue what that meant.

I tucked some cash into my pocket, hoping I could get my fingers in there to retrieve it again. I rifled through our CDs and found something suitable for walking, donned my sunglasses, and set off with no particular destination in mind.

We live in a small town, and our house sits on a large lot two blocks back from the main street. I descended the porch and turned left, walking briskly to the music—some disco mix. I tuned into my breathing and soon felt the burn in my calves. Turning toward Main Street, I headed for the park.

Winded by the time I reached the corner of Main and Parker, I started to think this hadn't been the best idea. Then I saw my oasis—Starbucks. I practically ran over an elderly woman with a cane to get to the door. Once inside, I stepped to the counter and salivated as I looked over the menu.

"I'll have a venti non-fat, decaf mocha latte with whipped cream." I then inched two fingers into my front pocket and jumped up and down, trying to reach the bills I'd tucked there. Just when I thought I'd have to go to the ladies restroom and unzip to get to the money, I snagged the corner of a bill and tugged. Thank God it was a five I'd reached.

The young woman behind the counter set the cup before me. "Anything else?"

"No, thank you," I said, passing her the five.

While she made my change, I looked at her carefully. "Shouldn't you be in school?" I asked.

She handed me the change. "Graduated last year."

"Oh. You look a lot like my daughter, and she's just fifteen." I took my drink, exited the store and waited for the walk figure to appear on the traffic signal so I could cross the street.

The park was two blocks long and one block deep. Neatly groomed flower beds were scattered in the grassy areas. Sidewalks wove throughout the park, and in the center stood a gazebo, something still utilized by bands for holiday celebrations. I liked our town because living here was like living in the past, in another time when life was simpler. And we were close enough to drive into the city in a matter of minutes.

I meandered along the walkways, settling on a bench near the gazebo where I sipped my brew, licking the whipped cream mustache from my upper lip. I watched a woman, overdressed for the weather and dragging one of those fold-up metal shopping carts. She picked up cans that had been carelessly discarded and dropped them into the cart, stopping to poke through trash receptacles with a long stick.

The woman stopped at the trash can a few feet from the bench where I sat. I smiled and said, "Good afternoon. It's a beautiful day, isn't it?"

She regarded me silently before responding, "Yes, it is. I feel sorry for people locked up in buildings on a day like this."

I was fascinated by this woman who appeared to be homeless, and I was struck by the fact that she seemed to be close to my age. I didn't know we had homeless people in our town. In the city, yes, but not here.

"Do you come to the park every day?" I asked.

She smiled. "I practically live here. Haven't seen you here before, though." She tossed a few cans into the cart, then sat on the opposite end of my bench. She removed her tattered gloves and ran a hand through her short, graying brown hair, pushing it back from her face.

"I used to be one of those people locked up in buildings on a day like this. I quit my job yesterday."

"Good for you. I quit, too."

"Oh? What did you do?"

She gave out a small laugh. "Life."

"Excuse me?"

"I'm playin' with you, honey. I quit doing life the way the rest of you do it. I live out here, most of the time."

"You live here? In the park?"

"You might say this is my living room. Oh, I sleep at the shelter in the city, but I can't stand the noise and exhaust. I take the bus out here in the morning and spend the day, then I catch the bus back to the city at night, when I have the money."

As I listened, I wondered how easily I could get those other bills out of my pocket. I transferred my drink to my left hand

and extended the right to her. "I'm sorry. I should've introduced myself. I'm… I'm Hope," I said shaking her hand.

"And I'm Joy. Hey, now all we need is Faith," she said, throwing her head back and laughing heartily.

"That's pretty good. Maybe if we sit here long enough, she'll show up. Can I buy you a cup of coffee?"

"Oh, no. Don't bother."

"It's no bother, if I can get my money out of this pocket. I guess I've put on a few pounds since I last wore these jeans." I set my drink down, stood and repeated my 'inching my fingers into my pocket' dance.

Joy watched with an amused smile on her face. "See, now that's why I don't keep money in my pockets."

"What would you like? Latte? Mocha? Vanilla? Regular or decaf?"

The amused smile stayed as she answered, "Just a cup of coffee… black."

"I'll be right back. Don't go anywhere," I said, turning toward Starbucks.

"Got nowhere to be," she said, settling back on the bench.

The girl behind the counter looked almost disappointed when I ordered then displayed the bills already in my hand. I think she must have enjoyed my dance.

She gave me the coffee and my change. "Decide you needed a little caffeine for the walk home?"

"This? Oh, no, it's for a friend I met in the park. Thanks."

I returned to the bench and handed Joy her coffee.

"Thank you." She reached into her coat pocket, extracting two tangerines and passing one to me. "Fruit? It's good for you."

"No, thank you. You hold onto it."

She continued to offer the piece of fruit. "I'll be insulted if you don't take it."

When I accepted the tangerine and thanked her, she said, "I was just teasing. Jack, the guy at the grocery store by the bus stop, gives me three or four pieces of fruit every time I get off the bus. I don't particularly care for that much fruit, but I don't want to hurt his feelings. So I give some of it away."

We sat and peeled our tangerines and sipped coffee, not unlike two women meeting in a kitchen somewhere for an afternoon visit, except we had fresh air and bright sunshine. It was April and still cool, but as the afternoon sun bore down, I wondered about Joy in her coat.

"It's getting warm," I said.

"Yes."

"Do you want me to hold your coffee so you can take off your coat?"

"Nope. Thanks," she said, stuffing a wedge of fruit into her mouth.

We sat in silence for several minutes, then Joy asked, "What was your job?"

"I was a bookkeeper. I did payroll for my husband's cousin's construction company. Let me rephrase that... I ran the company. The only thing Teddy ever did was sign the checks."

She wrinkled her nose. "Well, that sounds like fun."

"Oh, yeah. It was a lot of laughs. I quit some of my other jobs, too."

"How many'd you have?"

I laughed. "Too many. I resigned as housekeeper, chauffeur, cook and laundress. I decided it was time for my husband and kids to do more for themselves, and time for me to figure out what I want now."

"Hmmmph. Be careful. You could end up on the streets." She stood and dropped her empty coffee cup into the trash, then tossed the tangerine peelings on the grass. "I'm not littering. The squirrels love these, and the peels are organic."

"Joy. What did you mean… that I could end up on the streets?"

"Happened to me," she said as she worked her hands back into the worn gloves. "First I quit my job. Then I quit my home and my family. I just kept quitting until I had nothing to worry about but me, and here I am."

"Wow. So you, um, you…"

"I chose to be homeless. Wouldn't President Reagan loved to have had me on his campaign?"

"But why?"

She flashed a smile, and I noticed how blue her eyes were as the sun danced upon them. "That's a long story for another day." She took hold of the cart. "It was nice to meet you, Hope. Maybe I'll see you here again. Thanks for the coffee."

"You're welcome, and it was nice meeting you, too. Thanks for the tangerine."

I watched as she tugged the cart along the bumpy sidewalk, waving and calling to someone across the street. I shuddered as I thought, *there but for fortune go I.* Then I realized that Joy was a woman who'd walked away from her fortune, such as it may have been.

I pitched my empty cup into the trashcan and left the park.

My friend, Fran, ran a small antique shop along Main Street. The bell over the door announced my entrance and Fran looked up. "Well, what are you doing in here today? Aren't you supposed to be at work?"

"Not any more. I'll tell you in a minute. Gotta use the ladies room."

I hurried to the restroom in the back, then joined her for a cup of tea in her cramped office and told her about my retirement.

When I got to the part about renaming myself, she raised her eyebrows and looked worried. "Who are you, and what have you done with practical, down-to-earth Janet?"

"I've upgraded her to a new model, or at least I'm trying to. Fran, I'm bored with my life. I need something new and different. I want to do something of significance."

"The guys who work for Teddy would argue that you already did, especially on pay day."

"I know, but... when I was younger, I dreamed of doing something great, something that would change the world."

Fran looked into my eyes. "You did; they're named Michael and Gabriella."

I smiled, a little embarrassed by my declaration. "I love my kids, and I love Anthony. But I need something more for me. I just had coffee with a homeless woman in the park who told me she walked away from everything. Some days, I feel like that, like I'd like to just keep going."

"You met Joy?"

I had the tea cup in mid-lift and jerked my head abruptly. "You know her?"

"Everyone in town knows Joy. She comes out here on the bus almost every day. She's a very interesting person."

"How come I don't know Joy?" As the question escaped my lips, the double meaning sank in my stomach like a rock. "Omigod, that's it. I don't know joy."

"Your life is empty because you don't know the local homeless woman?"

My eyes misted, and my heart thudded. "No. That's what's missing. I've lost the joy in my life."

"Then why didn't you rename yourself Joy instead of Hope?"

"I guess I'm feeling hopeless, too. Good Lord, Fran, I'm a mess."

The bell rang, announcing a customer, and Fran stood. "Don't go anywhere. We're not finished here."

Fran returned and sat opposite me, her eyes bearing concern. "Now, Jan …Hope, whoever you are, where were we?"

"I know this sounds crazy, but I think I'm onto something. Janet was predictable and organized and lived for everyone else's needs. Hope is a clean slate. Hope can decide the kind of person she wants to be. Hope can…"

Fran held up a hand, palm out. "Okay. It was one thing when you started referring to yourself by a new name. Now you're talking about your newly-named self in third-person, and you're starting to scare me a little."

I jumped up. "I've gotta run. I've got a new identity to create. Thanks for the tea," I said as I started for the door. "Oh, and thanks for calling me Hope."

Fran grinned and shook her head. "Why wouldn't I? It's your name."

"I'll talk to you later," I said, giving a backward wave with my fingers. *The best best friends are the ones who play into your fantasies with you.*

I walked home with renewed energy, imaging Hope—what she looked like, how she dressed, her personality, her new hobbies and interests. *Yep, Janet, your train has left the track and rolled into insanity gulch. Yeehaa!*

Four

My eyes surveyed the supplies spread along the kitchen countertops, awaiting my less-than-eager students. Gabby and Michael were upstairs pretending to study. Anthony was due home any minute. I'd planned a simple menu: meatloaf, mashed potatoes and steamed green beans. How hard could that be?

Anthony came in the back door and went straight to the fridge, pulling out a cold beer and popping off the top with his thumb. He took a long draw and swallowed. "You're really going to make us do this, huh?"

"I'm not making you do anything. I'm offering instructions that will assist you all in becoming more self-sufficient. You may choose not to participate."

He turned, walked to the bottom of the stairs and boomed, "Gabby! Mike! Get down here. It's time for cooking class."

I bit the inside of my cheek and turned toward the sink so he wouldn't see the laugh I stifled.

Michael was the first to reach the kitchen; Gabby stomped more loudly than necessary down the stairs and walked in, arms folded across her chest, scowl on her face.

I refused to be drawn in by her sulking. "Okay, everyone's here so let's get started or we'll be eating at midnight. Rule number one: always wash your hands before handling food," I said cheerfully, directing them to the sink. I watched as they obediently scrubbed and dried their hands.

"Good, now here's the recipe for meatloaf. I made a copy for each of you to follow. I already turned on the oven. Who wants to volunteer to mix up the meat loaf?"

Gabby looked at the ground beef and raw eggs and scrunched up her face. "Eeeww. I'm not putting my hands in that. I just had my nails done."

Anthony and Michael engaged in a staring match. Anthony won. I handed Michael two plastic baggies. "Here, slide one over each hand if you want."

He looked at the mixture, then at the baggies and said, "Nah. I'll pretend it's Playdoh." He poured the eggs into the bowl of beef and dug in, kneading until the eggs were mixed through.

Anthony leaned back against the sink, sucking on his beer and grinning. I pointed into the sink. "Honey, you can wash and peel those potatoes, then cut them into small pieces and put them in that pot of water to boil?" He looked at me with dark eyes, chugged the beer and set about peeling. He mumbled something unintelligible. I think it was an Italian curse.

"What's that?" I asked.

"Nothing."

I asked Gabby to read off the rest of the ingredients and add them to the bowl while Michael continued to mix. When the mixture was complete, Michael shaped it into the loaf pan, smiling proudly at his accomplishment. He looked at the directions, checked the oven temperature, and then set the pan inside. *I love my son.*

"I suppose we have to shuck beans, too," Gabby grumbled.

Michael laughed. "You don't shuck beans—you shuck corn. You snap beans. Right, Mom?"

"Exactly," I said, handing them a bag full of fresh green beans. "Start snapping, then put these in the steamer, but don't turn it on yet. The meat loaf won't be ready for a while. I'll set the table."

You may not agree, but I think there is an art to making mashed potatoes. Anthony doesn't have the knack for it. He does, however, have the knack for lifting the mixer while in motion and sending a spray of potatoes around the kitchen. This was going to be a bigger challenge than I'd thought.

The meatloaf was perfect, the potatoes—what was left of them—were lumpy, and the green beans slightly over-steamed. I praised their efforts all the same.

As the meal came to an end, I set down my fork and cleared my throat. "While we're all here, I think we need to discuss a few things."

They looked at me expectantly, probably thinking 'now what'?

"I want to be fair, so I'll take my turn, just like each of you. We need to set up a schedule for cooking, food shopping and laundry, and we need to divide up the household chores. I've made a calendar so we can fill in who will do what chores for the next month."

"Month?" Gabby exclaimed.

"Yes." I smiled. "We'll do the calendar a month at a time."

Once we got all of the 'I have play practice that night,' and 'me and the guys are going to a concert' excuses out of the way, we settled on a schedule. To my surprise, Anthony didn't offer a single excuse. Come to think of it, he didn't offer anything, just sat there, frowning.

"Great. Okay, so I took care of dessert for tonight. Let's see…" I looked down at the calendar. "Michael, it's your turn to clear the table. I'll get the ice cream."

"Wow. You slaved over that one, Mom," Gabby said.

"Gabriella!" Anthony said sharply.

"Sorry," she mumbled.

Michael cleared the plates and I set bowls of ice cream on the table, along with jars of chocolate and caramel toppings that I'd warmed in the microwave.

"See how well this is working? It's not going to be so bad, is it?" I asked.

Six eyes glared at me over spoonfuls of ice cream.

"By the way, there is one other thing I want to ask of you. I've decided to change my name."

Anthony groaned audibly. The kids stared, open-mouthed.

"I'd like to be called Hope from now on."

"You mean... by everybody?" Gabby asked.

"Well, you can call me Mom, of course. But if you introduce me to someone, my new name is Hope."

Anthony stared at me and I could see the color changing in his neck as the deep red flooded toward his face. A nerve twitched in his clenched jaw. "Would you kids excuse us? I need to talk to your mother... alone."

Michael and Gabby stood and, before leaving the kitchen, Michael took their dishes, rinsed them and put them into the dishwasher. If I hadn't been mesmerized by my husband's twitching, I'd have laughed.

He waited until both the kids were out of earshot, then exploded. "What the hell is going on with you? Two days ago I had a wife. Her name was Janet and she worked, not my idea I might add, for my cousin. Then she came home and cooked dinner and... and... " he lowered his voice, " ...and sometimes let me make love to her. Now I have this stranger who looks like my wife, sort of, but has lost her mind completely!"

I clasped my hands in my lap to control their shaking. I wasn't afraid of Anthony. He was a yeller, and I knew that when I married him, but he was never abusive. Still, I'd never seen him so exasperated.

"Anthony, I'm still your wife. I'm just not working anymore, and I'm making a few changes. You know, you might really like Hope, once you get to know her better," I said, grinning.

He failed to see the humor in this, and glared at me. "I think you've gone stark raving mad. I think you need to get your head examined. That's what I think."

"Honey, relax. I know this seems a little weird, but…"

"A little weird? You're quitting the family and calling yourself by a different name, and you expect us to call you that, too, and you say it's a *little* weird?"

"Yeah, I can admit that. It's a little weird. But since you seem to think I'm dangerously insane, I'll sleep on the couch tonight so you won't fear for your life. How's that?" My frustration took over.

He leaped to his feet. "Fine. That's just fine." He grabbed his car keys and headed for the door. "I'm going out and talk to sane people."

I jumped at the 'bang' of the door slamming. *Oh, Hope, now look what you've done. Omigod, now Janet's talking to Hope! Maybe I am crazy.*

I cleared the last of the dishes and finished cleaning up the kitchen. Then I took a beer from the fridge and went to the patio. I soon heard the door slide open, then close.

"Mom? Are you okay?" Michael asked.

I turned and smiled. "I'm fine, honey. You know your dad's just loud."

"Oh, I know that. I mean, are *you* okay? What's this all about?"

I sighed. "I'm not all that sure, Mikey. Come here, sit."

He walked over and sat in the chair next to mine.

I looked at him, his father's dark curls, solid build and Roman features.

"When you were a little boy, about four, you wanted to be Darth Vader. You remember that costume we got you for Halloween? The one you wore all the time?"

"Yeah, that was a terrific costume." He put a hand over his mouth and deepened his voice, speaking in a monotone, "Luke, I am your father."

"Then, when you were ten, you wanted to be a pilot and you started that collection of model airplanes that hung all around your room."

"That was great until I realized I wasn't too crazy about heights."

"Here's the thing, Mikey. I can't remember what I ever wanted to be." I felt a lump form in my throat and my vision blurred. I swallowed hard.

He waited and, when I didn't speak, he asked, "Did you want to be a mom?"

My head swiveled, and I faced him. "Oh, Michael. I wouldn't change that for anything." I reached out and ran my hand through his thick curls. "You and Gabby are the best things I've ever done. Don't you ever doubt that."

"So, who's Hope?"

"I think maybe she's the girl who imagined what she wanted to be once. I know it sounds crazy. Maybe it's because my mother died when I was just starting to plan my own life, and I didn't have anyone to encourage me. Aunt Edna and Uncle Henry took care of me and loved me, but nobody ever asked me what I wanted to do with my life."

"Maybe you should go to college with me next year," he said.

"Yeah, right. You just want someone to do your laundry," I teased, tugging at his hair.

"You know what, Mom. I think it's kinda cool that you can just make yourself into another person."

"Is that what it seems I'm doing?"

"Well, yeah. You never wear jeans. I've never seen your hair like that. And I have to introduce my friends to my new mom, Hope. And all this stuff about cooking and laundry and everybody taking turns. It's different."

"Some day, some lucky girl is going to thank me for teaching you these things."

He grinned at me. "I was planning to find a girl like my mom, who did all those things."

I shoved him playfully, and he rolled out of the chair laughing, then stood. "Goodnight, Mom." He bent and kissed my cheek.

I held his bristly man-boy face between my palms and kissed him. "Goodnight, Michael. And thank you."

"Sure, Mom," he said, pulling free and going back inside.

I heaved another sigh and swiped at the tears that slid from the corners of my eyes. Anthony pulled into the driveway, and the Explorer screeched to a stop. He walked across the patio, stopped and looked at me, then silently went inside. A moment later, the door opened and a blanket dropped around my shoulders.

"It's getting cold out here," he said, his voice husky.

I pulled the afghan around my shoulders and reached for his hand. "Thanks. Sit for a minute. Please?"

He dropped into the chair Michael had vacated, and I got a glimpse of what my son would look like in twenty-five years …heartbreakingly handsome.

"I'm sorry," I said, squeezing his hand.

He didn't say anything, but squeezed back. Over our eighteen-and-a-half years together, I'd learned to read my husband's nonverbals. This was 'I'm sorry, too.'

"You know I love you and the kids more than anything," I continued. "Can you just go with me on this? Michael was out here earlier and, when I explained to him what's going on, I started to understand it myself." I told Anthony what I had told our son about not remembering ever having a dream for my life.

He slipped his hand out of mine and leaned forward, clasping both his hands together, his arms resting on his thighs, his head bent. "You never cease to amaze me. Just when I think I have you all figured out …wham!" He turned his face towards me and smiled. "You're crazy, you know that?"

I smiled back. "Is that a compliment?"

"I hope so. If not, I'm sleeping alone for sure tonight, huh?"

"I want to breathe a little, play with a fantasy about what I could do with my life. That doesn't mean I plan to discard the best of the life I have… you and the kids. Think of how exciting it might be to explore this new person with me."

His interest wasn't the only thing that piqued. In the light that splashed across his face from the kitchen window, I could see his eyes soften and a goofy grin appear, the one he got when he was turned on.

"Come on, big boy," I said, standing and tugging at his hand. "Let me introduce you to Hope."

Five

Anthony nuzzled my neck, said something about feeling more *hopeful* now and reminded me that we had laundry class in an hour. By the time he'd emerged from the shower, I'd stripped the bed and sorted my clothing. He looked at me, at the pile of his clothing and back at me.

I grabbed my things and said, "See you in the basement." As I walked the hallway to the stairs, I tapped on Gabby's bedroom door, then on Michael's. Gabby responded with an irritated groan; Michael called out that he was awake.

After starting the coffeemaker, I carried my clothes downstairs and dumped them into piles beside the washer. I lined up the products... detergent, spot remover, fabric softener, bleach ...and waited for my students to arrive.

"Look out," Anthony called from the top of the stairs. His clothing, which he'd stuffed into a pillowcase for easy transport, arrived with a loud thump at the bottom of the steps. "You want coffee?" he called to me.

"Yes, please, with cream."

He carefully carried two mugs of steaming coffee down the stairs and handed one to me, kissing me lightly on the cheek. "Did I tell you how much I like Hope? I mean, I really like Hope." He took the coffee from my hand and set both mugs on the dryer, then pulled me against him. "You didn't tell me Hope was so sexy, and so imaginative."

I blushed, remembering last night, and pressed against him. We were interrupted by feet clomping down the stairs and argumentative voices as Michael and Gabby headed for the basement.

"My clothes don't stink," Michael said. "They're dirty clothes, what do you want them to smell like?"

"They do stink. I'm walking behind you and the wind is carrying the smell this way. Trust me, they stink. Unless that smell's coming from you."

Michael dropped his clothes on the floor and began to sort, holding up questionable colors for my direction.

"Are we each going to do our own laundry?" Gabby asked.

"We are for today, just so you get the hang of it," I said. I sure wasn't having any of them wash my clothes until I was convinced they knew what they were doing. "Why don't you go first?"

Gabby separated her clothing, her bottom lip hanging halfway to her knees. She is such a drama queen.

I passed out a card with written directions for sorting, reading labels, determining load capacity and the choice of hot versus warm or cold water. After reviewing the basics, I told Gabby to go ahead with her wash.

She looked at the card and began to toss delicate underwear into the washer. "You don't all have to stand there and watch. I think I can read directions on my own."

I shrugged. "Okay, then. I'm having breakfast." Michael and Anthony followed me up the steps, leaving Gabby to her laundry.

"Who wants eggs?" Anthony asked, pulling a skillet from beneath the counter.

"I'll have some. I need to keep my strength up for my next class... Housecleaning 101." My grin wasn't returned.

"Me, too, Dad," Michael said.

Anthony groaned. "I'm gonna need a bigger skillet. Gabby," he called down to the basement, "would you like scrambled eggs?"

"No, thanks. I'll just have a bagel," she answered as she climbed the stairs. "Hey, Michael. Will you take me and Megan to the mall later?"

"Can't do. I have plans, and they're in another direction."

Gabby gave me her 'mommy, please' soulful eye look and asked, "Mo-om?"

I smiled and silently prayed for the man she would eventually marry. He was doomed. "Actually, I'm going to the mall to shop later. But you and Megan have to be ready to come home when I am."

"Okay. Thanks. I'm gonna call Megan," she said, hurrying from the room. She stopped abruptly and turned toward me. "Do you mind picking up Megan on the way?"

"I'll be happy to," I responded, pleased that she'd thought to ask first. I was enjoying this new way of doing things. I took orders for toast and popped four slices into the toaster.

Anthony spooned scrambled eggs onto our plates and set the skillet in the sink. "Jan...uh, Hope, I have some errands to run. I'll do my laundry later, when I get home."

"Are you going to miss Housecleaning class?"

"You forget. I had my own apartment when we met."

"Yes, I remember. As I recall, your mother came and cleaned once a week. By the way, what's for dinner?"

His head jerked up. "Ah, um, I hadn't thought about that. I'll pick up something," he said with a satisfied smile.

"Count me out for dinner. I have a date," Michael said.

When Gabby returned, I told them about Great-grandma Carmela's birthday party. "We're all going. It's her eightieth birthday."

"Aw, Mom. I made plans to go to the movies with friends," Gabby whined.

Anthony pointed his fork at her. "Well, you can unmake them. You're going with us for dinner and that's final." He then looked at me, his eyes narrowed. "You're not going to tell my mother and the rest of the family to call you Hope, are you?"

"Why wouldn't they call me Hope? That's my new name," I said happily, standing to carry my plate to the sink.

His fork hit his plate with a resounding 'clink,' and he sighed loudly. "Do you have to? Ja... Hope, they're all going to think you're crazy. They already think you're strange just because you're not Italian. This'll put them over the edge."

"I can't help that. I have to be who I am."

"Oh, for..." He slapped his napkin down onto the table. "Okay, this was fun last night, but..."

The kids raised their heads and Gabby asked, "What was fun last night?"

Michael flushed and nudged her hard in the side with his elbow.

"Are you two finished yet?" Anthony barked.

Michael carried his plate to the sink, shoveling the last of the eggs into his mouth. "I am now."

Gabby jumped up. "I think the washer's off. I better check."

They both disappeared quickly.

"Nice, Anthony. Talk about our sex life in front of the kids."

"I didn't say anything about sex. Jan...Hope... look, I'm begging you not to make this an issue with my family. You know what my mother will do with this."

"Yeah, well, it wouldn't hurt your mother to fantasize a little. She's been a widow for, what, seven years, and she stills runs around draped in black."

"She likes black. She says it makes her look slimmer. That's not the point."

A scream loud enough to rattle the glassware rolled up the basement steps.

"Gabby, what's wrong?" I called as I flew down the steps.

She held a bra in one hand and panties in the other. "Look! Look at this! Everything's pink!"

I bit the inside of my lip to keep from laughing. "You must have put something red in with your whites."

She bent over the washer and pulled out items, one by one, all the same shade of pink with brighter blotches here and there. At last she held a red midriff top by thumb and forefinger.

"There's your culprit," I said.

"What am I going to do? I can't wear pink underwear. Look, even my socks are pink, and my camisole. Everything's ruined, and it's all your fault."

And the winner for best dramatic performance is...

"It's not all ruined. Now's a good time to learn about bleach." I helped her sort, putting the things that would withstand bleach back into the washer. I showed her how to measure out the bleach and set the washer for soak. "Be careful not to spill any of that. It'll take the color out of anything else it touches."

She handled the bottle of bleach as if it contained nuclear waste, placing it carefully back on the shelf and checking for spills. "Okay, now what?"

"Now," I said, gathering up two buckets, cleaning rags and a mop, "we learn to clean a bathroom. Follow me."

By the time I finished my instruction, there had been a fight over the one pair of rubber gloves, a bucket of water had been upset in the powder room, soaking the edge of the carpeting, and Michael had cleaned the bathroom sink with toilet bowl cleaner because, as he said, "It's bowl cleaner."

I was more exhausted than I'd ever been when I'd simply done it myself, but I was determined. I called to Gabby, who'd gone to her room to put away her freshly laundered and still slightly pink underwear. "I'm leaving for the mall in fifteen minutes."

She appeared at the top of the stairs, damp hair sticking to her face. "Fifteen minutes? I can't be ready in fifteen minutes. I have to shower and do my hair and repair my nails…"

"Well, I'm leaving in fifteen minutes," I said and headed to my bedroom to freshen up and change.

Gabby flew out the back door and onto the front seat of my car just as I started the engine. "You were really going to leave me?"

"Told you… fifteen minutes."

She called Megan on her cell and asked her to be outside and ready when we arrived. When Megan jumped into the back seat, Gabby turned and said, "Megan, I'd like you to meet my mother, *Hope* DeMarco."

Megan didn't respond, but wrinkled her forehead in confusion.

"Pleased to meet you, Megan," I said with a smile, glancing at her in the rear view mirror.

"Nice to meet you, too… I guess," she said, shrugging with her palms up to Gabby.

Saturday afternoon is not the ideal time to shop at the mall. Add after-Easter sales and you have a mob scene. I parked at the far end of a row near the food court entrance. "Okay, synchronize watches. We'll meet right back at this entrance in two hours."

"Three?" Gabby asked.

"Two, and don't be late. The taxi leaves at four o'clock sharp."

The girls spied friends and ran off, waving and giggling. I elbowed my way through a mass of bodies clogging traffic at the smoothie stand and headed for Macy's.

What would Hope wear?

I was amazed to find the choices in jeans. The last time I'd purchased them, I had two choices, zip front or elastic waist. I faced shelf after shelf of boot cut, flare leg, button-fly, relaxed

47

fit… the variety seemed endless. It took me nearly an hour to try on and select three pair of jeans. I then moved on to blouses and tee shirts and made a few quick selections. A denim jacket caught my eye. It looked more appropriate for Gabby, but I slipped it on and pulled my hair back. I liked the way the look subtracted a few years.

On my way back to the food court, I was drawn to The Shoe Warehouse. I bought new sneakers and a pair of boots that I knew would look great with the jeans. Even laden with packages, I felt as though I could've skipped back to the food court. I was excited about creating my new identity. I set my bags on a table and ordered a strawberry-banana smoothie. I was sipping it slowly when Gabby and Megan appeared.

"Jeez, Mom. You've been doing super shopping. Did you get me anything?" she asked, snooping through the bags.

I reached over and pulled the bag from her hand. "These are all mine. Do you girls want a smoothie before we go? My treat."

They accepted the offer, and I handed Gabby a ten. The girls helped me carry my purchases to the car and we headed home.

"Can Megan come for dinner?" Gabby asked.

"I don't know. You'd better call the cook."

Gabby flipped open her cell phone and called her father. "Daddy, can Megan come for dinner? Yeah. Yeah. Okay. Are you sure? Okay." She clicked the phone shut.

"Dad said that would be fine. He also asked if I would ask you to stop for pizza and loan me some money to buy it, then he'll give it back to you when we get home."

I presented my open hand. "Give me your phone."

I took the phone, flipped it open and pressed 'redial.' Anthony answered. "Nice try at an end run. Order from Pizza Palace. They deliver," I said, then clicked the phone closed and handed it back to Gabby.

"Maybe I should just go home," Megan said slowly.

I smiled at her in the mirror. "No, not at all. You like pizza, and you're more than welcome to join us."

Gabby looked back at Megan. "Tonight's Dad's night to cook... hence, pizza. Mom's making some changes."

Oh, honey, you ain't seen nothin' yet.

Later that evening, I stood before the full-length mirror and studied my image. The jeans, probably because they fit properly, showed off the curve of my hips and allowed me to breathe. The denim jacket covered a rose-colored tee shirt bearing a flying unicorn on the front. Okay, so that may be a bit young, but I liked how it made me feel. The boots added an inch to my height and looked great beneath the boot-cut jeans.

I pulled my ash brown hair into a pony tail. It was a good look, but something wasn't yet quite right. Then I realized the problem... Hope is blonde! Not a platinum or brassy blonde; more of a honey blonde, with highlights.

~ * ~

As we drove to church the next morning, I could feel Anthony's tension sending a current across the seat of the car. "I'm not going to get up at the pulpit and announce my list of changes. You can relax."

"I wasn't worried," he said, but I could see his shoulders ease. "Mom called and invited us to dinner this afternoon. Want to go?"

"I can't. There's a new book club starting up at the book store this afternoon. I thought I'd join. You and the kids can go, though."

"I have plans," Michael said from the back seat.

"Me, too," Gabby chimed in.

"Guess you're on your own," I said to Anthony.

"Great. I get to play thousand questions with Angela the Inquisitor." He looked into the rear view mirror. "Don't ever let me hear you call your grandmother that."

When we returned home, the kids made a beeline to change clothes and headed out to meet their friends. Anthony settled with the newspaper. I went upstairs and put on the outfit I'd modeled for myself the day before.

As I descended the stairs and entered the living room, Anthony glanced up, then did a double-take. "What the...? Well, this is a new look." He smiled. "I think Hope is a good influence on you." He started to get that droopy-eyed leer. "Are the kids gone already?"

I reminded him that his mother expected him for dinner and that I was going to the book store. "I'll see you later. I may stop by to visit with Fran after the book club meeting, and we'll probably pick up some dinner."

"So you don't want me to bring Angela's leftovers?"

"Are you crazy? Of course bring Angela's leftovers. Don't tell your mother I said this, but she makes the best sauce I've ever tasted. I just wish she'd share the recipe."

He threw his head back and laughed. "Not even on her deathbed. I'll see you later, Hope." He planted a kiss on my cheek before going out the door.

I arrived early for the book club and purchased a vanilla latte in the café, then browsed the bookshelves. A man about my age and wearing a lanyard with a plastic card identifying him as the store manager asked if I needed any help.

"Oh, no. Just browsing. Thank you. I'm killing time before the book club meeting."

"You're here to join? Wonderful. It meets in the back, at the comfortable seating area. I think there are a few folks back there already. Have a nice day."

I thanked him and returned his wishes, then navigated the maze of bookshelves until I came to an alcove furnished with overstuffed chairs. A man and woman were seated and leaning forward in rapt conversation. They stopped talking and smiled up at me as I approached.

"Here for the book club?" the man asked.

"Yes. I'd like to join."

He stood and extended his hand. "Garrett Ryan. But everyone calls me Gary. I'm facilitating the group. This is Sue Lingood. Have a seat."

I set my latte on the table in the center and my purse on the floor, then settled into the third chair. "I'm Jan...um, Hope DeMarco. It's Hope. Tell me what the book club does."

Gary looked up and waved to someone, then excused himself. "You want to explain it, Sue? I have to take care of something."

"We make a list of the books everyone would like to read, and we meet once a month and have a discussion. So we end up reading a book a month. What do you like to read?"

"Oh, well... when I read, I enjoy books about strong women, maybe a little romance..."

"Who are some of the authors you read?"

I named the only person I could think of. "Elizabeth Berg. I really like her books."

"Yes, she's great. We've done a few of her books in the past."

A few others arrived and everyone made introductions, then Gary returned and passed a sheet of paper around. "Would you print your name, address, phone number and email address on here?"

I raised my hand, as if in fourth grade, and he nodded. "What if you don't have an email address?"

The gasp was audible. That was, obviously, taboo.

"Just make sure you have a phone number where I can reach you if there's a change in a meeting date or time."

Note to self—Hope would have email. The kids both had computers and Internet access, but I'd only used it at work. I may have to get my own computer.

There were seven of us in the group. Since I'd not been an avid reader for the past, oh, twenty years, I agreed to whatever books the others suggested.

Sue turned to me, asking, "Hope, is there a book you'd like to suggest?"

I stammered, "Oh, I, uh…I'm sure the list we have will be fine."

"Well, I was thinking of Lizzie Berg's latest book. Let's add that one." She winked and smiled.

We all trooped to the fiction shelves, like highschoolers on a field trip, to get copies of the first book to read. I stayed to browse for other books on the list. I'd just bought the Berg book and read a few chapters, but most of the other authors were unknown to me. I carried my stack of six books to the register, where I also purchased a discount card that, in the long run, would pay for itself and could be used in the café.

As I drove across town to Fran's house, I couldn't stop smiling. I was getting to know Hope, and the more I got to know about her, the more I liked her. *Let's see—Hope is youthful, she's a casual dresser, she likes to read, she enjoys being with people, she's sexy—according to Anthony. She needs to get a computer and…*I ran a hand through my hair…*oh, yes, she's blonde, or will be by Friday.*

Six

I called my hairdresser first thing Monday morning and made an appointment for a cut and color on Wednesday. Teddy phoned at ten o'clock to ask where I'd stored the toner cartridges for the copier. He called again at ten thirty to ask how to access contracts that were saved in the computer.

When the phone rang at a little past eleven, I let the machine pick up. Sure enough, it was Teddy. "Hey, Jan. Come on, I know you're there. Pick up." Silence. "It'll just take a minute." Silence. "Okay, so call me back. I hired a new office person, and I want you to come in and show her the ropes. I'll pay you, of course."

I grabbed the phone. "I'm not coming back in there. I'll talk to her on the phone, but if she's worth what you're paying her, she should be able to figure out simple bookkeeping. It's not rocket science."

"Jan, I said I was sorry, and I paid you a month's severance. This is the least you can do for me."

"Correction. You only said you were sorry to try and smooth things over so I wouldn't quit. *I* paid myself the severance, and coming in there isn't the least of anything. What's the new woman's name?"

"Penny... Penny something. She's a friend of Mack's wife. She'll be here tomorrow, and I'm gonna have her call you. I gotta run."

"Why? Is it post time?"

"You know, it hasn't been all bad without you here. See you at Grandma Carmela's party on Sunday."

"Goodbye, Teddy."

Dressed in one of the new jogging suits I'd purchased, I pulled on my sneakers, fixed my hair in a ponytail and donned one of Michael's baseball caps. After attaching the CD player to my waistband and sticking the little foam pads into my ears, I headed out for a walk.

Spring was making a grand entrance, and the sun glinted off the windows of cars parked along the street. Daffodils waved in the breeze like golden flags announcing the new season. I followed the route I'd taken the week before, heading first to Starbucks.

When I stepped up to the counter to place my order, the same young woman who was working last week smiled, said 'hello' and asked what I'd have.

I looked at her name tag... Ricki.

"Hi, Ricki. I'll have a venti regular, non-fat vanilla latte without whipped cream, and a large regular coffee, black."

"Counting calories, huh?" she asked as I paid her and she made change.

"Yes, well, I don't want to have to jump up and down to get my money out of my pockets," I replied.

She handed me my drinks. "Aw, shucks. And that was my entertainment for the day."

"Sorry. I'll see what I can come up with next time. Thanks."

I headed across the street to the park, a drink in each hand, hoping I'd see Joy again. I walked the perimeter of the park, then cut through the path that traversed the center, but she wasn't to be found. Settling onto the bench near the gazebo, I waited and watched two squirrels play tag around a tree.

I was sitting with my eyes closed and my face raised to the sun when I felt someone sit on the other end of the bench. I opened my eyes and glanced sideways.

"Joy. I was hoping you'd be here. I brought you coffee. I think it's still hot," I said, handing her the cup.

"Thank you," she said, a look of surprise on her face. Her coat was folded inside her cart. She rummaged in the pocket, presented two apples and handed one to me. "Here. Fruit of the day."

"Thanks," I said, taking the apple. We each rubbed our apple on our pant leg, then took a bite. "I was talking to a friend of mine the other day who says she knows you."

"And who might that be?"

"Fran Taylor. She has the antique shop down the street."

"Oh, yes. Nice person. She lets me browse the shop. She has such lovely things in there, and I enjoy antiques. Used to have a house full... once."

I cocked my head and looked at her. "Where did you live?"

"You know those big houses they built in that plan off of Hargrove, behind the high school?"

"You lived there?" I asked with surprise.

"Yes, I did. My husband and I built one of the first houses in the plan. It was a monstrosity, seventy-two hundred square feet. I don't know what we were thinking. He'd made all this money on some stocks, and I guess we thought we had to show it."

"How long did you live there?"

"Two years or so. My family still lives there, I think."

"Your family? You have kids?"

"Two. My daughter would be nineteen now, and my son is twenty-two. He's in medical school."

"Do you ever see them?"

"I thought I saw Tina once going into the drugstore. It's been so long since I've seen her that I wasn't sure." She looked away and fixed her gaze on the squirrels.

I thought about Gabby and Michael and how impossible it would be for me even to think of leaving them, of just walking away from them and from Anthony. "Joy, do they know you? Do they know you come here?"

She turned to face me, setting her coffee cup on the bench. "I left nine years ago. The kids were both old enough that I'm sure they remember, but... the last time I saw my son, David, was at his high school graduation. He was so handsome. He got his looks from his father. Tina was there, too. She looked beautiful."

"That must have been a great day for you, to be with your family again."

"Oh, I wasn't with them. They had the graduation on the football field. I stood by the fence and watched. I sent David a card, but I don't know if his father gave it to him."

A lump the size of a softball formed in my throat. I bit my lip to stop the quivering.

Joy reached over and patted my hand, smiling. "Now don't you go bawling for me. Things are what they are. I can't live the kind of life they live. That's just the way it is."

"But it's so sad that you have to watch from a distance."

"My choice, honey. Not theirs. It would be more unfair of me to move in and out of their lives and embarrass them with their friends. I mean, imagine, having to tell your friends that your mother is the local homeless woman who picks cans out of the trash for pocket money. No, it's best this way."

I pulled a crumpled tissue from my pocket, wiped my eyes and then blew my nose. "I'd die without my family. I'm not judging you, but I couldn't survive without my husband and my kids."

"You'd survive, if you had to. You may not like it, but you'd survive."

"What made you walk away from your life?"

Joy laughed. "See, now that's what everyone asks. And everyone assumes that, because I live on the streets and carry everything I own in this cart, I have no life. I didn't walk away from my life. This is my life. I walked away from *that* life. Just couldn't do it all."

She stood and removed her stretched-out sweater. Beneath it, she wore a soft blue tee shirt with khaki slacks. I thought that, aside from hair that needed a decent cut, and skin roughened by the elements, she and I were not so very different. She had created a new life for herself, and I was doing the same thing, but in a different way.

Joy folded the sweater and set it atop her coat in the cart. She sat again and took a swallow of coffee. "You probably won't believe this, but I was the president of the PTA once. I baked cookies and made Halloween costumes and fed my kids chicken noodle soup when they had sore throats. I was super-mom. I accompanied my husband to cocktail parties and hosted dinners for his colleagues. Then, one day, I couldn't get out of bed. I couldn't lift myself up and do one more thing."

"Were you sick?"

"In a manner of speaking. I had a nervous breakdown and fell into a deep depression. I was locked up in a hospital for months, medicated, talked at, talked to and talked with by a string of doctors and therapists. When it was decided that I wouldn't hurt myself or anyone else, and they couldn't do anything more for me, I was released to go home and assigned an outpatient therapist." She tossed the empty coffee cup into the can and grinned at me. "I'd guess you've never been to a therapist."

I shook my head, unable to speak. I was completely captivated by Joy's story.

"I lived on the sofa in my bathrobe for over a month. I would lie there after Harold and the kids left and try to figure out what I could do to make the hurting stop. It was like a toothache that hurt all over. Then one day I went upstairs, took a shower and dressed. I threw a few items of clothing into a bag and walked away."

"Just like that? You walked out? Did you leave a note or say 'goodbye'?"

"I walked all the way into the city. I had about twenty dollars on me, and I went to McDonald's, got a Happy Meal," she said, smiling at the memory, "then I asked a cop if he could tell me where there was a shelter. I went there and slept that night, and I've been on the streets ever since."

The idea that she'd never said 'goodbye' to her children horrified me. "You left your kids wondering what happened to you?"

"I called two days later after I saw my picture on a TV screen in the window at Kendall's. I talked to Harold and then to the kids. I knew they'd be better off without me the way I was. The funny thing is, as soon as I closed that door behind me and started walking, it was like the sea parted and weight lifted from me. I can't do schedules and routines and responsibilities. I can do this," she said, waving her hand from herself to the cart. "This is simple."

"Don't you ever wish you could go back?"

"Oh, sure, I wish. I wish I could've been different, stronger. I wish I could live the life you read about in books where you grow old with a husband you've known forever, and you watch your kids grow up and give you grandchildren. But I don't dwell on those wishes too much, because I can't live like that."

"Joy, this is going to sound like a strange question, but I have to ask. When you were younger, what did you want to be when you grew up?"

"Let's see, when I was twelve, I wanted to be a ballerina, but that was only until I tripped during a dance recital and took out half the line of dancers. Ended that dream. At fifteen, I wanted to be a nurse, but I'm squeamish about blood and puke. When I was six, my grandfather read me a story about Howie the Hobo and his adventures. I decided I wanted to be a hobo. I guess I nailed that one, huh? Why do you ask?"

I looked up at the sunlight piercing through newly-budded trees. "I've been thinking about that a lot lately. I can't remember what I wanted to be; I can't remember having a dream of being anything."

"Did you ever want to be a cop?"

"A cop? No. Why?"

She grinned. "Because you sure have the interrogation skills."

I felt myself flush, and I smiled. "I'm sorry. I had no right to keep asking you such personal questions."

"It's okay. People are generally curious about us homeless folks. Everybody wants to know why. I don't mind. It's kind of nice to have someone to talk to about it."

I stood and tossed my empty coffee cup into the trashcan. "I'm going home and make lunch. You want to join me? It would just be the two of us, and it's only a few blocks from here."

Joy hesitated, then said, "Maybe another time."

"Sure. Anytime. Do you... need anything? Is there anything I can do for you?"

"You already have. You treat me like a human being."

Her response hit me dead in the center. "I like talking with you. I promise not to interrogate you next time."

59

"You got that right. Next time, I want to hear all about Hope."

"I'll see you again. Have a nice afternoon."

"You, too," she called after me.

As I slowly walked home, Joy's story resounded through my mind, and sadness made my heart ache.

It was my turn to cook. I made a special dinner and baked brownies. After dinner, the kids went to their rooms, and I sat watching TV with Anthony. I settled close to him on the sofa and snuggled against his shoulder. "You know I love you, right?"

He tilted his head and looked down at me. "Right. Did something happen today?"

"Nope. Just wanted to be sure you knew. That's all." I stood and stretched. "I'm going upstairs. I want to read for a while."

"I'll be up soon," he said, squeezing my hand.

I knocked on Gabby's door and, when she didn't answer, I opened it and peeked inside. She was sound asleep with the earphones to the MP3 stuck in her ears. She looked so much like the little girl I used to tuck in, and my heart skipped. I smoothed hair from her face and kissed her forehead. "I love you," I whispered.

Music wafted from Michael's room as I tapped on the door. He turned down the volume and called, "Come in." He was seated at his desk, working at the computer. He looked back over his shoulder and smiled.

"Hey, Mikey. Just came to say 'goodnight.' " I saw him wince. Just like Anthony, who hated to be called Tony, Michael disliked any abbreviation of his name. He hadn't been Mikey since he was four years old.

"Goodnight, Mom. Everything okay?"

"Why do people keep asking me that? I just want to let my family know I love them, and everybody thinks something must be wrong."

"Um ...sorry."

I bent and wrapped my arms around my son's broad shoulders, resting my chin in his mass of dark curls. "I love you, Michael."

"I love you, too, Mom."

I released my hold and ruffled his hair. "Sleep well."

I was already in bed when Anthony came into the room and stripped to his boxers, then settled in beside me. "What're you reading?"

I turned the book so that he could see the cover.

"Is it any good?"

"So far. I've only read one chapter."

" Goodnight," he said, turning onto his side, away from me.

"Goodnight." I continued to read.

Anthony lifted up and turned, dropping onto his back and staring at me. "Are you going to read the whole book tonight?"

"I'm sorry... the light's keeping you awake. I'll go downstairs and read." I stuck my finger in the book to hold my place and looked at him. *Uh-oh, the droopy-eyed leer.*

"That wasn't what I meant. I was wondering if Hope wanted to come out and play." He ran his fingers along my arm.

The book landed on the floor with a loud thud. *Hope is a slow reader and very easily distracted.*

Seven

I stopped by Fran's shop on my way to the salon. "Take a last look. The next time you see me I will be Hope DeMarco, blonde bombshell."

Fran raised an eyebrow. "Are you sure you want to do that?"

"Absolutely."

"What's next? Botox?"

I pouted my lips and looked into an antique mirror hanging on the wall. "There's an idea."

"You wouldn't."

"You're right. I'm not putting poison in my lips or anywhere else. Why don't you come with me and get a new hairdo, too. It'll be fun."

"Can't. I'm working alone today. Besides, I don't want a new hairdo. Why? Is my hair that bad?" she asked, joining me in front of the mirror.

"No. It would just be fun. You'd look great as a redhead," I said, looking at her mirror image.

She ran her hands through her brown hair flecked with gray. "You think so?"

A customer came into the shop, and Fran straightened her hair and asked how she could be of help. I waved to her as I exited and mouthed, 'I'll be back.'

The salon was in the next block. A woman was leaving as I reached for the door to go in. Inside, an older woman sat beneath a dryer, and another woman I'd seen there before was in the midst of a haircut.

"Hi, Jan. Have a seat. I'll be with you in a few," Grace said.

I sat and picked up a two-month-old issue of *People* magazine, tuning into the three-way conversation taking place among Grace, the woman in the chair, and the other woman who kept ducking her head out of the dryer and asking, "What'd you say?"

Grace has been my hairdresser for the past fifteen years. She runs a one-woman operation and provides snacks and cold drinks for her patrons. The shop is in the basement of her house just beyond the park. I like the homey atmosphere and the family feel of the place. I am always amazed at how much Grace knows about the lives of her customers and what she can remember from one visit to the next. She also gives the best haircuts and has the most reasonable prices.

I set the magazine down and picked up a book of hairstyles, flipping through it and thinking I might try a new style while I was at it.

Grace shouted over the blow dryer, continuing her conversation with the customer in the chair. When she finished, she accepted payment and said goodbye to the woman, then turned to me. "Let me check Mrs. Dombrowski, and I'll be right with you."

She determined that Mrs. Dombrowski needed a little more drying time and angled her curler-laden head back under the silver dome. "Okay, Jan. What can I do for you today?"

I plopped myself into the chair, looking at both of us in the mirror. "For starters, you can call me Hope."

She raised both eyebrows and stared at me.

"Long story. I'll tell you while you work. Now, I want to be blonde, like this," I said, pointing to a picture in the hairstyle book. "I don't want my hair cut too short because I've been pulling it back into a ponytail at times and I like that, but I think it needs some shaping up."

"Honey blonde it is… Hope. Come over to the sink and let's get started. I can't wait to hear this story."

While she lathered shampoo into my hair, I rested my neck on the lip of the sink, closed my eyes and told Grace the details of my resignation and my emerging new identity. It would, no doubt, make national news by nightfall.

"So this is part of a complete make-over?"

"I guess you could say that. I don't know how complete, but…"

"Leave it to me."

She mixed color and put it in my hair, then covered my head with a shower cap. I sat and chatted while she unrolled and brushed out Mrs. Dombrowski, to whom I'd introduced myself. The timer dinged, and Grace excused herself to rinse my hair. She wrapped my head in a towel and finished styling the older woman.

As Mrs. Dombrowski left the shop, she thanked Grace, then looked at me and said, "It was nice to meet you, Hope."

I smiled and nodded. "Nice to meet you, too."

Grace removed the towel and combed through my hair, snipping and shaping. She then put another shower cap on my head and used what looked like a crochet hook to pull strands of hair through the holes in the cap. She mixed foamy liquid in a bowl and brushed it onto the strands with a toothbrush. I laughed as I looked at myself in the mirror. I looked like the doll I'd had when I was seven. It was one that had hair and, as bits of hair were pulled loose and fell out, the remaining strands stood up and revealed tiny holes in the doll's head.

When Grace was satisfied that the application had enough time to take, she removed the cap and rinsed, then applied conditioner. She kept me turned away from the mirror while she worked my hair with a round brush and blew it dry. Finally, she returned the blow dryer to its holder and set the brush on the table.

Stepping back, she looked at me and smiled. "Wow. I've outdone myself this time. You look ten years younger and positively radiant." She spun the chair, and I faced the mirror.

My jaw dropped, and my eyes widened. "Oh, my. This is incredible. This is just what I wanted. Grace, you are an artist."

She stood behind the chair and pulled my hair back from my face. "When you want to wear it back, just pull the front and the sides down a little to frame your face, like this," she said, demonstrating.

"I love it. I really, really love it. Thank you."

"You're welcome. So, I take it this will be a surprise for the family?"

I dug into my purse to get my checkbook. "Yep... for the whole family. Carmela's birthday party is on Sunday. Everyone will be there."

"Do they all know about Hope?"

"Not yet. Anthony's convinced they'll want to have me committed. I think he's just afraid of what his mother will think."

"I'd be afraid of Angela, too."

I wrote out a check and included a healthy tip. "Angela's not so bad. She has a good heart. She's just set in her ways."

"Yeah, well, when she comes in here for a haircut, she tells me how she wants me to cut each and every strand of hair, just so. I have to bite my tongue not to tell her if she's so good at this, she should cut it herself. But, frankly, I need the business and if Angela got pissed off at me, I'd lose at least ten customers, between her family and her friends."

I grinned. "I promise not to tell her you did this, then. I'll see you in a few weeks for a touch-up. Have a nice day, Grace."

As I rushed through the park to get back to Fran's, I heard someone calling my name. "Hope, is that you?"

I turned to see Joy tossing fruit peelings to the squirrels.

"Hi. I thought I heard my name."

She stared at me. "Nice hair."

I touched my hair lightly. "Do you like it? I just had it done."

"It's a good color for you. Makes your eyes stand out more."

"Really? I think it'll take some getting used to. I'll probably wonder who that woman is in the mirror when I get up in the morning."

"It suits you."

"Thank you. I'm sorry I can't stay and chat. Want to meet for coffee here on Monday morning?"

"Uh, I… I may be here. I can't say for sure."

"Oh, well, if you are. I'll be here in the morning. See you."

I stopped in Starbucks to get a couple of lattes to take with me to Fran's. I thought of purchasing a coffee and taking it back to Joy, but I didn't want to be insulting with my charity.

Ricki stood behind the counter taking drink orders. A baby sat parked in a stroller off to the far side of the counter, away from the machinery. She looked to be about six months old and had a head full of golden ringlets and piercing blue eyes."

Just as I stepped up to place my order, the baby broke into a loud wail. Ricki rushed over and shoved a pacifier into the baby's mouth, then returned to the counter. "Sorry. What can I get you?"

"I'll have two grande, non-fat, decaf vanilla lattes. She's beautiful," I added, nodding to the baby. "Is she yours?"

"Yeah. My mom usually takes care of her while I work, but she has an appointment today, so I had to bring the baby in for a couple of hours. She's usually quiet."

While I waited for the drinks, I walked over and stooped before the stroller. "Hi, sweetie. Aren't you pretty? What's her name?" I called to Ricki.

"Hannah."

I stroked her tiny hand with my finger. "Hi, Hannah. That's a beautiful name."

Her eyes fixed on mine and held there, her mouth continuing to work the pacifier.

"Here you go," Ricki called out, placing the two lattes on the counter.

"Thanks," I said, feeling the catch in my back as I straightened… a reminder that I need to exercise a little more often.

Ricki stared for a moment, then asked, "Is your hair different?"

"Yes. I just had it colored and highlighted. Do you like it?"

"I do. I used to have highlights put in my hair. But, now, with Hannah, I can't afford those little extras. It'll have to wait. Well, have a nice day."

"Thanks. You, too. And you have a nice day, Hannah," I said, waving to the baby.

When I walked into Fran's shop, she turned and barely glanced at me, asking, "Can I help… oh, it's you! Oh, my goodness!"

I set our drinks on the display case. "What do you think?"

"I think I need to make an appointment to see Grace. Jan… I'm sorry …Hope, that is fantastic. I think all this time you've been a blonde trapped in a brunette's body."

"Well, I don't know about that. I'm not blonde all over. Here, I brought you a latte."

"Thanks. Let's go in the back and sit. Did you tell Anthony you were doing this?"

I followed behind her and dropped my purse onto the floor next to a chair. "Nope. It's going to be a surprise."

"You can say that again. I hope he likes it."

"It'll be his problem if he doesn't. I like it, and that's all that matters. Fran, I am loving my life right now. I can be whoever I want to be. I feel so much lighter. It's not just hair color or not having a job. It's more than that."

Fran nodded. "I know what you're saying. You seem happier these days. By the way, I like the jeans."

"Thanks. I went shopping on Saturday. Do you know how many different styles of jeans they make? It took me an hour to wade through them to find the ones I liked. Things sure have changed."

Fran laughed as I told her about the classes I'd held for Anthony and the kids. "I would've paid to see it," she said, wiping tears of laughter from her eyes.

"Hey, I could've been onto something there, a whole new reality TV show: *Changing the DeMarcos*."

"Now that would be entertainment at its best."

I finished my drink and picked up my purse. "I'd better be going. I offered to pick Gabby up from school because it's her night to cook." I stood and rolled my eyes. "Pray for me."

I walked the two blocks to our house and ran inside to use the bathroom before getting my car keys. My own image in the mirror had me mesmerized. I ran my fingers though my blonde tresses and looked at how my eyes sparkled. Smiling, I said, "Hi there, Hope."

School buses idled along the curb in front of the high school. I eased into the line of cars in the circular drive.

Moments later, the doors opened and a river of students gushed through. I saw Gabby standing and talking with Megan. She spied the car, waved and headed my way.

Gabby opened the car door and bent to toss her backpack into the back seat. As she slid onto the seat, her eyes fixed on my head. "Mom? What'd you do to your hair?"

"Color and highlights. Do you like it?"

"It's, uh… um …different."

"Well, I like it."

"Daddy's gonna burst an aneurysm when he sees you."

I eased from the line and pulled out of the drive. "Is that a good thing or a bad thing?"

"It could go either way. Just make sure I'm there when he sees you."

"What's the big deal? It's hair."

Out of the corner of my eye I could see her head shake. "Some day I'm gonna come home, and I'm not gonna know you at all, Mom ...Hope."

"You have to be open to change, Gabby. I've been meaning to ask you something. What do you want to be?"

"What? You mean, like, when I grow up, which I already am?"

"What do you want to do with your life?"

"Do I have to decide right now?"

I laughed. "No. I know you'll change your mind a few times. I'm just wondering what you're thinking about for your future."

"I'm going to New York after high school and studying drama. I was thinking of Julliard. And I could, maybe, get bit parts on Broadway while I'm studying. And if that doesn't work out, I thought about Carnegie Mellon University. They have a great drama department, too." Her eyes flashed and her hands emphasized her speech, something she'd inherited from her father.

"That's great, Gabby," I said, my voice thick.

"Mom, are you crying?"

I swallowed and continued to look straight ahead. "No, I'm… well, maybe a little. I'm happy for you, honey. I love your enthusiasm for life. If you want to be an actress, I think you'll be a great one."

"You always tell me I'm a *drama queen*. I might as well make the best of what I've got going for me."

I laughed and reached for her hand. "You have a lot going for you. Don't you ever doubt that. Now, what're you cooking for dinner tonight?"

"I'm making spaghetti and meatballs, with garlic bread and salad."

"Uh-huh. And I suppose this would include Grandma Angela's sauce and her meatballs?" I asked, turning into our driveway.

"Sure, but you use her sauce all the time, so that's fair. Right?"

"I didn't say it was unfair. I was just asking."

She grabbed her backpack and hurried to the door. "I want to call Megan before I start cooking."

I went through the house and opened the front door, pulling envelopes from the mailbox. Gabby's certainty about her future and her excitement touched a tender spot. *How did I miss that?* I wondered. *How did I bypass having a dream?*

Gabby bounded down the steps, the phone to her ear, chatting rapidly. I heard reference to 'mom,' 'blonde' and 'gasket.' I wove it into a probable sentence, 'My mom died her hair blonde and my dad's going to blow a gasket.' She had a lot to learn about men. Anthony might 'burst an aneurysm' and 'blow a gasket,' but it would be in an entirely different context than my daughter imagined... and long after she and her brother were asleep.

Soon the clang of pots and pans rang out from the kitchen. I waited a respectable amount of time before casually wandering in there to get a glass of water... and to snoop and see what was going on. Surprisingly, she seemed to have everything under control. The garlic bread was wrapped in foil and ready to go into the oven. The sauce and meatballs simmered at a low temperature on one burner, and the pasta pot filled with water was set on high on another burner. Gabby had the phone tucked between her ear and shoulder and continued her conversation while she washed lettuce for the salad.

I was duly impressed and had the sudden urge to work with her, to be my daughter's friend. I motioned to her, and she asked Megan to hold for a minute.

"Want me to help with the salad?" I asked.

"Isn't that against the rules?"

"Not if I volunteer," I said, taking the lettuce from her hands. "I'd like to help you with dinner."

"Megan, I've gotta go. I'll call you back later." She snapped the cell phone shut and set it on the counter. "Mom, I was doing fine here. What am I doing wrong?"

"You're not doing anything wrong. I just want to spend some time with you, that's all."

She looked at me warily, narrowing her eyes. "O-kay. Then I guess I'll set the table until the water comes to a boil."

We didn't talk about anything. We were just two women in the kitchen preparing a meal together. Gabby and I had so few moments like this, moments that weren't edged with conflict and differences. Okay, so maybe I was trying harder to understand her because I'd had to work harder to understand myself these days.

Michael walked in the back door and straight to the refrigerator, grabbed a can of soda and carried it upstairs, calling 'hello' on his way through.

"I can't believe he didn't even comment on your hair, Mom. It's like he didn't even see you."

I smiled. "Gabby, let me give you a lesson on life. Men are very single-minded creatures. Your brother came in the door with one thought on his mind... to get a soda from the fridge."

"Huh, that explains a lot."

"It does?" I asked, surprised by my own wisdom.

"There's this guy at school, and he always acts like he doesn't even see me when I'm, like, right in front of his face. Maybe he's just thinking of something else, and it doesn't have anything to do with me, the fact that he ignores me."

"Is this a boy you wished would notice you?"

"Well, yeah. He's so cute, and he's on the basketball team, so he's really tall."

I set down the knife I'd been using to cut tomatoes and turned to face her. "Gabby, how come we never talked like this?"

"Because you were my mom, and that makes it kind of, like, strange."

"I'm still your mom," I said with a laugh.

"No, you're not. Now you're Hope, and she's different."

I resumed cutting up vegetables for the salad. "Different how?"

"You're, like, easier to talk to, and more fun. You laugh a whole lot more than you used to."

"Hunh."

Anthony came in the back door, started into the kitchen, then stopped dead in his tracks.

"Hi, honey. How was your day?" I asked.

He stared, his jaw slack.

72

"What's the matter, Dad?" Gabby asked.

"Huh? Uh…" He looked from Gabby back to me. "Smells good in here. Is that Grandma Angela's sauce?"

Gabby laughed and looked at me. "You were right, Mom. One thing on his mind."

"What's that supposed to mean?" Anthony asked Gabby. Then looking back at me, he said, "Your hair's blonde."

"I know. I paid Grace to make it that color."

"It's …nice."

"Thanks. I'm glad you like it." I smiled at him. There it was, the goofy grin. "I wonder how the family will like it when they see it on Sunday?" There it went, the goofy grin.

"Oh boy. They're gonna think I'm cheating on my wife with Hope, the blonde bimbo."

"Hey! Hope is not a bimbo. I'll have you know she is a very respectable and intelligent woman." Then I smiled and asked, "Do I really pass as a blonde bimbo?"

"You don't have to look so hopeful about that," Anthony said. "No pun intended."

I followed Anthony into the living room. "You hate my hair."

He pulled me to him, looking down into my eyes. My head came up to his chest, and his muscular arms completely encircled me. "Trust me," he said, his eyes twinkling. "I don't hate your hair. I'm starting to enjoy this game a little."

Poor choice of words. I wriggled free of his hold. "Game? You think this is a game?"

He heaved a sigh. "Oh, brother. Here we go."

My chin quivered, mostly because of disappointment. I thought Anthony had gotten on board and finally understood what I was trying to do.

"Oh, jeez. Don't cry. Please don't cry."

I played what I'd come to know as the Angela DeMarco trump card. I funneled all of the hurt and disappointment I felt into my eyes and looked at him, then said softly, "I'm sorry, Anthony. I guess I expected more from you."

His pressed his lips together tightly, and his face reddened. "I didn't mean that the way it sounded."

"Yes, you did. This is all just a game to you. That's probably my fault. I've allowed you to tease and joke about Hope, but no more. That's it."

"Okay."

"And I expect you to stand up for me with your family."

"Okay."

"Even with your mother."

This, for some reason, struck him mute.

"Anthony, did you hear me?"

"Can I just kill myself now and get it over with?"

"No. If I have to face your family, you have to face them with me."

Gabby called from the kitchen, "Dinner's ready… I think."

I locked my eyes with Anthony's for a moment to emphasize my point, then went to the stairs to call Michael for dinner.

When my son came into the kitchen, he looked at my hair and smiled. "Wow, Mom, your hair looks great. Sorry I didn't notice sooner. It's a very nice color for you."

Did I say how much I love my son?

Eight

Dinner at my mother-in-law's house on any given Sunday was a major production. Great-grandma Carmela's eightieth birthday meant the entire family would be there, including a few relatives who'd arrived the day before from Italy.

"Gabriella, get off the phone and get down here. We have to get going," Anthony called to Gabby. "What'd we get for Grandma?" he asked me.

"I got her a sweater. I don't know what you bought."

"You always get the gifts from both of us. Oh, I see. This is about Hope."

"It has nothing to do with Hope. This is about me not assuming responsibility for everyone else."

He went back to the stairs. "Gabriella, get a move on. I have to make a stop on the way."

I handed him the card I'd gotten. "Okay, you can go in with me on this one. Here, sign the card."

He smiled, looking as though he thought he'd won.

"You owe me twenty dollars," I said tucking the card he'd signed back into the envelope.

Gabby clomped down the stairs and sulked her way through the kitchen. We followed behind and trooped to the car.

When we arrived at Angela's, the house was bursting at the seams. Several men, and one woman I'd never met, were smoking cigars and drinking wine on the porch.

Anthony's brother, Dante, opened the door just as I reached for the doorknob. "Hey, check it out. Janet's gone blonde."

"Thanks, Dante, for the announcement."

"Anthony, you sleepin' with a blonde these days?"

Anthony stepped up beside me, a weak smile on his face. "Knock it off, Dante."

"Hey, Jan. This'll explain all those blonde moments you have."

Anthony took one step closer to his brother. "Dante, I said knock it off. Okay?"

I turned to Dante. "If that's my excuse, what's yours?" I asked, moving my eyes from his and up to his blue-black, wavy hair.

"Ouch," he said, still teasing.

Anthony put a hand on my shoulder and directed me into the hallway. We walked into the living room where Grandma Carmela was seated, accepting birthday wishes. I made my way over to her and placed our gift on top of the stack beside her chair.

"Happy Birthday, Carmela." I leaned and kissed her cheek.

"Janet, look at you. You're a blonde."

"Yes. Do you like it?"

"I love it. It's very becoming. I been thinking maybe I'd have Grace do something with my hair. What do you think, maybe some of that blue tint?"

I smiled. "I think you'd look great with blue tint. Carmela, there's something I want to tell you."

"You and Anthony gonna have a baby?" she asked, her eyes gleaming.

"No. Oh, no. I'm making a few changes, and I've decided to change my name. I want to be called Hope now. What do you think?"

"That's a nice name. It's so full of... hope. Okay, Hope. Why you want to be called Hope?"

In between well-wishers and sticky kisses from great-great-grandchildren, Carmela listened to my story about becoming Hope.

Angela came in to announce that dinner was ready. She scanned the room, then brought her eyes back to me. Her eyes widened, and she opened her mouth, but, for once, nothing came out. She stared at me as if I'd turned into Sigourney Weaver with an alien sticking out of my chest.

I stood and walked to her. "Hi, Angela. This is a lovely party," I said, leaning in to kiss her cheek.

Anthony crossed the room in five quick steps. "Hey, Mom. Doesn't Hope's hair look great?"

She looked at me and then back to Anthony. "Hope? Who is Hope? What's going on?"

I took her arm and turned her in the direction of the kitchen. "Come on. I'll explain everything."

I heard my husband groan. "Oh, boy."

~ * ~

The family gathered around the dining table, with the children seated at card tables in the living room and the den. I took my place beside Anthony. Angela called upon her brother-in-law to say grace.

We sat, and I looked down the long table to where Teddy and his wife, Stella, were seated. He looked at me hard, then whispered to Stella, who looked at me as well. One by one, heads turned in my direction. Heat crept up my neck, and my ears burned.

Grandma Carmela came to my rescue. She clinked her knife against her water glass and commanded everyone's attention. "I want to thank you all, my family, for coming to celebrate my birthday. Some day, when I'm an old lady, I won't be able to enjoy a party like this, so I'm glad you all came today. I'm happy my brother, Silvio, and his wife, Lena, could be here from Italy."

She raised her wineglass, and everyone followed suit, offering a toast to Silvio and Lena. Then Carmela continued. "I'm the oldest person in this family. You know what that means. I'm like… the godfather, only the god*mother*. I was talking with my grandson Anthony's wife, Janet, and she told me she's making some changes. I think change is good. It keeps us young. Janet asked me to call her Hope now, and I will respect her wishes. I think you will, too."

Dante, who was seated beside Grandma Carmela, cleared his throat. Carmela smacked the back of his head without missing a beat, then looked at me and smiled. "Now, I'm eighty years old. I've lived all these years because I always saw something new in life. So, I think I'm gonna change my name, too. From now on, I wanna be called Sofialoren. Just like that… all one word."

Angela's groan could be heard all the way down the table. She made the sign of the cross and mumbled something about the mother of God.

Carmela proposed another toast, "To me, Sofialoren, and to Hope. Two people in this family who know how to live."

I bit my lip, torn between laughter and tears. Carmela gazed around the table and, one by one, each person raised their glass.

Dante lifted his glass and said loudly, "Here's to Sofialoren and Hope." His tone was mocking.

Carmela flicked him again on the back of the head.

"Ouch. What'd you do that for?"

"Don't be disrespectful, Dante. Don't make your grandmother ashamed."

He reddened and lowered his head. "Sorry."

I'd always liked Grandma Carmela. When Carmela Assunto came to the United States at the age of eleven, she had only three changes of clothing and was the youngest of seven children. She went to work at fifteen and never finished high school. When she was seventeen, she married the son of a produce market owner and gave birth to three children. Carmela moved in after Angela's husband died, telling Angela she couldn't live alone any longer. I knew it was because Carmela worried about her daughter, who had been consumed with grief over her husband's death.

Carmela was the life of every party at the DeMarco house. She would become animated, telling stories about the old country, teasing the children, whipping her grown grandsons into line… all of it with a radiant smile. Carmela just loved life. She went to church every Sunday morning and to bingo every Friday night. She played cards with friends most Saturday afternoons. She'd weathered her share of grief and, yet, faced life with enthusiasm.

After dinner, guests returned to the living room where Carmela assumed her throne as queen of the party once again, and the younger children took turns handing her gifts to open. I was distracted by Angela's cold stare. Anthony was right… his family thought I'd lost my mind.

I felt a hand on my arm and turned to see Teddy. "You look good a blonde, Hope," he said, emphasizing the name.

"Thanks, Teddy. How's the new girl working out?"

"She's okay. She's not you, though. She won't make the coffee. She doesn't run errands. She refuses to clean up anything. And she keeps the bathroom locked. We have to get a key from her, and she checks it when we leave. She won't tell a little fib now and then. 'It's not in my job description,' " he said in a mocking tone.

I grinned, remembering the conversation I'd had with Penny, and the suggestions I'd offered when she called with a few questions. "Sounds like you've met your match, Teddy. I wish I'd thought of putting a lock on the bathroom."

"Yeah, well. She can be replaced if she don't work out."

"Uh-huh."

When I went to say 'goodnight' to Carmela, she grasped my arm and pulled me close. "You come by one day, and we'll go to lunch. I want to talk to you some more. Maybe you'll take me to Grace's to get my hair done?"

"I will, Car…" She looked at me with amusement, and I corrected. "I'll see you, Sofialoren."

"Goodnight, and thank you for the beautiful sweater, Hope."

I moved away to let Michael and Gabby say goodnight.

When Anthony leaned over to kiss his grandmother, she grabbed his face in both her hands and squeezed his cheeks. "You're my favorite grandson, Anthony. Now, you be a good husband, and you be nice to Hope."

"Okay, Grandma," he said through puckered lips.

She released him and patted his face. "You're a nice man, Anthony. You remind me of your grandfather."

As we walked to the door, various family members called out, "Goodnight, Anthony, Janet… uh, Hope."

Once we were in the car, I smiled at Anthony and the kids. "There, now that wasn't so bad, was it?"

Anthony grimaced and looked sideways at me, mumbling. "See what you started. Now I have to call my grandmother Sofialoren. Maybe I'll change my name to Antonio Banderas."

"Honey, he's Spanish."

"Hmmph."

"Won't work, Dad," Gabby piped in from the back seat. "You know Mexican food doesn't agree with you."

Anthony raised his eyes from the road to the rear view mirror, flashing a look of warning to her.

Michael asked, "Did Great-grandma Carmela really look like Sophia Loren when she was young?"

"How do you know who Sofia Loren is?" I asked.

"I saw an old movie. Man, she was hot."

Anthony glanced at me and grinned... like father, like son.

~ * ~

I wakened to a spring thunderstorm. I wondered if Joy would be looking for me at the park. Surely she wouldn't leave the shelter and hop a bus to have coffee in the rain. It had been a lot of years since I had nothing to do with my day. I sorted my laundry, all the while resisting the magnetic pull towards Anthony's clothes hamper. *It wouldn't kill you to do his laundry, you know.* This thought was followed by, *No, it wouldn't, but it might kill Hope.*

I did go through each of the bathrooms and collect towels. Based upon the odor and the stiff feel of his bath towel, Michael had obviously found a solution to weekly laundry ...do it every two or three weeks.

The rain eased some in the afternoon, and I headed for the mall. I had one goal in mind... to get myself a computer and establish an email account. The money I'd earned over the years had been placed into two accounts: a college fund for the kids and a little for my use. I hadn't spent a whole lot on myself. It mostly went for haircuts, clothing, a spa visit once or twice a year.

I knew a bit about computers from having used one at work. The problem was, I didn't know about many of the features the newer computers included. I stopped at Computer World, where a salesman not much older than Michael showed me rows of computers, monitors and printers, explaining the difference between the systems. I decided a laptop would better serve me, as if I was going to go somewhere and type. Besides, I liked the sleek, compact nature of a notebook computer.

I walked out an hour later with an HP notebook that, I was told, had wi-fi. I'd have Michael figure it all out and explain it to me in language I could understand. After locking the equipment in the trunk, I parked and went into the mall. On a Monday afternoon, the place was nearly deserted.

My thoughts turned back to Joy as I leisurely browsed and sipped a latte. I couldn't help myself. I wanted to rescue Joy from the life she'd chosen because I thought it was sad. *Is that what Hope is doing for Janet?* I shuddered.

The twenty-percent off signs in the book store window drew my attention. I went inside and roamed the aisles, when a book title caught my eye: *So You're Forty: Now What?* I picked up the book and skimmed the index. I carried the book to a chair in the corner and read the first chapter. Apparently, it's not unusual for women my age to lose their minds and change their lives. I purchased the book and drove home, humming along with a tune I didn't really know that was playing on the radio.

We had established an office of sorts in the den, where Anthony occasionally worked and where I sat to pay bills. I carried the computer and printer to the den, unpacked the boxes and set the equipment on the desktop. I followed the directions for hooking it all up and installing the printer to the notebook.

I was sitting there, smiling at the *Welcome* screen when Michael and Gabby returned home from school.

"Michael, will you come into the den, please?" I called out.

"Okay, just a minute."

He appeared a moment later with an apple in one hand and a glass of milk in the other. "Hey, Mom. What's this?"

"It's my new computer. I need your help to set up an email account."

I moved from the chair, and he dropped into it. "Wow, this is nice. It's wireless, too. We should be able to get you right onto the system with me and Gabby."

He typed away, then asked, "What name do you want on your email account?"

"Name?"

"Yeah, like mine is 'emdeem17'."

"What's that stand for?"

"MDM—Michael DeMarco, 17."

"Oh. What's Gabby's?"

"dramaqueen2. Apparently she's not the first," he said, grinning.

"I need to think about this. I want it to be something special or unique, something that has meaning for me."

"While you think about it, I'm going to the bathroom. I'll be back."

I stared at the computer screen with the little blank box requesting my unique identity. When Michael returned, I told him what to type—hope4janet.

"Hey, that's a good one." He set up the account and had me write down my email address and my password to sign on, then showed me how to do that. "You're all set."

"Thanks, Michael. Are you on for dinner tonight?"

"Yeah. We're having a cookout."

"Well, if you need any help, let me know. I owe you one."

He towered over me and dropped an arm across my shoulders. "Nah, thanks. I can handle it. You don't owe me anything."

I encircled his thin midriff, feeling his ribs against my fingertips, and I hugged him. "You're a wonderful son. You know that?"

"So you tell me. I'm gonna pick up Lori and bring her over for dinner. Is that okay?"

"Of course. I like Lori. She's a nice girl."

He stopped at the doorway and smiled, color rising in his cheeks. "Yeah, I know. She reminds me of you."

I played with the computer until supper time. I could hardly wait until the next meeting of the book club to give Gary my email address. I wished I had someone to email so I could see how it worked. Then I remembered Gabby and Michael's addresses. I clicked on compose and typed in dramaqueen2. In the subject line I wrote 'a note from mom,' then composed a message to Gabby. When I finished, I moved the cursor and clicked on send.

A minute later, Gabby flew down the stairs and into the den. "Mom, how'd you do that? Hey, we got a laptop!"

"Correction. *I* have a laptop. So I guess my email went through."

"Cute, Mom."

We were exploring the features of the computer when Anthony appeared in the doorway. "Dinner's ready, you two."

Gabby left the den, and Anthony came to look over my shoulder at the computer. "This is new."

"Got it today. My book club asked for an email address, and I was the only person who didn't have one."

"So you bought a computer?"

"Yes. I like it. It's cute, don't you think?"

"Cute?" He shook his head. "You know, you could've set up an account and used one of the kid's computers."

"I know. I wanted one just for myself. If you're really nice, I might let you use it, too."

"Honey, I sit in front of one of those all day long. It's the last thing I want to do when I come home. Come on. Michael slaved over a hot grill for the last twenty minutes. Let's eat."

We gathered around the table, and I welcomed Lori, Michael's girlfriend this year.

"Hi, Mrs. DeMarco. Thanks for having me for dinner."

"You're welcome any time. And you can call me Hope."

"Oh." She glanced at Michael. "I thought you told me your mom's name was Janet," she said, nudging his rib.

"It was. Now it's Hope. Want some salad?" I passed the bowl.

Across from me, Anthony shook his head as he speared a hamburger from the platter.

Nine

On Wednesday morning, I rang Angela's doorbell, then let myself in. "Hello. It's Hope."

"I'm in the kitchen," Angela called.

I followed the aroma of sauce simmering on the stove. "Mmm. It smells good in here. How are you, Angela?" I asked, giving her a hug.

"I'm good, and you?" she responded, her eyes moving from my face to my hair.

"I'm great. Did Carmela, uh, Sofialoren tell you I'm taking her out this afternoon?"

She glared at me, then said, "My mother is upstairs getting dressed. Sit down. You want a cup of coffee?"

"No, thanks." I sat at the table, watching her mix and roll meatballs and place them on a plate. "Angela, the birthday party was wonderful. You worked really hard to make everything nice."

"Ah, what work? It was just dinner for family."

"A lot of family and a fantastic dinner. I, um, I hope I didn't disrupt things too much. I realized I should've come by before the party and told you about …the changes."

She continued to roll the ground beef in her hands as she spoke. "Is everything okay with you and Anthony? Are you unhappy?"

"No, oh, God, no. I love Anthony and our kids. I'm not unhappy. I'm just... I don't know. I'm not ...fulfilled."

She dropped the meatball she was rolling back into the pan, wiped her hands on a towel and sat across from me. "What does that mean? Not fulfilled? That's the same as unhappy. You've got a good family and a nice home. I know working for Teodoro wasn't the best thing. It's good you quit."

I shifted nervously and folded my hands together, mostly to control the tremors. "Angela, you and I are very different. Maybe if I were more like you, I'd be content, but... "

Just then Carmela walked into the kitchen, having heard the last of our conversation. "If you were more like Angela, you'd be miserable."

Angela's head jerked around, and she looked stunned. "Mama, how can you say that?"

Carmela sat at the table. "It's true. Hope wouldn't be happy staying at home all day, cooking, cleaning things you cleaned just yesterday, making pans of food that you give to everybody in the family. She wouldn't be any happier than you are. She'd just be busy."

"I'm happy," Angela said, her voice rising an octave.

Carmela made a 'tsk' sound and waved her hand in front of her face. "You're not happy. You're just... stuck. You don't have a sense of humor, and you never have any fun. You just work, work, work. You should come with us today, get a new hairstyle, have a few laughs." She grinned at me, her eyes sparkling. "I always laugh when I'm with this one," she said, pointing to me. "You could learn something," she said to Angela.

I slid my chair back from the table. "I think we should be going. Grace will be waiting for you." I needed to stop this before it got really ugly. I could see Angela building up steam.

Angela resumed making meatballs, now rolling the beef between her fingers with a vengeance and muttering in Italian.

I didn't have a clue what she was talking about, but Carmela looked at her sternly and said, "You don't talk like that. Not in my presence." Then she turned to me and said, "Come on, Hope."

When we got into the car, Carmela laughed. "Did you see the look on her face? She always looks like somebody peed in her oatmeal."

I pressed my lips tightly to suppress a laugh. "I don't think it's good to tease Angela, do you? She's a good woman, and she's worked hard to care for her family."

"Yes. And she needs to care for herself now. She wasn't a very happy child. At one time, I thought it was my fault. Now I know; she chooses to be unhappy. You may not have noticed, but Angela is very critical."

Oh, I'd noticed. "She just has her way of doing things," I said.

"Well, I can't help her. She walks around like a black ghost in those clothes, picking about everything other people do wrong, like she's a saint. My other children were happy, but they all died young, may they rest in peace," she said, making a sign of the cross. "Maybe Angela knows something we don't. But me, I'd rather die right now with a smile on my face."

"I'd rather you didn't. Angela would blame me, for sure. Put your seatbelt on, please."

She pulled the seatbelt across her petite frame and snapped it into the lock. "You know something? You're good for this family. I worried when you were working for Teddy. He's a greasy little sneak, that nephew of mine. But I knew you could handle him, if you had to."

"Teddy's...um...," I searched for a kind word. "Okay, you're right, he's a sneak. Carm... Sofialoren?"

From the corner of my eye, I could see the broad smile that creased her face. "Yes, Hope."

"When you were a little girl or a teenager, do you remember what you wanted to be when you grew up?"

"I sure do. When I was a very little girl in Italy, I wanted to be a nun. Oh, I loved the nuns. I followed them around our little town and tried to talk to them. They were hard to talk to. Just nodded a lot. They didn't seem to be so happy or to like people very much, so I gave up on that."

"What about after you came to America?"

"I wanted to be a singer. I would go around our house all the time, singing as loud as I could. Finally, one day my mama took me aside and asked me not to sing so loud anymore. I guess I wasn't very good at it, and the neighbors complained. We lived in a tiny apartment in New York back then. The walls were like paper. Boy, the things I could hear! You know what I mean? I got a good education early."

"When did you meet your husband?"

"Ah. My father introduced us when I was sixteen and Dominic was twenty. He was the son of a friend of my father's and had just come from Italy. We got married a year later. He was some guy, my Dominic."

I was moved by the wistfulness in her voice as she remembered.

Carmela continued. "I worked in my father's restaurant. It was a small place, not too far from Broadway. People would come in there after the theater for my papa's spaghetti and meatballs. I used to stare at the ladies all dressed up in long gowns and jewelry that glittered in the candlelight. I wanted to be one of those ladies."

"What happened?"

She sighed. "I married Dominic. One time I told him about my dream. You know what he did? He bought me one of those long dresses, and he set our table with candles and put music on the record player and gave me a necklace and earrings to wear. He made my dream come true, for one night."

I blinked back tears and glanced at her. Her eyes glimmered, and a faint smile tugged at her mouth.

"That's a beautiful story," I said.

"Yeah, well. That was before he got a girlfriend and then up and died on me. It just goes to show, nobody else can make your dreams come true. You gotta do that yourself. Oh, look, we're here."

I gulped back a response and eased the car into a space along the curb in front of Grace's salon.

I took Carmela's arm as we walked to the shop, then held the door open for her to enter.

"Carmela, it's good to see you," Grace said.

"Good to see you, too. Oh, and would you call me Sofialoren?"

Grace's eyebrows raised and she looked at me. "This sounds like your doing, Hope."

"Hey, it was all her idea."

"Yeah," Carmela said. "When I was younger, everyone said I looked like Sofia Loren. When this one," she motioned toward me, "told me she was changing her name, it sounded like a good idea. I'd like to be Sofialoren for a while."

"Okay, Sofialoren. Have a seat, and tell me what you want done with your hair today."

Carmela sat in the chair and looked in the mirror. "I want some color. What do you suggest?" she asked, fingering her white curls.

Grace ran her hands through Carmela's hair. "I'd suggest a tint, just something to even out your color."

"I was thinking something blue or purple, maybe. Something to make me stand out. If I was younger, I'd have you die it dark brown, just like the other Sofia Loren. But I think that would be too much, don't you?"

Grace laughed and looked at me. "That would definitely be too much. How about a rinse with a little silver highlight?"

Carmela thought for a moment, then said, "How about a rinse with purple highlights. I know you have those. I see old ladies at the senior center with purple hair all the time. I kind of like it. It reminds me of that poem. You know the one about being an old woman wearing purple."

Grace looked at me, and I shrugged. Grace led Carmela to the sink to wash her hair and begin the color rinse process.

When Grace had finished, Carmela's satisfied smiled radiated across her face as she looked into the mirror. "Now, that's a good color for me."

"Are you sure that's not too …purple?" Grace asked.

"It's perfect. A real eye-catcher. Thanks, Grace."

Carmela slid from the chair and steadied herself, then asked me, "What's next? I'm having fun."

I rolled my eyes at Grace. "Why do I think I'm gonna pay for this? Come on, Sofialoren. Let's get some lunch."

With my arm linked through hers, I suggested we go to the café across from the park for lunch. "It's a nice day for a short walk, don't you think?"

"Yeah. I can show off my new hair. Do you like it? You didn't say much."

"I love it. It's very becoming and very… eye-catching."

As we made our way through the park, Carmela said, "You know, I admire you. You don't settle for things. You're smart and funny and a good person."

"Thank you for saying that."

"What are you gonna do now that you don't work any more?" she asked.

"I hadn't thought about it. I joined a book club, and I bought a computer. That's as far as I've gotten."

"I should get a computer," she said. "I could, what's it called, surf the net. Yeah, I could surf the net. It could open up a whole new world. They have classes at the senior center. Will you take me to buy a computer?" she asked eagerly. "I have the money."

"Maybe we should save that for another day," I said, hoping she'd forget about it. Angela was already going to kill me.

I kept my eyes open for Joy as we crossed the park, but there was no sign of her. The café was not yet crowded, and we took a booth along the front window. Carmela wanted to be seated where passersby could see her new hair.

We enjoyed soup and sandwiches, and Carmela waved to few senior citizens who'd come in for the special. Each one had commented on her hair, and she'd beamed radiantly. I thought, with her mass of curls, it looked a little like a bunch of grapes atop her head—not quite as dark, but close. Of course, I didn't tell her. Who was I to judge?

As we walked back to the park, Carmela said, "I can't wait to go to the senior center tomorrow and show off my hair and tell them my new name."

Oh, good Lord, they'll think she's gone senile, and it'll be my fault.

"This is a nice little park," she commented.

"Yes, it is. I've been coming here a few days a week in the morning to walk. I get coffee back there at Starbucks, and I sometimes talk to a friend I met here. I thought she'd be here today and I could introduce you, but I don't see her."

"I'd like to come to the park sometime. Do you think I could come with you? That'd be nice, get me out of the house for a while."

I stifled a laugh. Carmela was out of the house more than she was in. Angela finally put a calendar on the refrigerator and asked her mother to mark down where she was going and the date and time, just so she could keep track of her. At eighty, Carmela had a more active social life than any of us.

"Sure, you can come. I'll call you the next time I'm coming to the park, and I'll pick you up."

"Thanks. I like being with you, and I can use the exercise. I'm not getting any younger. I need to keep these old bones moving. Now, if I could get a driver's license, I could come to your house myself."

All I could think was that, if her old bones moved much more, Angela was going to have to put computer chip in her mother's ear to track her down. And as for driving… God help us all.

Angela was standing inside the door and looking out when I returned Carmela home.

"You want to come in?" Carmela asked.

I looked at Angela in the door frame, then at Carmela's purple hair. "No, I don't think so. You go ahead."

She stepped out of the car and grinned back at me. "Chicken."

"You got that right. I enjoyed our day, Sofialoren. I'll call you later in the week to go to the park with me."

"Thanks, Hope. You're a good girl. I hope my grandson appreciates you."

"He does, most of the time. The rest of the time, he's just confused. Bye, now." I waited until she made the top step of the porch, then pulled away from the curb. I could've sworn I heard Angela cursing in Italian, but it was probably my imagination. Probably.

I checked the calendar when I got home and saw that it was Anthony's turn to cook. I got my book from my night stand and went to the den, firing up my laptop. The book club was scheduled to meet on Sunday afternoon, and I wanted to finish the novel so I'd be prepared to discuss it. First, I signed online and looked up a few websites of interest... Amazon books, eBay. I had a few hours before anyone would be home, so I poured a glass of wine, put a CD of classical music into the computer and settled back in the chair to read. *Hope is a woman of culture and varied interests.*

The kids came in the back door, stopped briefly to say 'hi,' then went to their rooms. It was nearing time for dinner, and still no Anthony. I set the table and paced from the front door to the back, worrying that something had happened. At six-thirty, he pulled into the drive. I watched from the kitchen window as he rounded the vehicle and opened the passenger's door, removing a rectangular object in a brown paper bag.

He came into the kitchen, set down the bag and stared at me. "Do you know my grandmother has purple hair?"

Unable to resist, I replied, "No, but if you hum a few bars, I might remember it."

"Very funny. My mother is having a fit and says it's all your fault, that you're a bad influence on Grandma."

"What? Your grandmother is eighty, and you and I both know Carmela is not that easily influenced. She's having fun. What's wrong with that?"

"She has purple hair!"

"Yeah, so what's your point? And what's in the bag?"

"Stuffed shells, for dinner."

"Anthony Michael DeMarco. I can't believe you had your mother cook dinner for you to bring home. You should be ashamed."

"You said we were each responsible for providing dinner. You didn't say I had to cook it myself. Don't eat it if you don't want to."

I sniffed the steam emanating from the bag. "Are you kidding? Not eat it? These are Angela's stuffed shells we're talking about."

He removed the baking dish from the bag and set it in the oven, which he'd turned to a low setting. "I'll make a salad and dinner will be ready. So, other than turning my grandmother's hair purple, how was your day?"

I poured a glass of wine and handed it to him. "I didn't turn her hair purple, and my day was great. I enjoyed being with Sofialoren."

He shook his head. "My mother says you told her you're unhappy."

"I did not! She said that, not me. I told her I'm unfulfilled."

"What the hell does that mean? That sounds worse than unhappy."

Gabby came into the kitchen, and Anthony leaned close to me, whispering, "We're gonna talk about that later."

"Talk about what?" Gabby asked.

"It's a miracle! You're cured! The last time I asked you do something, you seemed to be deaf. Praise the Lord!" My comment drew a look from Gabby that said 'Oh, Mom. You're so lame!'

She walked to the stove and sniffed. "Mmmm. I like it when Daddy cooks."

"Yeah, right. It's Grandma Angela's take out. Maybe your dad can install a sliding window in the side of her house. Then he won't have to get out of the car to pick up dinner."

95

Michael bounded down the stairs. "Hey, do I smell Grandma's cooking?"

"How come none of you gets this excited when I cook?" I asked.

Three heads turned and six eyes just stared. Nothing needed to be said.

I was scheduled for clean-up after dinner, but Anthony stayed in the kitchen and helped me.

"You don't have to do this, you know. It's my turn."

"I thought we could finish that conversation." He tossed the dish towel onto the counter and sat at the table, motioning for me to join him. "Is that what this is all about? Are you unfulfilled?"

"I didn't mean that the way it sounded," I replied as I sat across from him. "It's like I missed something along the way, and now I have to go back and find it to complete my life. I think, maybe, that's what I expected working for Teddy to do, but it didn't."

"You expected working for Teddy to be fulfilling?"

I thought for a moment, then looked him in the eye. "Do you enjoy your work? Is it fulfilling?"

"I don't expect that much of my job. I like my work, and it's interesting."

"Do you look forward to getting up in the morning and going to the office?"

"Yes, most days." He grinned and his eyes crinkled. "Sometimes I'm with this hot blonde, and I don't want to leave."

I smiled. "Seriously. You have a job you enjoy. You feel good about yourself when you've done a good job, right?"

"I suppose so. But, this isn't about me."

"No, it isn't. I'm just proving a point. If you had to quit your job tomorrow and just hang around the house, would the kids and I be enough for you?"

He narrowed his eyes. "Is this a trick question?"

"Nope. Any answer is a good one."

"I guess I'd want to do something."

"I do, too. I just have to figure out what that is. I feel like something's out of sync or out of balance."

"Don't say that to my mother. It'll confirm her suspicions about you." He smiled.

"What suspicions?"

He stood and rounded the table, kissing the top of my head. "That you're unbalanced."

Ten

I arrived early for the book club meeting and went to the café to get a drink. As I turned from the counter, I noticed Sue seated at a table in front of a laptop computer. I headed her way, then hesitated, not wanting to interrupt, but she saw me and waved me over.

"Hi. You looked deep in thought. I didn't want to distract you," I said.

"Oh, please, distract me. Sit down. I need to stop now, anyway. I'm working on a paper for my class and it's driving me crazy. I can't get it just where I want it."

"Class? You're in school?"

"Yup. My youngest went off to college last fall, and I decided it was my turn. I'm taking classes in journalism. I got a bachelor's in communications, then started a family and got sidetracked. I'm going for my master's degree."

"That's wonderful."

She snapped the laptop screen down and picked up her coffee. "What do you do?"

"I used to be a bookkeeper, but I quit a few weeks ago. Right now, I, um, let's see… I go to the park a couple of days a week and have coffee with a homeless woman. I bought a new computer so I'd have an email address. Oh, and the other day, I took my husband's grandmother to have her hair dyed purple."

Sue laughed. "Your life sounds much more exciting than mine."

"My son thinks I should go to college with him next fall, but I'm convinced it's just that he wants someone to do his laundry and clean his room."

"If you did go to college, what would you study?" she asked.

I stared at her, dumbfounded. "I...uh ...oh, I don't know. I never thought about it. I have an associate degree that I got at the community college and that's in accounting, not something I'd want to pursue at a higher level."

"You should give it some thought. You'd like college," she said as she tucked the laptop into a bag. "Well, looks like it's time. We should head to the other side of the store."

As we stood, I said, "Sue, I want to thank you for the last meeting, for coming to my rescue by suggesting the Berg book. It's been so long since I've read consistently. I'm a little behind in the literature department."

"Most of the people in this group don't know one writer from the next. We just know what we like, and go with that. Otherwise, it would be too much like work. Last year, we had a woman who'd been home-schooling four kids between the ages of five and nine. We ended up reading Dr. Seuss for one discussion."

The book discussion was light and easy, no pressure. I enjoyed hearing everyone's take on the story and what the author was trying to accomplish, and even dared to share a few of my thoughts. *Hope is self-confident and a risk-taker.*

After the meeting, I stayed and browsed the shelves. I loved the look, the feel, even the smell of the book store and wondered, briefly, if they were hiring. I came upon a book titled *Find the Career for You*. I took it from the shelf and sat down to skim through it. The book had descriptions of different careers and a CD of quizzes to help you determine which career was the right one for you. I paid for the book, and went home and straight to the den, my new haven.

Anthony had gone to his mother's for Sunday afternoon family dinner. As usual, the kids had other plans and had disappeared right after church. Anthony came home laden with pans and containers. "Mom made this stuff for me to freeze and use when it's my turn to cook. If you're nice to me, I'll share."

"How *nice* do I have to be?" I asked, sniffing the containers.

He didn't respond and, when I looked at him, I saw he was wearing his droopy-eyed look and grinning.

"Okay, but I get the baked ziti for my cooking night. Oooh, and the cookies."

"I got pizza sauce, too," he said, waving the container in my face.

"Hmmm. I don't know if I have the energy to be that nice. I'll just take the ziti and the cookies."

His grin faded, and he put the containers in the freezer, then faced me. "Later," he said with a wink.

I returned to the den, turned on my computer and removed my new book from the bag. After skimming the entire book, I selected three careers to test. I popped in the CD and rolled the cursor along the index to Teacher. I scored sixty percent on that one, not a good choice. My next effort was Writer. Although I did better, I didn't break any records with my score. The last career I'd chosen was Social Worker. I got caught up in the questions and, when I totaled my score, I had ninety-five percent.

I sat back in the chair and stared at the screen. "Huh. A social worker?"

The kids came home, one by one, said their goodnights and headed to their rooms. I ventured to the fridge and made a sandwich, then returned to the computer.

Anthony appeared in the doorway, stretching and yawning. "It's past eleven. I'm going upstairs."

"Okay," I said, returning my attention to the screen.

He hesitated, then asked, "Are you going to be long?"

"What? Uh, no, I don't think so. Why?"

He flexed his eyebrows a few times. "Ziti and cookies."

"I'll be there in a few minutes," I said, sounding as enthusiastic as Eeyore.

"Jeez, don't sound so eager. I might get all excited. If you're not there in fifteen minutes, I'm coming back down here and having my way with you on the desk."

I played that scene out in my head for a minute and smiled. *Hmmm.* But what if one of the kids came downstairs for a snack? I removed the CD, turned off the laptop and headed upstairs. Anthony was undressed, in bed and waiting.

I went into the bathroom, brushed my teeth and slipped my silk nightgown over my head. I brushed my hair, admiring the color once again, sprayed some body oil on my arms and neck, then slipped into bed.

"Can we talk for a minute?" I asked just as he turned and reached for me.

"Oh, brother. This isn't going to happen tonight, is it?"

"Promise me we can talk after."

He rolled towards me. "We can talk after."

I leaned back and looked him in the eye. "You promise? I'm gonna hold you to it."

"I promise, we'll talk. And you still get the ziti and cookies."

Hope likes bargaining for food.

Anthony ran his hand along my arm and looked down at me. I put both arms around his neck and pulled his lips to mine. It amazed me sometimes how, after all these years, his touch still gave me shivers. *Thank God for the ziti. And cookies— hallelujah!*

~ * ~

Once we'd both caught our breath, I turned to face him. "Can we talk now?"

"Can I stop you?"

"Nope. Anthony, I think I want to go to college. I want to study Social Work."

"What did I do to deserve this?" A grin spread across his face. "I get to sleep with a blonde and a co-ed?"

"I'm being serious, and if you don't get serious, too, you'll be sleeping alone and on the couch."

"I'm sorry; you're just so cute right now. I'll be serious. Talk to me."

"I think I want to go to college and get a degree. I took a test in a career book and it says I'm suited for social work."

"You probably are. You can be very convincing and get people to cooperate with you. You're a good listener. You're resourceful, and you're conscientious. Not to mention that you can keep a secret better than anyone I know."

I was stunned into silence. I didn't expect this kind of clarity, especially when his mind had just been disengaged for an hour.

"If that's what you want to do, I think you should look into it."

I rolled onto my back and tucked the sheet under my armpits. "But what about the cost? We have Michael starting college in a few months, and Gabby is just two years behind him. That's a lot of books and tuition."

"Could you go to school part-time and work part-time? Not for Teddy, but work at something else? That would help with some of the cost. We'll get a loan for the rest if we need to."

My thoughts immediately went to the book store, and my mood lifted. "I could do that. I'm not in a rush. It's not like I have to graduate in the next three or four years."

"I doubt if your courses from the community college will apply after all these years, but you could ask."

The excitement of possibility rippled through me and a giggle escaped. I turned to Anthony and grabbed his face between my hands. "I love you," I said, then kissed him deeply. Before long, he owed me a pan of Angela's lasagna and garlic bread.

~ * ~

With the phone book open to the University of Pittsburgh School of Social Work, I picked up the phone and dialed. I hung up after one ring. Maybe I wasn't ready for this. *Maybe Hope doesn't really know what she wants, either.* I picked up the phone and hit the redial button, then listened to the automated menu. When a live person came on after I'd pressed 1-2-4-4, I asked about applying for admission. The woman took my name and address, promising to send me an information packet. Nothing to do now but wait.

My walk to the park that morning seemed shorter. Starbucks was crowded, and Ricki looked frantic as she hurried to fill orders and keep an eye on Hannah in her stroller. Since I had to wait anyway, I waved to Ricki, then walked over to the baby and popped her pacifier back into her pink bow mouth. She sucked earnestly and stared at me with huge blue eyes. As soon as I stood and walked away to get into line, she spit the pacifier out of her mouth and wailed. I went back to her, lifting her from the stroller and bouncing her in my arms. Her face relaxed and broke into a wet smile.

I walked to the counter to order. "I hope you don't mind that I picked her up."

"Are you kidding? I appreciate it. My mom's in the hospital, and I don't have anyone else to watch her. She's been pretty good, until now. If we can get through the next two hours, it'll be a miracle."

"I can watch her for you until your shift's over," I offered.

Ricki looked hesitant, and I realized I was still pretty much a stranger to her. "I'm sorry. Why would I presume you'd just hand your baby over to me? Look, let me see if my friend is in the park. I'll ask her to come back here, and I'll sit right here with Hannah until you're finished."

"You'd do that?"

"Sure. I'm not doing anything else. I'll be right back." I settled Hannah back in the stroller, exited the café and crossed the street. As I approached the gazebo, I saw Joy settled on the bench.

She waved when she saw me. "Hope. Hello."

"Hi." I sat on the bench beside her. "How are you?"

"On a day like this? I'm great. And you?"

"I'm good. I was hoping I'd see you today. I don't suppose you'd join me in the café for coffee? I promised Ricki, the young woman who works there, that I'd look after her little girl until her shift's over."

"Okay. But, you know, you don't have to buy me coffee every time you see me."

"I don't do it because I have to. I enjoy the company."

We walked to the café, and Joy held the door for me to enter first. She followed me up to the counter.

"I'll have my usual latte and a blueberry muffin. How about you?" I asked Joy. "The muffins look really good."

Ricki smiled. "They're fresh from the oven."

"You talked me into it. Regular coffee and a muffin," Joy said to Ricki.

We carried our drinks and muffins to a table, then I returned to the counter and pushed Hannah's stroller over and placed it between us. Her eyes widened, and she twisted her head, looking for her mother.

Ricki came over and gazed down at the baby. "Hey, sweetie, I'm right here. You be a good girl for Hope and her friend."

"I'm sorry, I didn't introduce you. Ricki, this is my friend, Joy."

Joy extended her hand to Ricki. "Your daughter's beautiful. She looks like you."

"Thanks." A customer entered and approached the counter. "I'd better get back to work."

Hannah began to fuss, and I lifted her from the stroller and bounced her on my knee.

"Did you go to college?" I asked Joy.

"Yes, I did. I have a degree in English. I never used it, though, except to write letters with impeccable grammar and punctuation. And we're supposed to talk about you this time," Joy said, blowing on her coffee.

"I'm thinking of going to college."

Joy smiled as Hannah grasped her finger. "What are you planning to study?"

I told her about the career book and testing high on the social work questionnaire.

She studied me for a moment. "I can see that. You'd make a good social worker."

"You think so?"

"Trust me, I'm an expert on social workers. I've had more than my share."

"Joy, I don't understand… "

Ricki came over, carrying a warmed bottle of formula. "She's fussing because she's hungry. Do you want me to feed her?"

I shook my head. "I'd love to, if you don't mind."

She handed me the bottle. "Be my guest."

Hannah lay in my left arm, her head resting against my breast. I brought the bottle to her lips, and she hungrily pulled the nipple into her mouth.

"So, Joy, how did you… "

"We're talking about you this time. Remember?"

"That's only fair, I suppose. So, where should I start?"

"Wherever you like."

I told her about my earlier years, growing up in the shadow of the steel mills in Homestead. "I could see the rollercoaster at the amusement park from our yard. It was torture to stand there and watch, unable to go to the park."

Joy nodded. "We used to go to that park several times throughout the summer. My brother and I loved the coasters."

"After my father died, my mother and I moved into one of the city housing complexes. She died when I was eighteen and in my first year at community college."

"That's so sad. It must have been terrible for you."

"I had one more year of school, so my mother's aunt and uncle took me in and let me live with them. I finished school and worked for an insurance company. That's where I met my husband, Anthony. We got married, and now we have two children, Michael and Gabriella."

"How old are they?"

"Michael is seventeen and Gabby's fifteen. They're in shock right now because I've quit doing all of the cooking, laundry and chauffeuring. I'm teaching them to fend for themselves."

"That's a good thing. They'll learn to be independent."

"They're good kids. I just got tired of feeling like a utility and not a person. So, here I am, remaking my life. I guess this is as good a time as any to tell you that Hope is not my real name. It's Janet. I chose Hope because I've always liked the name."

"Hope is your alter-ego, then?"

"Maybe Hope is my primary ego and Janet is the alter-ego. I'm not so sure."

I looked down at Hannah. Her mouth slack, the nipple released, her eyes closed, she breathed evenly. I put my lips to her downy-soft head and inhaled the scent of baby, sweet and powdery. Joy adjusted the stroller to recline, and I settled Hannah into it. The baby whimpered once, made sucking motions with her lips, and continued to sleep.

"They're so sweet at that age, aren't they?" I tucked the light blanket around the sleeping child.

Joy smiled at the baby. "Yes, they are." Joy's eyes softened and I wondered if she was thinking of her son and daughter in their infancy.

"My husband's family thinks I've lost my mind, especially my mother-in-law. The hair color was one thing, but the name change was just too much. Anthony's really trying to understand and to be supportive, but I know it exasperates him at times."

"You know the difference between you and me?" She laughed. "Okay, there are a lot of differences. But one difference? You can change your name and create a new identity and, while your family might think you've gone off the deep end, they don't have you committed. If I did the same thing, I'd be hauled off to the psych ward and labeled as schizo or delusional."

I thought about how unfairly I assessed people at times. I'd assumed that, because Joy chose to be homeless, there must be something wrong with her, she must be crazy or desperately in need of help. That had been my initial assumption.

"It must be hard to live with people always looking at you differently, thinking they know you," I said.

"No, that's not so hard to live with. What's hard to live with are the people who pretend they don't see you at all."

"Oh, Joy…"

"Want to hear something really funny? My name isn't Joy."

"You're kidding."

"Nope. My name was Madeline. When I walked away from everything and, after all I'd been through, I decided I needed a name that would remind me to be happy. So, I chose Joy."

I stared at her, my mouth hanging open. "Do you think this happens more often than we can imagine? I mean, what if no one is who we think they are? What if half the people we know have changed their names?"

"That would be something, wouldn't it? Like that old TV show, when they'd say 'only the names have been changed to protect the innocent.' "

"Innocent, huh?"

"We all are, at one time or another," she said, gulping down the last of her coffee. "I've gotta catch a bus. I'll see you again, perhaps."

"Perhaps?"

"Well, you never know." She gathered her things and eased her cart past the stroller, careful not to bump into it and wake the baby. "You should seriously consider that social work thing, Hope. See you around."

Ricki came over to the table and placed another latte in front of me. "Here, on the house. Decaf, non-fat. Thanks for tending to Hannah today. I'm going to have to find a sitter soon."

"Is your mom's condition serious?"

"She's having liposuction. I don't know, is that serious?"

"Oh, well, I guess it could be."

"Yeah, well, her flat tummy is causing me a real pain. She's been told she won't be able to lift anything for weeks, including Hannah. That leaves me without a sitter, and the boss isn't crazy about me having Hannah here with me. He's worried about liability."

I looked at the sleeping baby and felt an ache in my middle. I didn't want another baby, but it was a natural reflex. "Ricki, I have an idea. Why don't I babysit Hannah for the next two weeks, until your mom can take over again?"

"Really? You'd do that?"

"I quit my job recently, and I don't have much to do right now. She's a sweet baby, and I'd love to take care of her. Here's my address. I live just a few blocks from here. Why don't you stop by and check me out, see the house, then you can decide?" I jotted down the address and phone number and handed it to her.

"I can stop by later. I need to go to the hospital as soon as I'm finished here, which is in about... " she looked up at the clock, " ...ten minutes."

"I'll be at home all evening. Come by any time." I stood to leave. "Thanks for the latte," I said, taking the drink with me.

Ricki appeared at seven o'clock, carrying Hannah in one of those slings so that she nestled against Ricki's chest. I showed her the house, introduced her to my family and offered her dinner, which she gratefully accepted. She'd fed the baby, but had skipped her own dinner.

"So, do I pass inspection?" The sleeping baby was draped over my chest, drool soaking into the dish towel I'd placed there.

"I remember your son from high school. Well, he's younger than I am, but I think he was a freshman when I was a senior. My mom says she knows your husband's family, too. I think

she knows somebody by the name of Stella. So, you pass."
Ricki hesitated. "You know I can't afford to pay much."

"I don't expect to be paid! I'm just offering to be of help.
That's all."

"Are you sure about that? I mean, I could pay you
something."

"No. Please let me help you out. You can drop Hannah here
on your way to work, and I'll bring her by before your shift
ends, unless it's raining. Then you can come for her. How does
that sound?"

"Okay, but I have to be at work by six-thirty to open the
café. Are you sure you want her here that early?'

"I'm awake, anyway. It'll be fun."

I helped ease the sleeping baby into the sling and watched as
she nestled against her mother. Ricki was so young, just a few
years older than Gabby. A lump formed as I imagined Gabby as
a single mother. Then I shuddered. That would make me a
grandmother. *Hope is not ready to be a grandmother.*

I wrote down Ricki's work schedule and her phone number.
"I'll see you in the morning."

"Thanks. I'll bring everything you'll need. She's used to
sleeping in the stroller, so she should be fine there or on a
blanket on the floor."

After Ricki left, I remembered that I'd given Gabby's old
playpen to Angela to use when the grandchildren were there. I
called to see if she still had it.

"Angela, it's Hope."

I heard silence, then, "Oh, yes. How are you?"

"I'm fine. I was just wondering if you still have that old
playpen I'd given you for the grandkids?"

"Playpen? Why do you need a... oh, my God, you and
Anthony are having a baby!"

"No, no, no. Angela, we are not having a baby. I'm going to babysit for a few weeks, and I could use the playpen if you still have it."

"Oh," she said with disappointment in her voice. "It's in the attic, I think. I don't go up there much."

"May I come over and get it now?"

"Sure. I'm waiting up for Mama to come home from a date. The light will be on."

I smiled as I grabbed my car keys and called upstairs to tell Anthony where I was going. I tried to picture Carmela on a date. *I hope that guy takes vitamins.*

Angela opened the door as I reached the top step. "Whose baby are you caring for?"

I told her about Ricki, leaving out the part about the reason for Ricki's mother's hospitalization. That would've started a monologue about plastic surgery that I didn't have time to hear.

I followed Angela up the stairs and pulled down the attic stepladder, flipped on the lights and climbed up. The playpen was folded and leaning against the far wall. I lowered it down to Angela, then backed down the stairs and closed the hatch.

"Thanks. It's old, but looks none the worse for wear. I'm glad you kept this."

"You never know with this family when another baby's gonna come along. Look at Teddy's daughter."

"What about Teddy's daughter?"

"She's pregnant. Teddy's acting like it was all planned and she and the boy were getting married anyway, but I don't think so. Such a smart girl and now look."

"Jaclyn's only seventeen. She's Michael's age, isn't she?"

"Yes. It's so sad. Like father, like daughter."

My face must have reflected my surprise at her comment.

"Oh, come on. You know Teddy's always out screw...running around on Stella. Why should he think badly of his daughter for doing the same thing? Stella called me in tears because Teddy was ranting and raving about Jaclyn ruining her reputation and his. I said Teddy couldn't blame that on her. He did that himself. Well, you know Stella …never a bad word. Apparently, Teddy called Jaclyn names, bad names I won't repeat," she said, crossing herself.

"That's awful. I feel bad for Jaclyn."

"I told her if her father treats her badly, she should come and stay here."

I was stunned by Angela's act of kindness and compassion. I stared at her and wondered, *who are you and what have you done with Angela?* "That's very nice of you."

"She's family. It's the right thing to do. No matter what you think, you stand by family. You want me to help you get that downstairs?"

"No, I've got it."

I went ahead of Angela, sliding the playpen down the carpeted stairs, careful not to scrape the wall.

Carmela came in the front door as I reached the bottom. "Hope! What have you got there?"

"It's a playpen."

Her eyes lit up and she smiled. "How nice. You're gonna have a baby?"

"No, don't say that. I am not going to have a baby. I'm babysitting for a few weeks, that's all."

"Oh." She sounded disappointed. Then she grinned. "I was out on a date."

I rested the playpen against the wall, and we moved into the living room. "So I hear. Is he someone special?"

"Nah. I met him at the senior center. His name's Victor and he's hard of hearing." Carmela walked to her favorite chair and let her backside drop into the seat, her feet lifting from the floor as she did so. "He's eighty-three, so his hearing is about the only thing that's hard any more. Know what I mean?"

I laughed and felt my face warm.

Angela made a loud 'tsk' sound and went into the kitchen, once again talking to the mother of God. She did that a lot, it seemed. "I'm making tea," she called out.

"Did Victor like your hair?" I asked Carmela.

"He insisted it was blue. I think his eyes are going, along with his ears and his memory. He called me Sofialoren all night and, by the time he brought me home, he couldn't remember my real name. I don't think I'll see him again. He probably won't remember who I am anyway."

"I wouldn't count on that. You're pretty unforgettable."

Angela called us to the kitchen for tea and Italian wine cookies. "We missed you at Sunday dinner," she said to me.

"I'm sorry. I joined a book club, and it meets once a month on Sunday afternoon."

"Anthony told me that's where you were. I just wanted you to know the family missed you here."

Carmela set her cookie down and grinned. "You missed all the fun this week."

Angela gave her a look of warning, but Carmela forged on. "Teddy and Stella stopped by, and Teddy was really giving it to Anthony about how he can't control his wife."

"They were just teasing," Angela said.

"Yeah, well maybe Teddy was. But Anthony got right in his face, told him to mind his own business and tend to his own wife. Anthony said he was proud of you and glad you quit working for Teddy. He said you're too good a person to run Teddy's errands and cover his… "

"Mama! That's enough!" Angela glared at her, then looked at me. "Teddy was just teasing, and Anthony wasn't in the mood. You know Teddy doesn't know when to quit."

My eyes felt moist. "Anthony said he was proud of me?"

"Yes, he did," Carmela said. "I don't think Teddy will talk about you again, not in Anthony's presence."

"Anthony didn't say a word about it. Thank you for telling me," I said to Carmela. "Angela, thanks for the playpen and for the tea. I should be getting home."

I hauled the playpen across the lawn and shoved it into the back seat of my car. Anthony was watching TV when I walked through the back door and into the living room. I went over to him, bent and kissed him.

"What's that for?"

"That's for putting Teddy in his place on Sunday at your mother's house." I kissed him again. "And that's for being proud of me."

He pulled me down onto the sofa beside him, and I rested my head on his shoulder. "I am proud of you, and I love you. I think you're as crazy as they come, but I love you …Hope."

"Thanks. I love you, too." I snuggled in and watched the news with him.

Anthony brought the playpen inside and set it up before going to bed. I stayed up and scrubbed it with antibacterial soap and hot water, then lined it with a quilt. It was all ready for Hannah. I headed to bed and reminded Anthony to make sure I was awake when his alarm clock rang at five-forty-five. Ricki would arrive at six-fifteen with the baby.

Eleven

Ricki dropped Hannah off each morning, along with diapers, formula, jars of strained baby food, a change of clothes and the car seat. Michael and Gabby were both fascinated with the baby, and I'd find one or the other of them leaning over the playpen, delighting her with a stuffed animal or rattle.

One morning, I asked Anthony to keep an eye on her while I took a quick shower. When I returned to the living room, I found him sitting with Hannah propped on his knees, facing him. He was talking to her the way he'd talked to our kids when they were that age.

He looked up when I walked toward them. "You know, I've been thinking."

"Uh-oh. That can't be good."

"Wouldn't it be great to have another baby?"

"Are you nuts?"

He smiled at Hannah, then turned to me. "Don't tell me you haven't thought about it. I've seen the way you look at this baby. You get all dewy-eyed and soft."

"That's true. But it doesn't mean I want to *have* another baby, not at my age. You pick her up and she smiles at you, so you decide you want one of your own. I'm the one who would get swollen ankles and hemorrhoids. I'm the one who would put on thirty pounds, at least, and change diapers and… "

He stood and handed the baby to me. "Okay, okay. I got the picture. It was just a thought."

"Besides, we have two kids approaching college and I want to take some classes, too."

He kissed my cheek and ran his palm lightly over Hannah's soft head. "Forget I mentioned it. It's just having her around, you know. You see one of these and they're so cute and cuddly, makes you want one of your own. I'll see you tonight. I took out a pan of Mom's stuffed shells to defrost for dinner."

"I thought it was Michael's turn to cook."

"He has a date, so we traded. See you later."

After Anthony left, I put Hannah down with her bottle and fetched the packet of information I'd received from the university. Uncertain if any of the course work I'd done years ago would apply, I made a note to call and schedule an appointment.

Hannah dozed, wakened and fussed until I changed her. I donned one of my new jogging outfits and settled Hannah into the stroller. "Hey, Hannah-banana, what do you say we go for a walk. We'll stop and say 'hello' to your mommy and go to the park. Maybe Auntie Joy will be there, and we can visit her, too. And we can see what Auntie Fran is up to."

We hit the café at lunchtime, and customers were lined to the door. I slid past the line and parked the stroller next to a table, out of the way of traffic. Once the line dwindled, I waved to Ricki and ordered a latte and a muffin.

Ricki brought my order to the table and bent to run her finger along Hannah's soft cheek. "Hey, how's momma's girl?"

I observed the way she looked at Hannah, the gentleness of her touch. "You're a good mother. You know that?"

Ricki reddened, embarrassed by the compliment. "Thanks. I have to be. I'm all she's got."

"It must be difficult, raising a baby all by yourself and being so young."

She straightened. "You grow up fast when you have to." A customer walked to the counter, and Ricki turned to wait on him.

I thought of what she'd said about growing up, remembering how I'd gone from being a little girl to being a somber adolescent after my father died. I'd made another leap from carefree teenager to responsible adult after my mother's sudden passing.

I was thinking about my niece, Jaclyn, when a light tap on the window drew my attention. I looked up to see Joy smiling through the glass, and waved her inside.

Hannah was all sloppy grin and giggles when Joy bent to caress her cheek and speak to her. "She's such a pleasant baby. My Tina was like that, always smiling and content, unless she was hungry or wet. So, how have you been?"

"I've been watching Hannah for Ricki and, with the rain we've had, I've not been coming to the park. Sit down, and I'll get you a cup of coffee."

"That's okay, I can get it," she said, pulling a bill from her pocket.

When Joy returned with coffee and a slice of carrot cake, she sat across from me and smiled. "It's the first of the month, and I got my check."

"Your check?"

"I get a disability check each month, because of my mental health diagnosis. It's not much, but if I'm careful, I can get a bus pass, have enough for meals outside the shelter and a haircut once in a while. I was hoping to treat you to coffee today, but you beat me to it. Maybe next time?"

"Sure."

She didn't offer more information, and I filed away the mention of a mental health diagnosis. I told Joy of my plans to make an appointment at the university.

"That's wonderful. Good for you."

We chatted for a while as we finished our drinks. I took Hannah and waved goodbye to Ricki. "I'm going to stop by Fran's shop on my way home," I said to Joy. "Would you like to walk with us?"

"I'd like that," she said, gathering her cart.

"You can leave that here, if you want, then get it on your way back to the bus," Ricki called to Joy.

"Are you sure that's okay?"

"Do you see anyone here but me? That means I'm the boss," Ricki said, grinning. "Just put it back here out of the way."

"Thank you."

I asked Joy to push the stroller, and I walked alongside. We were just two women, friends taking a baby for a walk on an early summer day. I glanced sideways at Joy. She looked so normal. I then chastised myself. *She is normal. She's just homeless.*

"Joy, do you think you'll ever move off the streets and out of the shelter?"

"I suppose at some point I'll have to, when I can't manage by myself anymore. I mean, there's no homeless old folks' home under the Sixth Street Bridge. Do I expect to wake up tomorrow thinking this is the day I return to a normal life, get a job, an apartment?" She stopped and looked at me. "I wouldn't anticipate that happening."

"Oh."

She resumed pushing the stroller. "You're having a hard time with the fact that you and I are about the same age, similar in a lot of ways and, yet, I live something so counter-cultural to what you see as normal."

I felt myself flush, and stammered, "No, I... um... well, yeah, I guess it's hard for me to accept. I mean, what's between me and walking away like you did?"

"One fragile moment when reality becomes blurred and distorted and your mind tells you it's not real, that there's something else that's so much easier."

"Oh, is that all?"

Joy laughed and shook her head. "You just can't help yourself, can you? The urge to take me home, clean me up and rescue me from this madness grates at you, doesn't it?"

"Is it that obvious? I just... I can't imagine living your life."

She stopped in front of Fran's shop and locked eyes with me. "And I can't imagine living yours."

I opened the door and held it for Joy to roll the stroller inside, then I followed. Fran called out a hello to each of us and came to stoop before Hannah, admiring her curls and her huge blue eyes.

We sat in Fran's cramped office, and I told her about my plans to take college classes in social work.

"Fantastic! You'll be good at that."

Joy snickered. "She's practicing already... determined to save me from myself."

"I just worry about my friends, that's all," I said in my own defense.

I smiled, but noticed that Joy's expression was tight, her lips pressed together. She stood quickly. "I'm going to browse. You two visit."

She left the office abruptly, and I looked at Fran. "Did I say something wrong?"

"You called her your friend."

"Well..."

"Well, people like you don't typically befriend people like Joy. I think that means a lot to her, and she doesn't know what to do with it. Just give her room."

We chatted for a while and, when I glanced at the clock, I saw it was nearly time for Ricki's shift to end. I checked Hannah, then stood. "I'd better get this little one back to her mommy. Ricki's finished at work in fifteen minutes." I turned at the door and asked, "Do you want to have a girls' night out on Saturday night? Pizza and a movie?"

"Sounds like fun. Pick you up at six?"

"Great. See you then."

Joy and I walked for two blocks in relative silence. "Joy, thanks for walking with me today. I enjoyed the company," I finally said, breaking the silence.

"Me, too."

"Joy, I... " I was at a loss as to what to say next. I heard Fran's voice telling me to give Joy room. "I'll see you again for coffee, maybe later in the week?"

"Maybe." We'd reached the café, and she held the door for me. I wheeled the stroller to a table where I waited for Ricki to finish up. Joy retrieved her cart from behind the counter, thanked Ricki, then said goodbye to me and left.

Ricki pocketed her tips and turned the register over to her replacement. She came toward me. "You'll probably be glad when this week is over and you have your life back."

"Not at all. Hannah and I have fun, don't we, Hannah-banana?" I replied, brushing the baby's chin with my finger and eliciting a slobbery grin. "Well, I'll see you in the morning."

"My mom wants to meet you some time. She said to thank you for your help, and that we'd like to have you over for dinner."

"It's not necessary to do that, but I'd love to meet your mom. Just let me know when."

I arrived at home to find Grandma Carmela sitting in my living room. "Sofialoren, how did you get here?"

"Michael stopped by the house on his way home from school. I asked him for a ride. I needed to get out for a while. Angela told me to call her if I need a ride home. Hey, I like that outfit you're wearing."

"Thanks. It's one of my new jogging suits."

She rubbed the fabric of the jacket between her thumb and forefinger. "It's nice. And I like that green stripe down the leg. Do you think I could get those in my size?"

"I'm sure you could. Do you want to go to the mall after dinner, and then I'll take you home?"

The smile spread across her aged face. "I'd like that, but I didn't bring any money with me."

"I'll get them, and you can repay me any time."

"Deal. So, it's going well with everyone cooking and cleaning?"

I laughed. "It's going well because Angela keeps giving Anthony Italian take-out. If it wasn't so darned good, I'd call a foul, but who would complain about Angela's cooking?"

"She gets that from me, you know. Hey, where's that computer you got? I'd like to see it."

"Come to the den," I said, offering my arm to help her out of the chair.

Carmela sat in the leather desk chair, her feet dangling several inches from the floor, and I turned on the computer. Once it booted up, I clicked onto the Internet and typed in Amazon. "See, if I want to look for books, I can look them up right here. I can even buy them and have them shipped."

"Wow, this is fantastic! I bet you can look up just about anything, huh?"

"Just about. Do you want to play around with it while I get us something to drink? You just type in here what you want to look up and then hit this button," I explained, showing her what to do.

"I can do that. Thanks, honey."

The phone rang, and I lifted it from the cradle, carrying it with me to the kitchen. It was Fran, calling to talk about a big sale she'd made just after Joy and I had left. We got to talking, and I peeked into the den to make sure Carmela was okay. She seemed to be fine, her eyes wide and a grin on her face as she clicked away on the computer. I hung up the phone after confirming my plans with Fran for Saturday night, then poured two glasses of lemonade and headed back to the den.

When I rounded the desk and glanced at the computer screen, I was sure I wasn't seeing what I thought I was seeing. I set down the glasses and stared at the screen in disbelief.

Carmela chuckled and pointed. "Look what I found. You're right about one thing, you can look up anything on this Internet. Check out that one. I'll tell you, my Dominic didn't look like that."

I tilted my head first to one side then to the other, my eyes glued to the naked man spread-eagled on the screen.

"How about Anthony? Does he compete with this guy?"

Her question snapped me out of my stupor. "Carmela! I'm not going to discuss that with you, and especially not about your grandson."

"Well, I changed his diapers when he was a baby, and I'd bet he's at least as good as this guy."

I grabbed the mouse and clicked on File-Exit, feeling flames consume my face.

"That was fun. I tell you, I gotta get me a computer," Carmela said, laughing as she reached for her lemonade.

"Carmela, you can't go looking up porn sites." I wondered if I needed to change my email address now, imagining the spam I'd be receiving.

"I didn't look for porn. I typed in Bad Boy, and that's what I got."

"Bad Boy?"

"Yeah. He's the horse that won the derby last year. I wanted to see how he's done since. I like to follow the horses. They're beautiful animals, don't you think? So graceful."

"Horses?"

"Although, you gotta admit, that guy and a horse have a lot in common."

Oh, good grief.

Michael stopped at the doorway on his way to the kitchen. "What are you two up to?"

"Your mom's teaching me how to surf the net. It's amazing, Mikey. Do you know you can look at… "

I gasped. "What time will you be home tonight?"

"Eleven o'clock too late?" he asked.

"Try ten. It's a school night. Have fun." I followed him to the kitchen and turned the oven on to warm, then returned to the den and picked up the glasses of lemonade. "Come on, Sofialoren, let's go and sit on the patio until dinner's ready. And don't tell people about that website. Especially not Angela. She already thinks I'm a bad influence on you."

I managed to keep Carmela's mind off the Internet during dinner, although the image of what I'd seen was forever burned in my mind. *Poor Anthony.* I passed him more shells. He was going to need his strength later.

Gabby cleared the dishes, and I ushered Carmela out to the car. "Is there anything else you want to shop for besides a jogging suit?"

"Maybe a pair of shoes like yours, to go with the suit."

I waited until she buckled her seatbelt, then backed from the driveway and turned toward the mall. "Have you seen your friend, Victor?"

"I saw him one day at the center."

"Did he ask you out again?"

"Yeah, but I turned him down. I think I need a younger man. You know, somebody who can see and hear and… you know."

I pretended I didn't know and skimmed on to other topics. "What's happening with Teddy's daughter, Jaclyn?"

"Hope, you should've heard it. He came by and yelled at Angela for offering to let Jaclyn stay with her. You don't yell at my Angela. She tore Teddy a new one. You know what I mean? Then Stella started yelling at Teddy. Jaclyn and her soon-to-be husband are going to live with Teddy and Stella until after the baby's born. Stella told Teddy if he didn't like that, he could move in with one of his little floozies."

"It's about time," I muttered.

I parked as close to the mall entrance as possible, and Carmela wrapped her boney fingers around my arm as we walked to Sears. I found the 'petites' department and searched for the rack of jogging suits. "What colors do you want?"

"I want one in purple, if they have it, to go with my hair."

I found a black suit with a purple stripe down the arms and legs. She took that to try on and, once we found the right size, she selected two more suits—dark green with an orange stripe and navy blue with a soft blue stripe, just like one of mine. I took the suits to the cashier and presented my credit card, then carried the bag for Carmela.

"These are great. Now, let's look at shoes." Like an excited ten-year-old, she tugged me along.

"Do you have socks?" I asked.

"What kind of socks do I need?"

We found the sock department where Carmela selected several pairs of white ankle socks just like mine. Next, we moved to shoes and she bought a pair of pink and white Reeboks with gel heels and glow-in-the-dark running stripes.

"I was tempted to get the ones that light up, but I was afraid people would think I was trying too hard to get their attention."

"Good point. You wouldn't want that to happen," I said, grinning.

Back at the car, I put the packages in the trunk while Carmela got into the passenger's seat and buckled up.

"When can I go to the park with you?" she asked. "I want to try out my new suits."

"I'm still babysitting this week. I'll pick you up on Monday morning if it isn't raining, and we'll go then." I wasn't sure I could keep up with a six-month-old and Carmela.

"Good. And you'll have to tell me which suit you're wearing so I don't wear the same color."

I grinned and eased out into traffic. I carried Carmela's packages inside when I took her home. Angela's eyes widened when she saw the jogging suits and sneakers, then they narrowed on me.

Carmela came to my rescue. "Angela, I'm gonna go walking with Hope on Monday. I got the shoes and socks and everything. Isn't that nice? The exercise will be good for me. You should come, too. I think they have these suits in a size sixteen."

Angela's left eyebrow raised and she stared at Carmela. "I am not a size sixteen."

"It's nothing to be ashamed of. You're Italian. We're full-bodied, until we get older," she said, looking at her shrunken frame, "then we shrivel up, just like a raisin."

I thought of the comparison between Angela and a good bottle of wine... full-bodied. I just couldn't wrap my mind around that one. "I have to get home. Angela, Anthony served your stuffed shells tonight, and they were delicious, as always."

"Hmmph. A man shouldn't have to come home from a hard day at work and cook a meal. Did he use my sauce?"

"Of course. They wouldn't be complete without your sauce. Some day you're going to give me that recipe," I said, smiling.

Another 'hmmph.'

"I'll see you Monday, Sofialoren. Goodnight, Angela."

~ * ~

When Anthony slipped into bed that night, I closed my book and told him about Carmela's adventures on the Internet.

"Omigod, you let my grandmother look up porn sites?"

"I didn't let her. She stumbled on it by accident." I then told him about the guy on the screen and Carmela's comments.

"You and my grandmother were discussing my... you know."

"We weren't discussing it. She asked, and I didn't answer, and she assumed and said something about changing your diapers."

His mouth slackened into the loopy grin and his eyelids drooped. "Well, how do I compare to that guy?"

I grinned and moved next to him, sliding my hand beneath the elastic of his boxers. "Honey, there's no comparison." *Why hurt his feelings?*

Twelve

A thunderstorm raged through the afternoon on Friday. I removed the quilt from the playpen and put it on the floor in the den. Hannah rolled around and played contentedly there with toys while I researched social work on the internet. I browsed the *Post-Gazette* employment ads. There were so many different opportunities for social workers, and excitement about my new career choice sent a shiver along my spine. I had to hope I could get through the coursework. My appointment was scheduled for the following Tuesday at the university.

Hannah was napping that afternoon when Ricki arrived, soaked despite the umbrella she carried.

"Come on in," I whispered, motioning to where Hannah slept. "Are you in a rush?"

"Not really."

"Want a soda or a cup of tea? It might be best to wait until this rain eases up before you drive home."

Ricki followed me to the kitchen after stopping to look at Hannah. "It's really coming down out there. The streets are a mess. I guess it's raining faster than the storm drains can handle. It's best if I wait a bit."

"What'll it be, soda or tea? We have Coke, Sprite and root beer."

"Root beer, thanks. I'll bet you're glad to see this day come. Now you can get back to your regular routine."

I laughed. "Oh, yeah. That's important."

"I really appreciate your help."

When I turned to give her the root beer, I saw she was crying. "Ricki, what's wrong?"

She shook her head and swiped the tears away. "Nothing. I… it's Hannah's father. All of a sudden he wants to be part of her life. I don't know how I'm going to deal with that. My mother's going to have a fit when I tell her."

I sat across from her at the table. "When did you find this out?"

"He came into the café today. He's graduating from college next month and has a job lined up and…" She broke into sobs that shook her shoulders.

I rounded the table and knelt next to her, taking hold of her hand. "Oh, honey, isn't it a good thing that he wants to step up and be a father to Hannah?"

"He's going to be living in Virginia, and he wants shared custody. That would mean he could take her there for weeks at a time."

"Oh, I see. Well, do you have a lawyer to help you with this?"

"I can barely afford baby food, much less a lawyer. I'll have to ask my mom for help and I just hate that. She's always willing to help, but it comes with a cost. I have to be reminded over and over how stupid I was to get into this mess in the first place." She shook and I pulled her against me, holding her while she cried.

Michael and Gabby came through the back door, gave the situation a quick assessment and continued through the living room and up the stairs.

Ricki pulled back and took a paper napkin from the table to wipe her nose. "I'm sorry. I shouldn't be telling you all of this.

It's not your problem. I've been holding this in all day, and I felt like I was ready to explode."

I smoothed her hair back, the way I'd done a thousand times with Gabby when she was hurt or upset. "It's okay." I eased into a chair, keeping a hand on hers. "Is he a good guy?"

She nodded. "He can be. I mean, when I told him I was pregnant, he wanted me to have an abortion. I know he was scared. So was I. He still had to finish college and, well, we'd never planned to get married."

"Is he doing this because he cares about Hannah or because he wants to get to you?"

"I think he cares. He came to the hospital after she was born, and he's sent her little gifts and sent me money now and then. I never pushed for child support because I figured we'd be better off without him being involved. I think he has a job lined up and figures he can be a dad now."

"Maybe you need to give him a chance, for Hannah's sake."

"I know, but... Virginia? That's so far away. What if he took her there and she got sick or she missed me? It's not like he's got a mother or a wife there to help him. How do I know that he'll know what to do?"

I smiled, remembering how Anthony was with Michael when he was a baby. "My husband was scared to death of Michael when he was first born. He was afraid he'd drop him or hold him too tightly. I had to teach him everything, and I wasn't all that certain myself. It was my first baby, too. Before long, he could feed, bathe, dress him and even change a diaper. He started taking him out on Saturday mornings for a little father-son bonding time when Michael was about Hannah's age."

"So you think Tim can learn those things?"

"I think that being a daddy has to come naturally. You can learn to do some of the father stuff. Give him a chance to be around Hannah and get to know her. Let him come to the house and spend time with her while you're there. Then you can see how he is with her. I was nervous about Anthony taking Michael out at first, too. You know what changed that? The day I came into the room and saw Anthony giving Michael his bottle. He was looking into Michael's face, and he had tears in his eyes. I knew, right then, that he'd throw himself in front of a train for his son."

Ricki sniffled and looked toward the living room where her baby lay innocently sleeping. "I guess she deserves to know her daddy, too. She looks like him, you know. She has his blonde curls and his smile."

"It'll be okay. You still might want to talk to an attorney about the particulars of visits, especially with the distance."

"Thank you," she said, squeezing my hand. "I think I know how I can talk to my mom about this now. And I think I can talk reasonably to Tim. As long as we can keep Hannah's best interest in front of us, it should be okay."

I leaned forward and gave her a hug. "You can talk to me any time. You know that."

The storm subsided and the rain became a drizzle. Ricki gathered the baby's things and I carried a bleary-eyed Hannah to the car. I kissed the baby's forehead and said, "Bye-bye, Hannah-banana. See you around." After snapping her into the car seat, I said to Ricki, "Call me anytime you need a babysitter. And I hope you will. I'm going to miss her."

"Thanks. I'll keep that in mind." She put the diaper bag on the floor and hugged me tightly. "Thanks for all your help. I'll see you at the café, I guess?"

"You bet. Probably on Monday."

I was in the kitchen preparing dinner when Gabby came down the stairs. "Did something happen to Ricki?" she asked.

"She just needed to talk something through."

"Well, she picked the right person," she said as she poured a glass of juice.

"What do you mean?"

"People always talk to you about their problems, Mom. It's because you listen, and you usually have some ideas that can help."

"Really? You don't talk to me about your problems."

She rolled her eyes. "Well, duh… you're my mother. I mean other people, like Aunt Stella and your friend, Fran. Remember when Megan was having that fight with her mom, and you talked to her and they got things all worked out?"

"I remember."

"Well, there you go." She turned and sprinted back up the stairs.

~ * ~

Carmela was waiting on the front porch when I arrived at Angela's house on Monday morning. She wore the black and purple jogging suit, her sneakers and a deep purple visor cap. Her lilac-tinted curls stuck out above the visor and around her ears. The over-sized sunglasses made her look like an aging Cabbage Patch kid.

"Good morning, Hope. What a beautiful day we have." She plopped onto the front seat and reached for the seatbelt. "I can't wait to hit the pavement."

"Well, don't hit it too hard. You'll get shin splints. I usually get coffee at the café and meet a friend in the park. Actually, I don't do all that much walking. Is that okay with you?"

"Hey, I'm just along for the ride. Well, the walk. And I'd love to meet your friend. I like meeting new people."

"We'll see if she's there today." I drove through town and found a parking space in front of the café. "You remember the baby I was caring for? Her mother works here."

"Oh, good. I can meet her, too. I brought some money, so the coffee's on me. My treat."

We went into the café and stood at the counter. Ricki came from the storage room, smiling when she saw me. "Hi. I'm glad you came in today. I wanted to tell you that my mom and I had a good talk. Tim is coming over tonight to see Hannah."

"That's wonderful. I hope it works out for the best."

"You having the usual?"

"Yes, and I'd like you to meet someone. This is my husband's grandmother, Car…"

Carmela raised her arm and stretched her hand over the counter to Ricki. "Sofialoren Mancini."

"That's an interesting name. Wasn't she an actress?"

"Yes and one of the most beautiful women alive. When I was younger, I was told I looked like her. That's why I borrowed her name."

"Well, Sofialoren, what can I get for you?"

Carmela stared up at the menu hanging behind the counter. "I didn't know you had so many kinds of coffee. What are you having, Hope?"

"I'm having a non-fat, decaf vanilla latte."

"That sounds good. I'll have that, too, and a chocolate biscotti. You want one?" she asked.

"No, thanks. We'll also have a large regular coffee, black."

Ricki made the lattes and asked, "Is the regular coffee for Joy?"

"Yes, have you seen her?"

"Oh, you didn't hear what happened."

"What? What happened?"

"Joy's in the hospital. She was hit by a car as she was going to the shelter on Saturday night. The guy who has the produce market down the street was in earlier. He told me about it."

My heart hammered in my chest. "Is she okay?"

"He said she's pretty banged up and has a broken arm and a broken leg. She's at Mercy."

Ricki handed us the lattes and a biscotti.

"Thank you for telling me. I'll be sure to visit."

"Please give her my best when you see her. She's a nice lady."

My hand shook as I set my drink on the table. Carmela sat across from me. "I'm sorry about your friend. Hey, maybe instead of walking, we should go and visit her in the hospital. We could take her some flowers."

I smiled. "That's a wonderful idea. Let's finish our coffee first. There's a flower shop down the street. I'll get a nice bouquet before we go into the city."

Mercy Hospital sat on a bluff across the city. I took the bypass, then picked up the parkway. The lower floors of the parking garage were filled, and I ended up parking on the roof.

"Hey, look. You can see the university from up here," Carmela said, pointing to the east.

"And I have an appointment there tomorrow." I linked my arm through hers as we walked to the elevator.

"I think it's just great that you're going to college. If I was a few years younger, I'd think of doing that, too. But what would I do with a degree at my age?"

"You could take a non-credit class. They offer those at the community college. What would you be interested in learning about?"

"Anything. I never graduated from high school. I got married. I'd like to learn about anything. Maybe history. You know, I'd have an edge in a history class. I've lived through most of it."

"Good point," I said, laughing. We stepped onto the elevator and I pushed 'G' for ground floor. Once inside the hospital lobby, I realized I didn't know Joy's last name.

I walked up to the receptionist and, feeling a bit foolish, explained, "A friend of mine was admitted on Saturday. She was hit by a car."

The woman smiled pleasantly. "Yes, and the name?"

"Her name is Joy… or Madeline …something."

A raised eyebrow reflected her doubt. "You don't know her name?"

"See, here's the thing. She's someone I met recently while I was walking in the park. We meet for coffee and talk, but I just realized when I walked in here that she's never told me her last name. She's… uh …she's a homeless woman. About my height …brownish hair. Does that help?"

"One moment." She picked up the phone and punched in a number, asked about a woman using my description and the admission information. "She's in room 410. You can use that set of elevators just ahead."

"Thank you so much."

Carmela followed me to the bank of elevators. "She's going to be so surprised. Those flowers are very nice. Should we stop at the gift shop and get her a magazine or anything?"

"Let's wait and see if she needs one. There's something I should tell you about Joy, but I'd appreciate it if you didn't tell her I told you."

Carmela made a zipper motion across her lips with her thumb and forefinger.

"Joy is homeless. She stays at a shelter here in the city and takes the bus to come to the park a few times a week."

"I heard you tell the receptionist. That's a shame."

"Well, she doesn't mind. She likes living a simple life."

Her eyes widened. "Living on a farm is the simple life; living on the streets can't be so easy. Hey, maybe we could help her find a place to live. She's not going to be able to go back to the streets for a while, I'd bet."

The same thought had crossed my mind. I knew from what Joy told me that the shelter sent the residents out in the morning, and they couldn't return until after five p.m. How was she going to manage with an arm and a leg in casts?

"Please don't mention that I told you. Let's see what she has to say first, okay?"

"Sure, no problem."

We followed the arrows on the wall to room 410. Joy was lying in the second bed, next to the window. Her right leg was in a cast and supported in a sling by an overhead cable. Her right arm rested close to her body in a sling. Her face was bruised and swollen.

"Joy?"

She turned her head slightly and looked at me, then recognition broke in a lopsided smile on her swollen face. "Hi, Hope. How'd you find me?"

"The produce guy told Ricki what happened, and she told us. This is my husband's grandmother, uh…"

Carmela stepped to the side of the bed. "I'm Carmela, but I like to be called Sofialoren."

Joy grinned and looked at me. "Too bad it isn't Faith," she said. She then looked back to Carmela. "It's nice to meet you, Sofialoren."

"Nice to meet you, too. I'm sorry for your accident."

I held the bouquet out to Joy. "We brought you these. Shall I put them on the windowsill?"

"Oh, thank you. They're lovely. Yes, that's a good spot."

I set the vase of flowers in the window and pulled a chair up for Carmela to be seated. I stood on the other side of the bed. "So, what happened?"

"I was crossing Fifth on my way to the shelter. It was just getting dark, and some kid decided to try to beat the light. He didn't."

"How bad is the leg?"

135

"I'll be in a cast for three or four weeks at least. Then they'll put on a walking cast. The problem is, with the break in my arm, I won't be able to use crutches for a while." Tears filled her eyes.

I rested a hand on her good arm. "What do you need in order to recuperate?"

"The doctor says I'll have to be off my feet for a few weeks, but there's a rehab facility he's talking about sending me to first. It's after that. I guess this is where things get complicated. There's no place to go."

Carmela stood and stepped closer to the bed. "Hey, I have a great idea. I live with my daughter, and we have a bedroom and bath on the first floor, no steps. I thought my grand-niece was going to move in, but she's not. You could come and stay with me and Angela."

Joy smiled. "Oh, thank you, but I don't think I could…"

I looked from Carmela to Joy. "Actually, that's not a bad idea. I was thinking of ways we could set up our den for you, but Angela's house would be even better. And I could come by every day." I looked back at Carmela. "Are you sure Angela would be okay with this?"

"Are you kidding? She's always looking for someone to take care of. Why do you think she jumped at the chance to make dinners for Anthony to bring home?" Carmela looked at Joy. "Angela tries to take care of me, but she can't keep up with me."

Joy and I both laughed and I said, "That's truer than you know."

"I could call my family, I suppose, but it's been so long, and I wouldn't expect…" Joy's chin quivered.

I squeezed her hand. "How about if Carmela and I talk to Angela and see what we can work out. Angela is my mother-in-law, and not nearly as tough as she'd like me to think."

"Thank you. I hate to be trouble for anyone, but I don't know what I'm going to do."

"It's settled, then," Carmela said, smiling broadly. "Hey, do you play cards? Or checkers? I love to play cards and checkers. We can play every afternoon."

I caught Carmela's eye, then looked toward Joy. "And I'm sure you'll have plenty of privacy and quiet time, if you need it. Isn't that right, Sofialoren?"

"Oh, sure. You just say the word, and I'll disappear."

Joy passed on our offer to get magazines, since she couldn't hold one with both hands to read it. "I got the TV turned on, so that'll entertain me."

"We'll go and let you get some rest. I'll talk to Angela tonight and come back tomorrow after my appointment at the university."

"Thank you. And good luck with your meeting."

We returned to the elevator and pressed the down button. "She seems like a nice person," Carmela said. "I've never met a real homeless person. I've seen them on the street, but she doesn't look like that. She looks just like you or Angela... like a regular person."

A few people got off the elevator, and Carmela and I stepped in. "Are you sure Angela won't be upset that you offered her house to a stranger?"

"She's not a stranger. You know her."

Yeah, I know that she's had a nervous breakdown and gets disability payments for a mental health diagnosis. Maybe this wasn't the best idea. I didn't really know Joy that well.

"Let's see what Angela thinks of the idea first. Maybe I can find some other solution for Joy."

I stopped at McDonald's where we had lunch before returning to Angela's. When we walked into the house, Angela was in her usual spot... standing over the range, stirring a pot of sauce. Anthony teased that her footprints would be forever embedded in the linoleum in front of the stove.

"Hi, Angela. Smells great in here, as usual," I said stepping beside her and kissing her cheek.

"Thank you. Did you two have a nice walk?"

Carmela responded before I could answer. "We had a great time. I met a friend of Hope's. She was hit by a car and is in the hospital, and she has nowhere to go while she recuperates, so I told her she could stay here in the back room. I knew you wouldn't mind."

Angela's head did her 'exorcist' impression, spinning around so fast I was sure it would do a full three-sixty. "You what?" She looked at me. "I'm very sorry about your friend. Mama, what did you promise?"

"Relax. She's a nice lady, about Hope's age, maybe a little older. She doesn't have anywhere to go after she gets out of rehab. She has a broken arm and a broken leg."

"Angela, I know that would be a terrible imposition. I'll fix up my den, or see if I can find a place for her," I said.

Angela set the wooden spoon in the spoon cradle and put a lid on the pot, reducing the heat. She wiped her hands on her apron, then turned to me. "We do have an extra room already set up and with a bathroom. Since Stella put Teddy in his place, it looks like Jaclyn won't be coming to stay."

"I don't know, Angela. Joy's going to need some assistance, and I don't know how mobile she'll be. I could come over here during the day and help out, though, I suppose."

She motioned for me and Carmela to sit, then poured each of us a cup of coffee. She sat and looked at me. "Tell me about your friend."

I told her everything, including the fact that Joy was homeless and had had some emotional problems. I figured she needed to know the whole story if she was going to open her home to this woman.

"Emotional problems... who hasn't? Does she want to come here?" she asked.

"Well, she doesn't have very many options."

"Does... does she have a shopping cart?"

I laughed. "Actually, she does, but not one of the grocery store ones. It's one of those collapsible kind, like the one you use."

Carmela interceded. "Just think, Angela. You'd have someone new here to appreciate your cooking. She's been living on shelter food. Boy, she'll love anything you make."

I saw the hint of a smile tug at the corners of Angela's mouth. "Why don't I go with you to the hospital and meet her? Then we can talk about it."

Okay, I was starting to believe in alien abduction. It was the only logical explanation for Angela's transformation.

"How about Wednesday? I have another appointment tomorrow. Let's say ten o'clock, but I'll call before I leave the house."

~ * ~

Anthony came home that evening to find me in the bedroom, viewing six different outfits and trying to choose one for my appointment the next day. "What do you think?" I asked. "Skirt or slacks? Jeans or khakis? How would a prospective student dress?"

"Honey, I don't think they select students based upon wardrobe. If that's the case, you need to rip the knee out of your new jeans and poke a few holes in them."

I picked up a pair of jeans, a soft blue tee and the denim jacket. "What do you think of this?"

"Cute. You'll look like a teenager."

"Is that okay?"

He pulled me against him and nuzzled my neck. "It's okay with me."

I pulled away and picked up the khakis and a short-sleeved sweater. "Maybe this would be better. Yes, definitely. This is it."

"Thank heaven we figured that out. Want to go out for dinner tonight, just you and me?"

I turned and smiled. "This is a surprise. What's the occasion?"

"No occasion. I just want to spend some time with my wife. Hunan Palace sound good?"

"I can be ready in ten minutes. Would you let Gabby know we won't be here for dinner? I don't think she'll mind. Michael's out, too. She won't have to cook."

During dinner, I told Anthony about Joy, and Carmela's suggestion to move her in with Angela.

"What'd my mother say about that?"

"She wants to go to the hospital with me to meet Joy and discuss it with her."

Anthony's eyes widened. "You're kidding."

"Nope. Believe me, no one was more surprised than I am."

He wiped his mouth with a napkin and looked at me. "You know, it kind of makes sense. Mom took care of my Aunt Carla before she died. Then my pop, even though she had to help him to the bathroom and bathe him. She's a caregiver. That's what Mom does."

"I hadn't thought of that, but say what you will about Angela, she is a nurturer. We'll see what happens when she and Joy meet."

"I've never heard you mention this Joy. Where'd you meet her?"

"In the park. She's, uh…" I knew my next sentence was going to make Anthony ballistic.

He blinked and waited. "She's what?"

"She's, um, homeless."

He smiled and shook his head. "You have my mother taking in a homeless person you barely know. And the best part is, you've got my grandmother on the bandwagon."

"I…" What could I say? He'd pretty much summed it up.

140

His smile faded. "What if this lady is psycho?"

"She's not psycho. She's been a little depressed in the past, but…"

He pulled the napkin from his lap and tossed it onto the table. "Great. Just great. I'm telling you, Jan, I don't approve of this for one minute, and I'm telling Mom that."

"Hope."

"What?"

"Never mind. I offered to have Joy stay with us, turn the den into a temporary bedroom."

His lips tightened, and he turned an odd shade of red-purple from the neck up. "Are you hearing yourself? We have two kids in the house. I'm finished eating. Are you finished?"

"Anthony, Joy's a good person. She's got a broken arm and one leg in a cast. What's she going to do? Chase them around the house with a butcher knife? Even Carmela can outrun her." My voice had risen, and the family in the next booth looked at me warily. I dropped my volume and said, "I promised to go there every day to care for Joy until she can manage again on her own. Besides, I don't even know if your mom's going to say yes."

He waved to the waiter for our check. "I don't like the idea. I'm just registering my opinion."

"Anthony, why was it okay until you found out Joy was homeless?"

"It has nothing to do with her being homeless, although you do have to wonder. It has everything to do with her mental state."

I laughed. "Her mental state? She's probably saner than either of us. Look, you know I would never do anything to put our family or yours in danger. I know people. I know Joy is a good woman who's had a hard time managing life, and she found her own way of being able to do that. It's not what I'd choose, but it works for her."

"Well, we both know I can't talk you or my mother out of anything either of you put your mind to. But I don't have to like it."

I picked up my fortune cookie and broke it open, removing the message inside. I read it silently and laughed aloud.

"What's so funny?"

"My fortune. It says 'small kindnesses reap great rewards.' See, it's a sign."

He opened his cookie, read the fortune then dropped the slip of paper onto the table. "Ready to go?"

"What does your fortune say?"

"Nothing. Let's go."

I reached across the table and unfolded his fortune: trust the wisdom of those you love.

"Okay, you don't see this as a sign? I thought Italians were superstitious."

"Over Chinese fortune cookies?"

Still, I tucked both fortune slips into my pocket and linked my arm in his as we walked to the car. "It's all going to be fine, honey. I promise."

"Hmmph."

Thirteen

I circled the campus three times before finding an open parking space. I had just one hour on the meter and hoped I'd make it back in time. The office I needed was on the twenty-second floor of the Cathedral of Learning in the center of campus. The elevator clanked and groaned in its ascent, and I wondered how hard it would be to walk twenty-two floors. I glanced at the students occupying the elevator with me. They all looked so... young. I caught a glimpse of my reflection in the shiny silver door. Next to them, I looked old...er. *Well, you could be the mother of any of them.* Then I noticed the girl with two metal rings in her lower lip and six studs in her earlobe. I shuddered, wondering if Gabby would come home from her first semester of college looking like she'd been in a nail-gun accident.

The car bounced to a stop, and the doors whooshed open. I followed the signs to the School of Social Work office. Behind the glass door, a young woman sat at a desk wearing a headset and chatting into the microphone. She looked up and smiled, waving a finger to indicate she'd be with me in a minute. I picked up a brochure and a copy of the School of Social Work newsletter from the counter while I waited.

"I'm sorry to keep you waiting. How may I help you?" the girl asked.

"I have an appointment …Hope, uh, Janet DeMarco. I'm here to see about registering for classes."

"Are you sure you're not looking for the graduate school? That's upstairs."

"No, no. I'm looking for undergrad."

"Okay. Have a seat and Mr. Robbins will be with you shortly."

She called and announced my presence. A few moments later, a man walked down the hallway and into the reception area. He looked to be in his mid-thirties, nice smile, expensive suit.

"Hello, Ms. DeMarco. I'm Greg Robbins, the admissions director for the undergrad program." He extended his hand and shook mine. "Please, come back to my office."

I followed him into a small office nearly filled by a desk and several file cabinets, taking a seat in one of the two available chairs. He edged behind the desk and into a large leather chair.

"You're interested in admissions information?"

"Yes. I… "

"Is this for your son or daughter?"

"Neither. It's for me. I'm thinking of pursuing a social work degree."

"I see. We have a lot of later-life students. Do you have any college background?"

"Not much. I went to community college to learn accounting, but that was, uh, twenty years ago." His words "later-life students" zinged through my head.

"Why social work?"

I relaxed in my chair. "I took a quiz in a career book and passed the test."

He laughed. "Well, then, it's meant to be. We do have a number of women who return to school once their children are grown. You can't have children that old."

"Thanks. They're seventeen and fifteen," I said, feeling heat rush to my face, and enjoying the compliment.

"Why now?"

I looked at my hands and entwined my fingers nervously. "I just figured out what I wanted to be when I grew up." I laughed at his look of surprise. "I'll bet you don't hear that one very often. You know the funny part? I quit my job and taught my family to take care of themselves because I was feeling taken advantage of. Now, here I am, looking at getting a degree in a helping profession so I can solve other people's problems. Which, by the way, I'm told I'm good at… that and listening."

He nodded and said nothing.

"So, what? Am I too old for the program or something?"

"No. I was just thinking that you'd be a welcome addition to the program. Let me give you an application packet. I don't think any of the course work you did twenty years ago will apply, so you'll be starting from scratch. How do you feel about that?"

"It's not like I'm in a hurry or anything. Actually, I'll probably need to take classes part-time and work part-time."

"Okay. Here's the application packet. Once you're accepted into the program, you'll be assigned a faculty advisor who will help you choose your courses and set your schedule."

I stood and tucked the packet under my arm. "Thank you, Mr. Robbins."

"You're welcome. You know where my office is located, if you need anything at all. I'll look forward to seeing you on campus, Janet."

"Hope," I said, excitedly shaking his hand again.

"I'm sorry. I thought your name was Janet."

"It is. But my friends call me Hope. Thanks, again," I said as I backed from his office.

Was he flirting with me? Nah, he was just being friendly— wasn't he?

I considered taking the stairs. A woman carrying a brief case exited an office and stepped into the open elevator. She held the door open. "You going down?"

"Uh,,, yes, thank you." At least I wouldn't die alone if the cables snapped and the box plunged twenty-two floors. By the time we reached ground level, we'd made four jerky stops and picked up waiting students. I was jammed in the back corner, breathing stale air and a faint odor of something sweet and smoky. I had vague memory of what it could be. It was emanating from the lanky, pimple-faced kid to my right with a glazed-over look in his eyes. *What the hell are you thinking, Jan? You don't belong here.*

~ * ~

I drove the short distance from the campus to the hospital and made my way to Joy's room. When I arrived, two women were seated next to her bed. Both looked unkempt and wore shabby clothing. One was wearing a long skirt and a pair of men's work boots that had to be at least two sizes too big. Joy beamed as I entered the room, and the two other women turned to look.

"Hope. Thank you for coming. These are my friends, Mary and Betty."

One of the women turned and smiled; the other lowered her head shyly. I walked to them, extending my hand to each. "Hello. It's nice to meet a few of Joy's friends." I looked at Joy. "If I'm interrupting, I can come back later."

The woman in the boots, Betty, stood, and the other woman followed suit. "We got to be going, anyway. You take care of yourself. Everyone at the shelter says to tell you they're praying for you." She turned to me and nodded. "It was nice meeting you. Say goodbye, Mary."

Mary lifted her face with a broad, toothless smile, and I could see that she had Downs syndrome. "Bye."

"Bye. It was nice meeting you both."

They exited the room, and I sat beside Joy's bed. "How are you feeling today?"

"Better. I don't think the hospital knows quite what to do with a steady stream of homeless people, though. A few of my friends weren't allowed inside. Mary and Betty slipped in through the emergency room and found their way up here. We're very resourceful people," she said, smiling.

"Is there anything you need that I can get for you?"

"No, thanks. I'll be okay. Got everything I need right here."

"Did you give more thought to Carmela's suggestion?"

"Don't see as how I have many options. Did you talk to your mother-in-law?"

"Yes. She wants to come with me tomorrow to meet you. Would that be all right?"

Joy nodded. "Fine with me; I'm not going anywhere."

"Joy, if for any reason it doesn't seem comfortable for you, I will happily set up our den and you can stay there. Angela can be a little... tough, but she's a good-hearted soul."

She grinned. "I live in shelters and on the street. How uncomfortable could it be?"

"Oh, you haven't met my husband's family. Loud, argumentative, opinionated... and they love one another fiercely. Sunday afternoons might be the one time you'll wish you could disappear. Angela has everyone there for mid-afternoon dinner. It sounds like a hockey match, and it could be overwhelming. Of course, you wouldn't have to join in."

"I won't pretend this whole thing doesn't have me in a tailspin. I'm scared to death wondering what's going to happen. But, heck, I'll catch up on my reading, I suppose."

"What do you like to read? I belong to a book club, and I have books I'd be happy to share."

"Thanks. I like mysteries, mostly. Sometimes I'll read a little romance."

"Uh, Joy, you should know that I had to tell Angela about your whole situation, about you being homeless."

"She didn't run the other way, huh?"

"No. She did ask if you came with a shopping cart."

She laughed. "Not any more. My cart and everything in it got destroyed in the accident. The cart actually kept the car from rolling right over me. So, how do you like this gown, 'cause it's what I got for now."

"What size do you wear?"

"A ten. Why?"

"You're in luck. I have size tens… and eights and twelves. I tend to fluctuate, and I can't part with things if I think I'll get back into them. Those are the eights. I keep the twelves because I know I'll get back into those. Don't worry. You're probably going to be wearing nightgowns for a while, anyway."

When she nodded and yawned, I took that as a sign. "I'm going to run and let you rest. I'll be here tomorrow around ten-thirty with Angela."

She reached for my hand with her one free hand and squeezed. Her eyes filled. "Hope, thank you for being so kind."

I swallowed hard and squeezed back. "That's what friends are for. You'd do the same for me, wouldn't you?"

"Oh, yeah. I'd be happy to share my cardboard box with you. Seriously, you have no idea what this means. It's not easy for me to accept help like this, but you make it easier. I'll try not to make your mother-in-law nervous or to be in the way too much."

"You won't be in the way at all, and I don't think Attila the Hun could make Angela DeMarco nervous. I'll see you tomorrow."

I went home, cleaned the bathrooms and the kitchen and pulled steaks from the freezer to grill for dinner, needing to do something special for Anthony and the kids. Anthony was still adamantly opposed to Joy living with his mother and grandmother, and not crazy about the suggestion she live with us. When I refused to argue the point, he let it drop. It didn't hurt that he had meat to chew on.

Gabby bounced down the stairs later. "Hey, Mom, guess what? The bathroom fairy cleaned the upstairs bathroom."

"Honey, you're old enough now to know the truth… there is no bathroom fairy. I cleaned the bathrooms this afternoon."

"But why? It's my turn."

I smiled. "I just felt like doing something nice." I pulled her into a quick hug before she could get away.

"Oh. Thanks." She grinned and went on through to the kitchen.

"Bending your rules?" Anthony asked.

"Rules are meant to be bent sometimes. I had one of those moments today, realizing again how much I appreciate what I have. That's all. And don't get that look."

"What *look*?"

"That *does Hope want to come out and play* look. Ain't happening tonight."

He feigned hurt, then grinned. "Okay. Is Janet available?"

I threw a toss pillow at him and retreated to the den. I emailed Sue and Fran to let them know I'd gotten my application packet from the university, and then checked my incoming email. As I connected with more people through the reading group, I received more email. I was up to at least three a day; fifteen, if you counted all the spam. Those included the 'hey, baby' email offers I'd gotten ever since Carmela's venture onto the naked man website. Okay, so I admit I was tempted to go back there for a second look, but I didn't.

Angela was sitting on the porch when I arrived the next morning. She descended the steps as I pulled up at the curb.

"I convinced my mother to stay here so we wouldn't overwhelm your friend. Does Joy know I'm coming with you?" she asked as she fastened the seatbelt.

"I told her yesterday. She's looking forward to meeting you." I pulled away from the curb. "Angela, you don't have to do this. I appreciate you considering it, but I know it'll be an inconvenience and…"

"What do I do all day? I clean things that are already clean, and I cook for everybody I know. My mother's right; I don't really have a life."

I was shocked into silence by her admission.

Angela exhaled and continued. "I take care of people. I took care of my husband and kids. My kids grew up and moved out and I nursed my husband until he died." Her voice cracked, and she cleared her throat. "I brought my mother to live with me, but she doesn't need care. A bodyguard, perhaps, but not a caretaker."

We both laughed at the truth in her statement.

"But this is a complete stranger, Angela."

"She is for now. That's why I want to meet her. I'm good at this one thing, taking care of a home and family, taking care of other people. It's what I do." She turned to face me. "I know you and I see things differently, the duties of a wife and mother. And I know you have to do it your way. I'm trying not to judge you for that."

"And I try not to judge you, Angela. I hope you know that."

"It isn't easy, though, is it?" she asked, a smile tugging at her mouth. "I know my ideas are old-fashioned. The truth is, change scares me. There, I've said it. Angela DeMarco *is* afraid of something. I was looking forward to having Jaclyn come and stay so I'd have someone to dote on. It's good she can stay with her mother to get through this pregnancy, but I was disappointed."

"But it could be a while before Joy's back on her feet."

"So? Where am I going? I've got nothing but time and plenty of sauce."

I turned into the parking garage at the hospital, pulled the ticket from the dispenser and found a space. "I don't think you like people to see it, Angela, but you're a good woman."

"Thank you. Don't tell anybody, or I'll never give you my sauce recipe."

"You're giving me your sauce recipe?"

"Maybe."

Joy's door was closed when we reached her room. I tapped and opened it a crack, peering inside. A nurse was tending to her and called out, "I'll be just a minute." Angela and I stood in the hallway, waiting to be admitted.

The nurse swung open the door. "She's all yours."

I walked to Joy's bedside. She appeared to be in pain. "Joy? Are you all right?"

She opened her eyes. "I will be. It's a bitch... uh, it's painful when they move me to change the bed. They say it's good that I'm feeling that pain in my leg, but I beg to differ."

Angela stepped up beside me. "Hello, Joy. I'm Angela, the mother-in-law. My son, Dante, had a broken leg once, and he cried every time I had to move him. I know how that must hurt."

Joy forced a smile. "It's nice to meet you. I'm sorry for the language."

With a dismissive wave, Angela said, "Ack. Don't worry about that. I can teach you a few words in Italian, and no one else will know what you're saying."

I pulled the two chairs up next to the bed and closed the curtain between the two beds. Angela sat closest to Joy. "My daughter-in-law has told me a little about you and your situation. I want to be of help, if you'll let me. I'm a person who, how do you say, cuts to the chase. I have two questions to ask you, if that's okay."

Joy nodded.

"Have you ever been violent to anyone or yourself?" Angela asked.

Joy shook her head. "Nope, never."

"Good, question number two… do you like Italian food?"

A smile creased Joy's face. "What's not to like?"

Angela looked from Joy to me, and back again. "I'm satisfied. Any questions you want to ask me?"

"Just one. Why are you doing this?"

"Because I can, and because, as I told Hope on our way over here, I'm meant to take care of others, and I have no one to take care of right now. You met my mother," Angela said.

"Sofialoren? Yes, I see your point. By the way, is Angela really your name?"

"It is," Angela said.

Joy grinned. "Just checking. So far, none of us is who we started out to be. My name used to be Madeline."

Angela pursed her lips, then said, "Well, maybe I'll change my name, too. I could be Gina. You know, like Gina Lollobrigida. Besides, what's so great about ending up as the person we started out being?"

I exchanged looks with Joy, raising my eyebrows and shrugging. Joy probably thought I'd lost my mind when I described Angela to her. The woman sitting in this room was *not* the Angela I'd known for twenty years.

Angela turned to me. "What do you think, Hope? Do I make a good Gina?"

"You make a great Gina," I said with a laugh. "Now, you know I'm going to be blamed for this."

"Or given the credit," Angela responded. She turned her attention back to Joy. "Here's what I think we should do. We can get a hospital bed for the downstairs bedroom. It's a good place because, once you're in the house, there are no steps. The bathroom has a walk-in shower, and I still have the shower seat my husband used. It's also right off the kitchen, so I can talk to you while I work. So, what do you think?"

"I think you people are all crazy, in the best possible way. I don't know how I'll ever repay your kindness." Joy's eyes filled.

"You won't. It doesn't come with a price tag. It's a gift. You only have to accept it." Angela patted Joy's hand. "Well?"

"How can I refuse?" Joy asked. "I'd be very grateful."

"Okay, so it's all settled. You'll let Hope know when you're ready to come. In the meantime, I'll get my sons to take the bed apart. The hospital bed will make it easier for you to sit up. I have a TV in there, so you'll have something to pass the time."

"Carmela's already planning card games and checkers."

"Do not let my mother sucker you into playing poker. She cheats," Angela said. She put a hand on Joy's arm. "I know we're strangers to you, and this may be overwhelming, but I think you'll be very comfortable."

"I'm sure I will be. Thank you both."

I stood. "Well, it's all set then. I'll stop by tomorrow afternoon. Can I bring you anything?"

"No, nothing."

A tap sounded on the door frame, and I turned to see Betty and Mary standing there. "Hi. Come on in. We're just leaving. Angela, these are Joy's friends, Betty and Mary. This is my mother-in-law, Angela."

Angela welcomed the women. "You can call me Gina," she said with a smile.

Uh-oh, I'm going down for this one. Wait till Anthony hears this news.

On the drive back to Angela's house, she laughed aloud. "Wait till I tell my mother to call me Gina. You know, Hope, Carmela's right about you. You're good for this family. I used to be a lot more fun before… " her voice faded.

"Before what?"

"Before I outlived my brother and sister. Before my oldest son died in a desert fighting someone else's war. Before I became a wife and mother, then had no one to hold onto at night and no one to mother during the day. Do you remember when you and Anthony were first married, and I was always singing while I cooked? I haven't sung for so long."

I turned the corner and pulled to the curb in front of Angela's house. "Angela, I never knew you felt this way."

"I know. Neither did I. Funny, isn't it? You get into a rut and you plod along, and then one day it all hits you in the face. You're walking around lost." She turned and looked at me, her eyes misted. "I used to feel like Gina. I want to feel that way again. Probably foolish for old lady, huh?"

I rested my hand on hers. "It's not foolish, and you're far from being an old lady. Just look at Carmela. I mean, Sofialoren."

"I'm no comparison to my mother." She laughed. "I'd better get inside. I need to call Grace and make a hair appointment." She pulled herself out of the car and turned, smiling in at me. "Do you have time to go shopping with me one day?"

"Absolutely. Call when you want to go. And, Angela, thank you."

"No, Hope. It's Gina now, thanks to you."

I left and headed straight for Fran's. I had to tell somebody about this. I also had to have someone pinch me and confirm that I was, in fact, awake.

Fourteen

"What have you done to my mother?" Anthony boomed the question at me as he came in the back door.

"Hello to you, too. I haven't done anything to your mother. Why?" I asked, continuing to shuck corn over the wastebasket.

He set his briefcase on the floor and went to the refrigerator for a beer. "I stopped by there on my way home. She said she's having your friend come and stay with her, then she started babbling about knowing her purpose in life and that everyone should call her Gina." He fixed his eyes on me. "That's when I knew you had something to do with it… Hope."

I set the corn aside, got a beer from the fridge and sat at the table. "You could just say thank you."

"I don't want to thank you." He was now up and pacing. "I want everybody to stop changing their names and turning into different people. Is that too much to ask?"

"I'm afraid so," I said calmly, taking a long gulp of my beer. "Anthony, sit down. You're going to give yourself a stroke. I'll admit the change in your mother is a little scary and I didn't trust it at first, either. What's the big deal? She's helping someone out. She's smiling and having a little fun, and she wants to be called Gina."

"And that seems perfectly normal to you? Of course, look who I'm asking!"

"You know what she told me today? She said she's afraid of change. I think she's just confronting her fear."

"Oh, now you're a psychologist?"

"Anthony, what are you so afraid of? Are you afraid you'll lose your mother? That she'll stop taking care of you?"

"I-am-not-afraid! I think you've all lost your minds. Notice it's only affecting the females. It must be some woman thing."

The kids came in the back door. Anthony looked at Michael. "What's your name this week, son?" he asked.

"Huh? Uh, Michael, same as last week."

Turning to Gabby, Anthony asked, "And what about you? Are you changing your name, too?"

Gabby smiled. "Well, I've always like Britney or Christina. But if I changed my name, it would be to something unusual, with mystique. I'll need a stage name eventually, but…"

"Your grandmother wants to be called Gina. How do you like that?" he persisted.

Michael shrugged, dropped his backpack and opened the fridge.

Gabby set her books on the counter and raised her shoulders as well. "It's not very imaginative, but it is Italian, like that other Italian actress, what's her name?

"Gina Lollobrigida," I said.

Anthony narrowed his eyes, shook his head and stomped off to the bedroom.

"Boy, this name thing sure has Dad's boxers in a twist," Gabby said.

I stifled a laugh. "It's confusing for him, honey. He'll get over it. Dinner will be ready in about a half-hour. Don't you two disappear."

They both headed up to their rooms. I finished shucking the corn and filled the stockpot with water to boil. The chicken would only take a few minutes on the grill. After turning on the burner beneath the pot, I headed upstairs.

"Anthony?" I called as I walked into the bedroom. He was stretched out on the bed, still in his work clothes, staring up at the ceiling. I sat next to him and put a hand on his arm. "Why is this so upsetting for you? When I made these changes, you treated it like a game."

"It's not a game, though. I have to call my wife of twenty years by a new name, my grandmother has purple hair and looks up pornography on the internet, and my mother is dancing in her kitchen and calling herself Gina."

"You mother was dancing in the kitchen?"

"I haven't seen her like that since…"

"Since when?"

"Since she and my dad danced together. He'd come in from work and grab her, and they'd dance around the kitchen, and she'd laugh."

"You miss him, don't you?"

His eyes misted, and I saw his Adam's apple move when he swallowed. He didn't speak, just nodded.

"Anthony, is this about your mother getting on with life again? It was bound to happen some time, you know. She's only, what, sixty-one? Don't you think she deserves to be happy?"

"Of course she deserves to be happy. She was happy. Everything was just fine."

"No, honey, it wasn't. Not for me, not for your mother, not even for Carmela."

He turned and looked into my eyes. "Why weren't you happy?"

"I wasn't *un*happy. I just needed to figure some things out, get a direction again. And that's what's happening with your mother. She needed to remember how to dance again, and to sing and laugh."

"Everything was different after Pop died. We all got used to that empty space at the table. I got used to carving the turkey and the ham on holidays. I got used to Mom wearing black all the time and cooking like the army was due in her kitchen any minute."

I brushed the hair from his forehead with my fingers, thinking of Michael when he was a little boy and afraid, but trying to be brave.

"Just because your mother sings and dances in the kitchen again doesn't mean she's forgotten your father. It doesn't mean you have to, either."

He stared at the ceiling, his jaw clenched. "Remember how Pop changed before he died? He was so weak; then he rallied. He laughed more and he told jokes and…" His chin quivered. "I went there a few days before he died. I looked in the window and couldn't believe what I was seeing. Mom was holding him up and they were dancing, very slowly, and he was leaning on her and crying, but with a smile on his face." A tear escaped the corner of his eye and streamed into the fine hairs at his temple.

"Anthony, look at me. Your mother is not dying. She's living."

He closed his eyes, then opened them and stared into mine. "She was dancing alone. I think I finally realized that Pop isn't coming back and that she has to dance alone from now on."

I laid down next to him and put my arm across his broad chest, my head resting on his shoulder. "Honey, she's not dancing alone. She's dancing with her best memories. As for becoming Gina… it's a name that lets her take that first step forward, out of the box she's been trapped in. Let her have that. Please."

He placed a hand over the top of my head, playing with my hair. "I'm sorry."

I hugged him. "It's okay."

"Promise me one thing."

"What?"

"Promise me I'll never have to dance alone."

"Oh, honey, that would be best. Have you seen yourself dance? I usually cover for you."

He laughed, and I hugged him again, then I whispered, "You'll never have to dance alone." I planted a light kiss on his lips. "I'm going to put the chicken on the grill. Dinner will be ready in twenty minutes."

As I stood, he grabbed my hand. "I love you… both of you."

~ * ~

The shopping spree with Angela the next week gave new meaning to the phrase "shop 'til you drop." She was a woman on a mission: slacks, blouses, a couple of dresses, one hot pink jogging suit with a thin black stripe, and several pairs of shoes, including one pair of sneakers which she wore out of the store.

We sat at a table in the food court, surrounded by bags. Angela stretched her legs out and looked at her feet. "Now that

I have the right shoes, maybe I'll go walking with you and my mother some time."

"That would be great, Angela. And once Joy arrives, I can sit with her if you and Carmela want to walk together."

"I want to thank you, Hope. I was turning into a dried up old woman locked away in my house, waiting for my family to come for Sunday dinners. I knew something was wrong when you came in with your new hair color and your new name and I felt jealous of you, of you and my mother, both."

"You felt jealous? Of me and Carmela?"

"Yes. You had the courage to change things for yourself, and I was still afraid to do that. I don't know what I thought would happen. I guess I thought I was putting my family first, doing things for their sake. It's like my mother was the sixty-year-old, and I was eighty."

"When I quit working for Teddy and then colored my hair and changed my name, I got a little scared by it. I wondered how far I'd go and if I'd get so far away, I wouldn't be able to come back home. But Anthony and the kids are my anchors. No matter what, I'll always know where home is. You have that, too."

"You chose a good name… Hope. It's a strong name. I think it suits you."

"Really?"

"Yes. Now," she gathered up packages, "let's take Hope and Gina home. We'll have a fashion show for Sofialoren."

I got a glimpse of the Angela I'd seen when I'd first married into this crazy Italian family.

Carmela came in from the senior center while Angela and I were admiring her new outfits. "Hey, look who's here," she said as she toddled over and kissed me on the cheek, then turned to Angela. "And look at you. What's all this?"

As Angela showed each of her new outfits to her mother, I noticed what a beautiful smile she had… straight, white teeth, full lips and laugh lines that deepened with her smile. She really was a strikingly beautiful woman and had kept that hidden for far too long.

"I'm going to make an appointment with Grace to have my highlights touched up. Does anyone want a hair appointment?" I asked.

"I do. I want to see if I can try blue this next time. Do you think Grace can change that?" Carmela asked.

"I want an appointment for the works: cut, color and style. She's gonna need a couple of hours, I'm sure. And I want a manicure, and…" Angela said, becoming animated.

I gazed at the two of them. "I have a great idea. Let's have a spa day. We can get massages, use the sauna and have manicures and pedicures. Then we can go to Grace's and get our hair done. It'll be a girl's day out."

"That sounds like fun," Angela said. Both Carmela and I looked at her with surprise.

"Okay. I'll call the spa and set us up for Friday morning, then see if Grace has the afternoon open. Angela, I enjoyed spending today with you."

Angela pulled me into a hug when I leaned to kiss her cheek. "Thank you, honey. You know, I may have never said it, but I consider you my daughter."

"You're welcome," I said with a smile, pulling back and looking at her. "I'm going to run. I have to finish my application for college." I stopped. "I can't even believe I just said that. I want to go to the book store, too, and apply for a part-time job."

I returned home and went to the den. After completing the initial application paperwork for school, I grabbed the CD player and clipped it to my waistband, then headed to the post office on foot. It was a wonderful early summer day, and the sunshine kissed the top of my head as I walked.

I thought about how my life had changed in the past weeks. I liked being Hope, even though I knew the name was just a password for *me*. I had become more of myself, not less. That was important for me to know. I considered the name I'd chosen for myself: Hope. *Was that the thing I felt I needed? Isn't that what we all need?*

Then I thought of Joy and how it seemed she'd lost the joy in her life, unable to find that even in her children. I shuddered at the thought that a woman could become so lost. She'd left and shed herself of everything she knew in search of that one thing… joy.

As I dropped the application into the mail slot and felt it slide from my fingers, a ripple of excitement rolled through me. It was quickly followed by a piercing doubt, and I wondered if I could get my arm into the slot to retrieve the envelope. I pulled down the tray on the mailbox and peered into it. *Nope, ain't gonna happen. What's done is done.*

~ * ~

Okay, so maybe spending time in a sauna with an eighty-year-old wasn't the best idea. It turned out Carmela had little modesty when in the company of women. It's frightening to see the future that close up. I found myself subtly checking my body to see if some things were sagging and others were wrinkling. I also double-checked the tuck on my towel to ensure it stayed put.

"This was a wonderful idea," Angela said, swiping damp hair from her face. "It's funny. For a few years, I spent my time trying to keep cool and not sweat through hot flashes. Now, here I am, in a sauna."

"I remember hot flashes," Carmela said. "I'd get up in the middle of the night and tear off my nightgown and stand in front of the fan." She looked at Angela. "Your father would grumble and complain that I woke him and that I was blocking the breeze. He didn't even comment that I was standing there naked. I don't think he even noticed."

I laughed. "I think if I stood naked in front of a fan, Anthony would definitely notice." They both stared at me. The heat of the sauna concealed my embarrassment. I'd forgotten who I was talking to. "I mean, I don't think he'd be able to sleep. Um, that is…"

Angela grinned. "We know what you meant."

I was saved by the bell as the timer indicated it was time for our massages. A few hours later, we left the spa, relaxed and renewed. I treated us to lunch before heading to Grace's for the rest of the transformation.

Grace's shop was empty when we arrived. She'd reserved the afternoon for the three of us. I was first, getting a wash, trim, and then having roots touched up and hair pulled through the cap to add highlights. I took a seat at one of the hairdryers while Grace tended to Carmela, explaining the potential risk of trying to change her hair from purple to blue.

Carmela weighed the risk, then said, "Go for it. Color is color. What's the worst that could happen? It'll be interesting."

"O-kay," Grace said. "But remember I warned you."

When she'd finished and set Carmela's hair in rollers, she seated her next to me, under a dryer. "Now, Angela. What am I going to do for you today?"

Angela had browsed the hairstyle books and lifted one to Grace, pointing to the page. "I want this style," she said, then turned the page. "And I want this color. Can you do that?"

Grace smiled broadly. "You have an eye for this. That's a perfect style for you, and the color will complement your complexion. Follow me. Let's get to work."

Local gossip flew back and forth while Grace worked on Angela's hair. While Angela waited for the color to set, Grace finished both my hair and Carmela's. I was happy to see that my color was subtle and caught the light in a golden glow.

Carmela, on the other hand, should have heeded Grace's warnings. Her hair had an odd bluish-purple hue and looked a little like a clown wig. Grace looked at her and said, "I can try to tone that down for you."

"Are you kidding? I love it. I'll be the only one at the center with this color. Boy, will I be the topic of conversation."

"Yeah, well, please don't tell anyone I did this," Grace said, adding hairspray to hold the curls in place.

When Angela's hair was dried and brushed out and she turned to face the mirror, she gasped. "Oh, my goodness!" So did I. She looked at least ten years younger. Her hair was the color of cloves, and her dark eyes were wide and warm looking.

"You look beautiful," I said, standing next to her chair. "The color is so warm."

"It's wonderful, Grace," Angela smiled. "I hardly know myself."

Carmela stood on the other side of Angela's chair. "Now that looks like Gina."

Grace looked confused and caught my eyes in the mirror. "Who's Gina?"

"Grace, you know Hope," I said, pointing to my chest. I pointed to Carmela. "And you know Sofialoren. Well, this," I said as I rested my hand on Angela's shoulder, "is Gina."

"You've got a crazy family here, but you sure make life interesting," Grace said with a shake of her head.

We paid, thanked Grace and headed for home. Angela lowered the visor and stared at herself in the mirror, lightly touching her hair.

My cell phone rang as I pulled up in front of Angela's house. "Hello."

It was Joy. "Looks like they're letting me out of this joint. I'll have one week at rehab, and then I'll be released."

"Wonderful. I'll let Angela know. She's right here with me. And I'll come by tomorrow and bring you some nightgowns and a pair of slippers for rehab."

She thanked me, and I hung up and relayed the message to Angela and Carmela.

"Perfect. The boys are going to take the bed down this weekend, and I have a hospital bed scheduled for delivery on Tuesday," Angela said.

As they got out of the car, Carmela turned and smiled at me. "Thanks, Hope."

Angela leaned in next. "Will I see you on Sunday afternoon for dinner? I'd like you to be here when the family sees my new makeover."

"I wouldn't miss it for anything. I'll make sure we're here early."

~ * ~

The kids grumbled when I insisted they go with us for family dinner on Sunday. "Your grandmother has a surprise for everyone, and it's important both of you are there. Michael, bring your car, and you and Gabby can leave after dessert, if you want."

"What's the big surprise?" Anthony asked as we got into his Explorer. "Is she getting married or something?"

"It's not my place to spoil her surprise. You'll see for yourself."

He cast a wary glance my way, then backed out of the drive. We were the first to arrive. I pretended to search for something in my purse so Anthony would go through the door first. I then followed as he walked the hallway toward the kitchen.

When Angela turned from the stove and smiled, Anthony stopped in his tracks. "Holy mother of… Mom, what'd you do to your hair?"

I punched his arm, and he rephrased. "I mean, wow, your hair looks nice. It's… different."

Angela beamed and put a hand to her hair. "Do you like it?"

"Yeah, it's… I've never seen it that color."

I stepped in beside Anthony. "Hi, Gina. I like the new outfit, and your hair looks great."

"Thanks, Hope."

Carmela shuffled into the kitchen. In the broad light of day that streamed through the window, her hair looked surreal. "Hi, Hope. Anthony, my favorite grandson! How are you?"

"Grandma, um, your hair's… unusual," he said, his eyes fixed on her head.

"Yeah, ain't it great?" she asked with a smile. "I'm the only one at the senior center with this color. I tell you, by next week, others are going to try to get this color, too. I've gotten a lot of attention, especially from the men."

The back door opened and Anthony's brother, Dante, stepped inside. He scanned every head in the room and brought his eyes back to his mother. "New look, Mom? What'd you do, join Hope's club?"

Angela waved a wooden spoon at him. "Do not start, Dante. I'm still your mother, and I can still swing this wooden spoon." She smacked his arm with the spoon.

Dante grabbed his forearm and feigned hurt. "Ow! Not so hard. That hurts." He bent and kissed his mother's cheek. "It's a nice look, Mom, really. You're gorgeous." He then stooped to kiss Carmela. "How's my favorite blue-haired old lady?"

"Watch who you're calling old," she said as she pinched his bearded cheek.

He then turned to me. "And how's my favorite blonde?"

"I'm good, Dante," I said, accepting a kiss on the cheek. "How are you? And where's your girlfriend?"

Dante pulled two beers from the fridge and handed one to Anthony. "She dumped me. I'm available again. I don't suppose Hope has a friend," he said, an impish gleam in his eyes.

"Not that she'd turn over to the likes of you," I teased.

"Ouch," he responded. "Come on, Anthony. Let's get this job over with, take that bed apart and get it stored."

As they headed into the back room, Angela called to them, "You two be careful not to scrape the paint or the woodwork."

"We got it, Mom," Anthony called back.

The sounds of hammering on metal and swearing emanated from the back bedroom. After a loud 'thunk' and the sound of the metal bed frame collapsing, there was silence, then laughter. Angela and Carmela both looked at me. I was elected to investigate. I found both men sitting with backs against the wall, beers in hand, laughing at the pile of rubble in front of them.

"Everyone okay in here?" I asked.

Neither could speak, both gasping for breath, but Anthony nodded and waved me away.

I returned to the kitchen. "I don't know what's so funny in there, but I can safely say the bed is down. So are the guys."

The two men carried the dismantled bed through the kitchen and out to the garage for storage.

Anthony stuck his head into the kitchen. "We're going to Home Depot and get plastic to wrap up the mattress and box spring. We'll be back in a few minutes."

The men soon returned and, with Michael's help, wrapped the mattress and box spring, secured the cover with duct tape, and carried the items to the garage for storage.

As other family members arrived for dinner, Angela beamed at their compliments of her new look. Seeing her so happy, Anthony caught my eye, smiled and winked.

Angela announced to everyone during dessert that Joy would be coming the following week and staying for as long as she needed to recuperate. She didn't go into the details about Joy's situation, just that she was a friend of mine who needed a place to stay for a while.

"I hope she's paying rent," Dante quipped.

Angela launched into a reprimand in Italian that sent blood rushing to Dante's face. She then switched back to English. "I brought you up better than that, to be so selfish and single-minded. You will be kind to her while she is a guest in my home, or you will not be coming here. Is that understood?"

169

The thirty-five year old, macho cop stood with his hands in his pockets and his head down, looking like a scolded ten-year-old. "Understood."

Dante wasn't a bad guy. With thick black hair, a broad smile and deep brown eyes, he was strikingly handsome. His tendency towards chauvinism eventually brought an end to every relationship he'd had. He was well on his way to becoming a life-long bachelor.

Michael and Gabby were the first to leave after dinner, soon followed by Dante. I gave Anthony my 'shouldn't we be going now' eye-blink.

Anthony stood. "We should be going. Thanks for dinner, Mom. I really do like your hair and the new clothes. You look great. Bye, Grandma."

I followed him, giving Angela and then Carmela a hug and kiss. "I'll be here on Tuesday when they deliver the bed so I can help with the set-up."

"Oh, they'll set it up. But I suppose we might want to rearrange some of the other furniture to make it more comfortable for Joy. Why don't you plan to come for lunch?"

"Thanks. I'll be here," I said.

I pulled the car door closed and reached for my seatbelt.

"You and Mom are getting chummy," Anthony said.

"What are you talking about? Your mother and I have always gotten along."

"The two of you don't usually go shopping together, have spa days and do lunch. What gives?"

"I think your mother identifies with me. You may have been right; it's a woman thing."

"Oh, brother."

Fifteen

The night before Joy was to arrive at Angela's, I went to the florist and got two bouquets to put in the room… Angela's suggestion. I delivered the flowers and helped Angela make up the bed.

"Is there anything else I can do?" I asked.

"Do you know what she likes to drink? Soft drinks, or anything?" Angela asked.

"I only know that she drinks regular coffee, black, and she likes the muffins from the café. I'll get some of those on my way over here in the morning."

"Good. Now, let's see. Do you think the TV is in a good spot for her?"

I lay on the bed and directed Angela in adjusting the angle of the television. "Where's the remote?"

"Right here in this pocket," she said, pulling the remote from a pocket fastened onto the bed rail by a Velcro strip. "This way it'll always be within her reach."

I hung some clothes that I'd brought along in the closet and put new underwear and a few more gowns in the dresser drawers. I placed two mystery novels and a few magazines on the stand beside the bed.

Angela had ordered a rolling adjustable bed tray and had this set with a call bell and a note pad for Joy's use. She stood in the doorway and looked around the room. "Do you think this is okay?"

"I think it's perfect. Thank you, again, for doing this."

"It's my pleasure. I'll have her in good health and back on her feet in no time."

"And I'll be responsible for getting her to any appointments. I'll be here in the morning with muffins. If you think of anything else you need, call me."

It was a warm evening, and I drove home the long way with the car windows open. The air smelled of fresh-cut grass and lilacs. I realized that I was happy, contentedly happy. Things were running smoothly at home. I was preparing, though with some trepidation, to start classes at the university, and I'd gotten a call that my application for part-time employment at the book store was accepted. I'd be working two nights a week, plus Saturdays and every other Sunday. With helping Angela with Joy's care and my classes, that would be enough.

The next morning, I headed to the café at eight o'clock. Ricki was behind the counter and smiled when I walked in. "Hey. I haven't seen you for a while. How have you been?"

"I've been keeping busy. I came in to get some of the muffins Joy likes. She's moving in with my mother-in-law today to stay for her recuperation."

"I'm glad to hear that. It sounds like you have your hands full. You having your usual?"

I nodded. "How's Hannah?"

"She's fat and happy. I was going to call and ask you to babysit on Saturday evening, but it sounds like you'll be busy."

"Are you kidding? I'd love to see her. I can take her to Angela's with me. This Saturday is good. I start work next week at the book store."

She handed me the latte. "Are you sure? I, um, I have a date, and my mom has something scheduled."

"In that case, I'm very sure. New relationship, or something serious?"

"Not so new. It's with Hannah's father, Tim. We met a few times and talked about Hannah and how we'd work out visits for her benefit. The next thing I knew, he asked me out to dinner and started talking about how we should maybe give things a chance."

"That's wonderful. What time do you want to drop Hannah off?"

"Is six o'clock okay? I don't like to be out late for Hannah's sake."

She bagged a half dozen muffins and, when I opened my wallet, said, "These are on the house. Tell Joy I asked about her, and I hope she's feeling better."

"Thanks. I'll let her know. And I'll see you on Saturday. You know, I could keep Hannah overnight if you want."

She grinned. "I'm not going to rush things. I'll pick her up by ten at the latest."

Angela, Carmela, and I were sitting at the kitchen table having coffee when the front doorbell rang. Angela answered and came back with the ambulance driver, showing him where the room was situated. He determined they could more easily bring Joy in through the kitchen door using a specially-equipped wheelchair that would keep her broken and casted leg straight. I followed him outside and waited to hold the back door open.

Joy smiled broadly when she saw me. "I'm glad you're here. Thanks so much for all of this."

"It's good to have you out of the hospital. Your room's all ready."

The driver maneuvered the chair carefully around the kitchen table and through to the bedroom. Angela welcomed Joy, as did Carmela. The ambulance attendant showed us how to help Joy stand on one leg to maneuver from the chair to the bed. He helped her settle into the bed, parked the wheelchair in the corner, and gave me a bag of Joy's belongings. I saw him out and thanked him, then returned to the bedroom where Angela was already taking charge.

"Is the head up enough for you?" she asked, adjusting the bed. "I'll get another pillow."

She left the room, and I pulled up a chair next to the bed. "Is it overwhelming for you?"

"Hope, life is overwhelming for me. This is fine, really. It's a relief to get out of the hospital and rehab. It's been a long time since I've had a bedroom all to myself, and such a lovely room. The flowers are beautiful."

"Thanks. I stopped at the café and got muffins, and there's coffee, once you're ready."

"I really hope this isn't too much for your mother-in-law. I can get from the bed into the wheelchair by myself, so I can probably get myself into the bathroom."

"She had my husband and his brother take the door off, and she got one of those raised toilet seats with railings. I'll check the wheelchair and see if it fits." I wheeled the chair over and it slipped through the doorway with a few inches to spare. "Looks like you'll just have to back out. How's the arm?"

"It's good," she said, slipping her arm out of the sling. "It wasn't a bad break, and it's mostly healed. I use the sling because it starts to ache at times, but I can use it enough to wheel around."

Carmela came into the room with a glass and a pitcher of water that she placed on the bed tray. "It's nice to see you again. Any time you want to play cards or checkers, you let me know."

"Thank you. I will," Joy said, smiling.

"And this is for you to ring, in case you need help and we're not right here," Carmela said, picking up the bell from the night stand and shaking it.

Angela returned with a spare pillow. "I see my mother is orienting you. Here, lean forward and I'll put this behind you." Angela lightly touched Joy's shoulder and slid the pillow behind her. "Is that better?"

"Yes, it is. Thank you so much."

Angela bore a satisfied smile. "Now, I'm going to get coffee and muffins, and we can visit for a short while. Then we're going to let you get some rest."

I pulled two more chairs into the room from the kitchen and we sat around the bed. Joy looked like a queen holding court as we sipped coffee, enjoyed the muffins and chatted.

Joy handed me some papers. "Those are my discharge orders. They told me a nurse would come by once a week, and a physical therapist will be in a couple of times to get me walking again. The cast should come off in a week or so. I guess I'll have to go to the hospital for that."

"Don't worry, I'll get you there. Everything's going to be fine."

When Joy sighed and stifled a yawn, Angela stood and collected cups and plates. "I think it's time for a nap. I'll take these to the kitchen, and my mother will help. Hope, say goodbye for now and let Joy rest."

Joy and I exchanged a smile as Angela ushered Carmela from the room. "Orders from the boss," I said. "There's a remote for the TV in that pocket, and I put some books and magazines here for you. My phone number is on the pad beside the phone, so call me any time. I'll be back later. I know you're in good hands."

"I'm sure. Thanks, Hope. Would you leave the door open just a little?"

"Sure. Rest well. I'll see you later. Oh, and Ricki from the café sends her best."

I returned to the kitchen and told Angela I'd come back after dinner. "You're welcome to, but don't feel you have to. I'm sure everything will be under control."

"Oh, it's not for you. I know you can handle things. I just thought Joy might feel more comfortable with a familiar face. Bye, Gina. See you, Sofialoren!"

~ * ~

Within two days, Joy and Angela had a system worked out and things were going smoothly. On Saturday, I spent the day with Joy, then returned home to babysit Hannah. At Joy's request, I asked Ricki for the car seat and packed Hannah off to Angela's for a short visit. She was entertainment for everyone, smiling, talking in jumbled baby language and staring wide-eyed at Angela's collection of snow globes.

Ricki brought Tim along when she came to pick up Hannah. He was handsome, polite and friendly, and his eyes lit up when he saw the baby. With his blonde hair and blue eyes, there was no denying he was her father. She was still awake and let out a delighted shriek when he walked in. This was a good sign in my book.

Tim carried Hannah to the car and Ricki stayed behind, gathering up her diaper bag and toys. "Thank you, Hope. I really appreciate this."

"You're welcome. How'd it go?"

She smiled. "It went well, I think. We'll see."

Michael came in from a date just after Ricki left. "Hey, Mom. Who was that?"

"That was Ricki picking up Hannah."

"Oh." He got a soda from the fridge and sat on the sofa. "Where's Dad?"

"He already went upstairs, and I'm not going to be far behind. It's been an exhausting day."

"Can I talk to you about something?" he asked.

I felt my chest tighten as I imagined what might be coming. *I'm not going to college. I wrecked the car. My girlfriend's pregnant.*

"What is it, Michael?"

"I've been thinking."

"Okay, now there's a news flash," I said.

"I've been thinking about how you're getting another part-time job so you can buy books for school. So, I got a job, too."

"You got a job? Where?"

"That's the thing you're probably not going to like very much."

"Why? Where are you working?"

"I got a job working for Uncle Teddy."

"Uh-huh. First of all, he's not your uncle, and you don't have to call him that. He's your dad's cousin, and that makes him your cousin, too. What's he got you doing?"

"Driving the truck and delivering supplies. Seems the other driver's in jail. He's paying me decent money. Well, I kind of told him if he underpaid me, you'd know." He grinned.

"You're a bright kid, Michael. But what about school?"

"He told me I can work on Saturdays until graduation. Then I can work full-time through the summer. It seems like the fair thing to do. You and Dad never made me work as long as I kept my grades up. But now you have to work in order to take a few classes. I want to do my share, that's all."

I moved next to him and put my arms around him. "Michael, you have got to be the best son ever. I was really scared when you said you needed to talk."

He grinned again. "You thought I got some girl pregnant or something, huh?"

"Of course not. I know you better than that. I thought maybe you wrecked the car."

"Sure, Mom." He stood, kissed me goodnight and headed up to his room.

Gabby had stayed with Megan for the night. I turned off lights and checked both doors, then climbed the stairs.

Anthony was awake and reading when I entered the bedroom. "Did I hear Michael come in?"

I told him about my conversation with our son. "I wanted him to have this summer before college, but he's insistent on taking this job."

Anthony dropped the magazine he was reading onto the floor. "It'll be good for him, and it will help financially. He can buy books or clothes for himself."

I changed and slid into bed next to him, where we cuddled for a while.

"We have so much to be grateful for, don't we?" I asked.

"I know that *I* do." He kissed my temple and his hand caressed my breast. "Want me to show you how grateful I am?"

I giggled and rolled towards him. "If I were standing naked in front of a fan, would you notice?"

He pulled me closer, and I felt his response.

"I'll take that as a yes," I said.

"Should I get a fan?"

"I don't think we really need one."

~ * ~

Tuesday afternoon, I reported for work at the book store at three-thirty. I was scheduled to start at four p.m., but I was nervous. I donned my 'Hello, I'm Janet, Trainee' tag. My trainer was Ashley, who looked to be about sixteen... black hair streaked with hot pink and a diamond nose stud.

"Ashley, do you think I can get another name tag?"

"Uh, why?"

"Well, because I prefer to be called Hope."

"Why?"

"It's just a preference. It's like a nickname that I go by."

"You'll have to talk to Walt, the manager."

"Okay, is he here?"

"Nope. He's off today, so I'm in charge."

"Then, can't you make that decision?"

She rolled her eyes. "It's a managerial decision. I can't do that."

"Oh. Never mind. This will be fine." *She's going to have a long and not so lustrous career at the book store.*

I spent that evening 'tagging' Ashley. That meant I followed her around like a puppy while she explained her every move as if I were brain damaged. It was sales, not rocket science, but, then, I guess I had to consider that it was also Ashley. The degree of difficulty is probably directly proportionate to the level of I.Q.

I went to the café on my break to grab a latte. Sue was seated in a corner in front of her laptop, so I stopped to say hi.

"Working hard, I see."

She looked up and smiled. "Hope. What're you doing here?"

I pointed to the name tag. "I'm working here now. This is my first night."

She squinted at the tag. "Who's Janet?"

"I am. Well, that's my real name. I mean, my given name. I prefer Hope, but apparently getting the name tag changed requires an act of congress, so…"

"I thought you were going to take classes," she said.

"I am, part-time. I'm working part-time to help defray the cost. We have a son starting college in the fall, as well."

"Will you still be able to participate in the reading group?"

"I'll try. I have to work every other Sunday, but I'm not sure of my hours yet. Well, I'd better get my latte and get back to work. Ashley is watching. It was good seeing you."

"Good seeing you, too."

I spent the better part of the evening stacking books on shelves. I didn't mind the physical labor and enjoyed being in the book store atmosphere. When closing time came, I went to the office to retrieve my purse and thanked Ashley for sharing her expertise.

"You did a good job today, Janet. I'll see you on Thursday?"

"Thanks. It's Hope and, yes, I'll see you Thursday." I left her standing with a confused look on her face, probably wondering who Hope was.

I was in the kitchen making a sandwich when Anthony came in. "Back from a hard night's work, I see. How'd the first day go?" he asked, kissing my cheek.

"It went fine. I'm not as tired as I expected to be."

"Really?" His eyelids drooped and his grin spread.

"Is that all you think about?"

"How do you know what I'm thinking?" He narrowed his eyes and stared at the name tag. "Oh, Janet's back."

"I know what you're thinking by the expression on your face. And as for my name tag, you don't even want to know the story."

He grabbed a cold beer and sat across from me while I ate. "I did some figuring today with our income, and you don't really have to work at the book store, unless you want to."

"I did some thinking today, myself. I'm not all that certain I want to enroll in college as a student. I think I just want to take a few classes here and there. I like the book store. Maybe when

I get really, really good at stacking books on shelves, Ashley will recommend me for a promotion."

"Who's Ashley?"

"Never mind. I was just thinking of how contented I am with my life right now. I'm happy."

"What about the social work thing, though? I thought you wanted to get a degree so you could help people."

"I've realized I don't need a degree to be able to help people. There're lots of things I could do without a degree. I think I'm going to take one class at a time for now."

"Whatever Hope desires is fine with me. I stopped at my mom's on the way home from work and I met your friend, Joy. She seems nice."

"She is. I think things are going well there, don't you?"

He stretched his legs out and leaned against the back of his chair. "I haven't seen my mother so happy in a long time. She just loves having someone to take care of. You were right; I was wrong."

"She's a natural at it, that's for sure. And would you put that last part in writing, please?" I got up, rinsed my plate and set it in the dishwasher. "I'm going to bed. It's been a long day."

"I'll be up soon. I'm going to watch the late news. Goodnight."

The evidence of my having lifted stacks of books appeared the next morning as I tried to sit up. An ache seized my lower back. Ashley had tried to tell me to sit on the foot stool rather than bending over to shelve books. *Maybe her I.Q. is higher than I thought.*

After a long, hot shower, I dressed and headed to Angela's. I walked in to find Joy in her wheelchair, sitting at the kitchen table and having breakfast. Angela sat across from her rolling meatballs.

"Good morning," I said.

181

"Good morning, Hope," Angela said. "There's fresh coffee. Help yourself."

"Thanks. How are you this morning, Joy?"

"I'm doing fine. My greatest concern at this point is packing on pounds because of Angela's…er, Gina's cooking."

"You could use a few more pounds. You're too thin," Angela said, smiling.

"Yeah, well, just keep in mind you're the one who has to pick me up if I fall down," Joy retorted.

It was apparent that Angela and Joy had found their comfort zone together.

I poured a cup of coffee and sat at the table, easing into the chair.

"Something wrong?" Joy asked.

"I'm a little stiff. I shelved books last night at the book store. It was my first day on the job."

"You shouldn't be doing that kind of work," Angela said. "I thought you were going to sell books."

"Yeah, well, you have to shelve them before you can sell them, and I learned that it's the newest trainee who gets to do the shelving."

"Joy has some good news to share," Angela said.

I looked from her to Joy.

"The nurse told me that I'll probably get a walking cast when I go to the doctor next week."

"That is good news. Your appointment's next Wednesday, right?"

She nodded. "At eleven a.m."

"I'll be here to take you. Then, if you're up to it, we'll stop by the café or go somewhere for lunch."

"That would be nice."

When Joy was finished with her coffee, she wheeled back to the bedroom and I helped her get into the shower.

I then rejoined Angela in the kitchen. "Angela, is this working out okay? It's not too much for you?"

She rolled the last meatball and set it on top of the stack on a plate. "It's working out fine. I love taking care of people, and Joy is no trouble at all. I probably drive her crazy, always asking what she needs, because I don't trust she'll ask."

"It's very good of you to do this." I added hot coffee to my cup.

Angela covered the meatballs with waxed paper and washed her hands, then sat across from me. "I'm worried, though. What's going to happen to her when she's better? Is she going to go back out onto the streets?"

"Probably. I know it's hard to accept, but it's her choice."

"It's not right. There's really no reason she couldn't live here. It's not any trouble, and we have all this room."

"You can make that offer, but don't be surprised if she doesn't take you up on it." I heard the shower cease and went to see if Joy needed my help, calling in around the door.

"No, I can get dried and dressed on my own. I'll need help to get back into the chair, but I can call you," she said.

I walked back to the kitchen. "Angela, has Joy talked with you at all about… family?"

Angela shook her head. "No. Why? Does she have a family?"

"Yes. Well, she did. It's not my place to discuss it. I just wondered if she'd mentioned anything to you. Don't say anything. Okay?"

"Okay. But, it's a shame that a woman has a family and lives like that."

"Angela…"

"I won't say anything. I promise."

Joy called from the bathroom, and I went to help her step from the shower and ease into the wheelchair.

"Whew. That's a lot of work," she said.

"Do you want me to dry your hair for you?" I asked.

"Oh, no, that's okay."

"I don't mind." I grabbed a comb from the counter next to the sink and combed through her hair, apologizing as the comb caught in tangles.

"It's okay. My hair's gotten a bit long and out of hand."

I stopped combing and looked at her in the mirror. "I have an idea. Would you like a haircut?"

Her eyes widened. "You know how to cut hair?"

"Oh, no. Not me. Heavens no," I said with a laugh. "I'll call Grace and ask her to come by. She came here to cut Carmela's hair once when she'd twisted her ankle and couldn't get around. I'm sure she'll do it."

"I don't know. I… my check doesn't come until the first of the month. I hope they forward it from the shelter. But, until then…"

"Don't worry. I'll pay her and you can pay me back anytime." I stood behind her and pulled the hair back from her face and up. "Have you ever considered having color?"

"That depends on the color. I've seen Carmela's hair, and blue and purple won't work for me." We both laughed. I felt as though I were sharing a moment with a sister, and it seemed so natural.

"I'm going to call Grace right now and see when she can come. It'll be fun."

I wheeled Joy to the bed and helped her from the wheelchair. Then I removed my cell phone from my purse and looked up Grace's phone number. When I explained the situation, Grace happily agreed to come by that evening.

"It's all set. She'll be here this evening, so I'll come back and make sure you don't end up with a green Mohawk. Be prepared. Grace is very talkative and will ask a thousand questions about who you are, where you come from and what you do."

I left Joy watching TV, told Angela I'd be back before Grace arrived and was just ready to leave when Carmela came down the stairs. The purple jogging suit clashed loudly with the bluish-purple hair.

"Hope, I didn't know you were here."

"I'm just leaving."

"Good. Can you drop me at the senior center?"

"Sure."

On the way to the center, Carmela said, "That Joy's a nice girl. She's a card shark, though. Beat me out of twenty cents yesterday playing poker. And she didn't even cheat. I'd know because I cheat, so I know the tricks. It's too bad she can't see her kids."

I nearly drove off the rode and into Mrs. McMillan's front lawn. "She told you about her kids?"

"Sure. We talk while we play cards. She has a boy in medical school and a girl who's in college. She hasn't seen them for years. Her husband's remarried, and she doesn't have any contact with him either. They live just outside of town, near the high school."

"Joy told you all of this?"

"Yeah, it's a shame, you know. I think she's ashamed to let her kids see her and know how she lives."

"I think she's afraid of embarrassing them."

"Nope. She's afraid they'll reject her, or they'll be angry with her because she left them when they were young."

The psychological assessment of Dr. Sofialoren. And she's probably right.

"Hope, I was thinking."

Uh-oh. This could be trouble.

"About?"

"Maybe you could look up her kids and invite them over, say for the Fourth of July."

"I don't think that's a good idea. If Joy wanted to see her family, she'd do something about it."

"But it isn't right. If you were in her shoes, wouldn't you want somebody to tell Michael and Gabriella where you were?"

"What if they think she's dead?" I asked, pulling into the lot of the senior center.

Carmela sat in thought for a moment. "I guess then it would be a shock. Maybe it would be best to talk with her husband first." She opened her purse and pulled out a slip of paper. "Here's his name and the place where he used to work. You can probably get his phone number from the book."

She handed me the paper and I dropped it like it was on fire. "I'm not going to call this man. Did you even ask Joy if she wants to see her family? And how did you get his name and where he worked?"

Carmela grinned. "Murder, She Wrote."

"Excuse me?"

"I watch 'Murder, She Wrote.' I see how Jessica Fletcher gets information from people while they don't know they're giving it. It's a gift."

"Uh-huh." I found myself replaying conversations I'd had with Carmela, wondering what I'd divulged in the process. "So, Joy told you about her family, her ex-husband's name, and where he worked?"

"Yeah, a little bit here and little bit there. I don't think she'd have told me any of that if she didn't really want me to know and do something about it."

I picked up the paper and looked at the name. "I'll tell you what, I'll talk to Joy and try to broach the subject with her. If she wants to see her kids, I'll make the call. I won't do it without her permission, though."

Carmela shook her head. "You'd be a terrible matchmaker, Hope." She opened the car door to get out.

"And that's why I'm not a matchmaker. Do you need a ride home later?"

"Nope. Irma's going to drive me home. She drives that big Cadillac over there. It's got plush leather interior. I sit in the back seat and pretend it's a limo. Thanks. I'll see you later."

She closed the door and shuffled into the senior center. I shook my head in disbelief, then looked again at the note... Dr. Harold Richardson. I knew this man's name from somewhere, but I just couldn't place it. The note said he worked at North Shore Medical Center. I stuffed the note into my purse and pulled from the parking lot.

~ * ~

I left Gabby to clean up the kitchen after dinner, and returned to Angela's. Once Grace arrived and I made introductions, I angled the wheelchair bearing Joy into the bathroom beside the sink. Grace brought her style book and Joy picked a short style that would require little care. Angela, Carmela and I watched as Grace worked her magic. Joy decided to forgo color until she could more easily recline for the rinse. I managed to keep the conversation going so that Grace didn't ask Joy any personal questions.

Joy admired the cut in the mirror. "That's perfect. Thank you so much."

"You're welcome. You be sure to call when you're getting around better so I can do color."

"Grace loves to do color," I said.

"Yeah, all kinds of color," Carmela added.

Grace shook a finger at her. "I told you not to give me credit for that," she teased.

I walked Grace to the door and paid her, thanking her again.

"That's a great haircut," I said as I returned to Joy's room. "How does it feel?"

"Wonderful. I usually get a haircut at the beauty academy downtown. It's like Russian roulette with clippers. I haven't had a really good haircut in years."

Angela and Carmela had left us, and I closed the door. "There's something I'd like to talk with you about."

"Is something wrong?"

I sat across from her and took in a deep breath. "Carmela has been doing undercover work, all on her own, I might add. She gave me this," I said, showing her the paper.

"I see. And she wants you to call?"

"She thinks it's a shame you have a family and you don't see them, especially your children. She wants me to call and tell your kids where you are. I told her I wouldn't do that without your permission."

Joy's eyes filled. "How would I ever explain my leaving to them? I just can't…"

"But if they wanted to see you, what then?"

"I don't know what Harold told them after I left. They may think I'm dead, for all I know."

"Your ex-husband's a doctor?"

She nodded, wiping her eyes.

"Where would I know his name from? It sounds very familiar."

"He's head of oncology at North Shore Medical."

Of course, that's where I knew the name. "Your ex-husband was the doctor who treated Angela's husband before he died. I knew that name was familiar. I remember him being very kind."

"He always was. But I don't think he'd be that forgiving if I showed up now."

"Your kids are all grown up now. They may feel differently. I won't say a word or do anything, but I hope you'll think about it."

Again she nodded, then grabbed my wrist. "It's been a long time since I had a real friend, Hope. I can't thank you enough."

"You're welcome. By the way, do you mind if I ask how old you are?"

"I'm forty-six. Well, I will be in a few weeks. And I'm not telling you the date because, knowing you and Angela, you'll throw a party, and I'm not ready for that."

"Okay. We'll just have a quiet lunch... you and me. Won't say a word to anyone else. I promise."

When I left, Joy and Carmela were engaged in a cutthroat game of checkers. Carmela had looked at me hopefully when I exited the room, but I refused to meet her gaze. I thought about Joy's comment about having a real friend, and it warmed me that she thought of me that way.

Sixteen

The next few days, I felt all out of sorts. At first I thought it was PMS, then concluded I was coming down with something. When that didn't happen, I decided to have a talk with myself. I walked to the café, got my latte and chatted with Ricki, then went across the street to the park. It was warm, and I searched for a bench in the shade. I watched squirrels chase one another around a huge oak tree and sipped my drink.

Okay, Hope, spill it. What's going on? I sat there staring at the tree until the vision became fuzzy. It had only been a few months since I'd quit my jobs and changed my name, and now it seemed those months were a blur. I'd lost sight of the 'why'…why I was making these changes. I'd managed to get just as busy doing other things. Some of those things were more satisfying, but I was still as tired as I'd been. But, was I fulfilled? That seemed to be the question.

Frustrated, I got to my feet and headed for Fran's shop, not even stopping for another latte. I walked in and waited for her to finish up with a customer.

"Hi, there," she said, walking to where I stood examining old framed photographs. "What're you up to?"

I turned and looked her in the eyes. "Fran, have I changed?"

"Uh, that depends. Who am I talking to, Hope or Janet?"

When I didn't smile, she apologized. "I'm sorry. That was a serious question. Let's sit down." She led me to the office and offered me a bottle of water from the small fridge.

"Thanks. Now, answer the question," I persisted.

"No, you haven't changed that much. You're busier than you were when you worked for Teddy. But, other than that…"

"See, that's the thing. I'm doing all this stuff and I feel okay with what I'm doing, but there's still something missing, and I'm starting to think there's something inherently wrong with me." I stopped and sucked in a breath.

"Slow down. Give me a minute to think." She took a long draw on her bottle of water. "Okay, let me ask you a few questions."

"Shoot."

"What was the reason you started all of this in the first place?"

I stood and paced the narrow space between the desk and file cabinet. "This started with a letter I wrote just to vent my frustrations, a letter I didn't even intend to deliver. It kind of snowballed from there when Anthony and Teddy made a joke out of my letter notifying Teddy I quit."

"So, where'd Hope come from?"

I stood behind the chair, my hands grasping the back, and stretched my arms taught. "See, that's the thing. I don't know. I needed something to be different. I knew what it wasn't; it wasn't Anthony and the kids. So, it had to be me. I guess I thought a new name would let me embrace other new things."

Fran nodded. "And why Hope?"

"I've always liked the name. It sounds positive and light and…"

"Hopeful?"

I rounded the chair and slumped into it. "I've been feeling so unsettled for the past few days. Everything was fine and then, boom, it's not, and I don't know what changed. I feel like I'm back to where I was when I quit Teddy's."

"You're not."

"And you know that because…"

Fran leaned forward, resting her arms on the desktop. "Because you've made a difference for one homeless woman, one young, single mother and your mother-in-law… and you have your husband and kids cooking and cleaning."

"Hunh."

"It doesn't matter what you call yourself. But, I think you chose Hope because that's what you felt was missing. You didn't have that when you were younger, at that time of life when we all set our course and steered into it."

"Hunh," I said again, mostly because I was speechless.

"Do you like working in the book store?"

"I like the book store."

"Interpretation: you took the job because you liked the atmosphere, and now you know it's not all it's cracked up to be to work there."

"Uh, yeah. But I've decided I don't want to go to school, either. I just want to take a couple of classes here and there."

"Stay right here. I'll be back." She went to the front, turned the sign to 'closed' and locked the door, then returned to her seat behind the desk. "I'm going to share with you a secret question a wise therapist asked me that got me started in the antique business. Are you ready?"

I sat up in the chair and folded my hands in my lap. "Ready."

"What's the one thing you are doing when you feel the happiest?"

I thought for a moment and ruled out the first answer. That involved Anthony and his droopy-eyed grin. "I like reading."

"How nice. You're not listening. How can I rephrase this? What makes you feel like smiling when you do it?"

I smiled and felt heat creep up my neck as I once again thought of Anthony.

"I know what you're thinking, and that's not what I meant."

"How do you know what I was...?" I stopped as I remembered Anthony asking that same question of me. "Okay, I'll try to be serious and shift my focus." I closed my eyes, took in a breath and exhaled. "I feel really good about being able to help Joy and becoming her friend, and I enjoyed babysitting for Ricki while her mom was sick."

"Good. You're on the right track."

"That's why I passed the social work test in the career book. I'm a helper... I think."

"I don't think you're a helper. I think you're a care-er, if that's even a word. Note I did not say caretaker or caregiver. There's a big difference."

"And who's going to pay me to care?"

"That's not the point. This is the one thing you do well, you care. Ironically, you give people hope, Hope."

"I remember when my mom died and I went to live with my great-aunt and uncle, how sad everyone was around me. All I wanted to do was tell them it was okay to smile again. I would do everything I could to get a laugh out of them. Then I started to think that maybe it was me, that my being there was too much for them." Tears welled in my eyes. "I figured I just had to get through school and get a job so I could move out on my own. I think that's when I lost any hint of a dream. I couldn't afford the luxury of dreaming."

Fran got up and knelt in front of me, taking both of my hands in hers. "And that explains the name and the feeling of being unfulfilled."

I laughed through my tears. "You're good at this therapy stuff, you know."

"I should be. I apprenticed across from one of the best for three years after my divorce. I should've been given a degree when that was over. Lord knows, I paid for one." She stood and pulled me up with her, then hugged me. "See, there's an advantage to having an older friend. We're wiser."

"You're just three months older," I said, slapping her arm lightly.

"And wiser. I've got to open the door again, just in case a customer accidentally wanders in off the street. Are you going to be okay?"

I wiped my eyes and sniffled. "I'm going to be fine. I just have to figure out my next step. I'm pretty sure the book store isn't it."

I followed Fran out of the office and into the store. She flipped the sign to 'open', unlocked the door, and turned to me. "Where're you off to now?"

"I'm going home. I need to think about all of this. Thanks, Fran. I'll call you. We're about due for a girls' night out, and this one will be my treat."

"Talk to you later."

I looked back after the door closed behind me and Fran waved. *Hope has good taste in friends.*

~ * ~

Maneuvering Joy into the back seat of my car was not a simple feat. Her casted leg could not be bent. Angela stood in front of her as Joy backed into the car and eased onto the seat, then supported her leg while I tugged from behind to slide her across the seat.

Once Joy was situated, Angela stepped back and wiped her forehead. "And we thought getting those clothes on you would be the hard part."

"I'm sorry to be so much trouble," Joy said.

"No, no. That's not what I meant. I was just joking. I hope your appointment goes well."

I got into the driver's seat and looked back. "All set?"

Joy gave me a smile and a thumbs up signal.

We drove for a few miles in silence. After I turned onto the bridge and into the city, Joy spoke. "I've thought about what we talked about, my kids. I won't lie. I'd love to see them, to know things turned out okay for them. But... I can't go back there. Not now. Not ever. I don't know how Harold explained my leaving to them. I don't know if they're angry with me, or if they even remember me at all. I'm not that woman. I never was that woman, that's why I had to leave."

"I understand."

"No, you don't, but that's okay. You don't have to understand it. Hell, when I really think about, I don't understand it, either. But it is what it is. Sometimes we make choices in life, and sometimes life makes choices for us. Life made a choice for me a long time ago. I can't change that now."

"Is it painful?"

"What? My leg?"

"No. Living with that choice."

"I can't afford to feel that pain. I ask you to accept that and leave it alone, please?"

I glanced in the rear view mirror to see that Joy was staring straight ahead, out the opposite window. "I won't push you to do anything you don't want to do. But I'll help you, if you ever want to pursue contacting them."

She nodded and continued staring straight ahead.

I reached the hospital outpatient entrance and pulled up to the door. "Sit tight. I'm going to get an attendant with a wheelchair."

"I'll be right here."

I went to the outpatient admissions desk and told the receptionist what I needed. She instructed me to go back and wait at the car, and she would page an attendant.

Joy inched her way across the seat and, when the attendant arrived with a wheelchair, eased herself off the seat and into the chair. The attendant took her inside to wait while I parked the car.

I returned to the lobby, wheeled Joy to the admission desk and registered her. We browsed magazines for twenty minutes until Joy was called back to the exam area. I wheeled her back, and a nurse appeared to take her inside.

"Do you want your sister to come in with you?" the nurse asked Joy.

"My sister? Oh, we're not..." She stopped and smiled at me. "No, my sister can wait here."

I returned her smile, feeling moisture brim in my eyes. I sat in the small waiting area reading a different six-month-old magazine.

An hour later, the nurse reappeared with Joy in the wheelchair, but now wearing a walking cast. "She's good to go," the nurse said, passing the wheelchair off to me.

Joy thanked her. "At least I'll be able to stand and move around now on my own."

"That's got to feel good."

"What really felt good was being able to scratch after the doctor took the other cast off. This one has a little more room in it."

I parked Joy at the entrance and brought the car around to her. She was able to stand and slide into the car with little help.

"Do you need anything while we're out, before we go to lunch?" I asked.

"Not a thing, thanks. I'd just like to go home, though. Let's go out to lunch another day."

"Home it is."

I pulled into Angela's driveway so Joy could go in through the back door. There was only one small step into the kitchen. She slid into the wheelchair, and I rolled her to the door and shoved it open. She eased up from the chair and stepped carefully into the kitchen. As she moved along the wall and into the room, I lifted the wheelchair over the step and pushed it inside.

Angela stood at the stove, and two women were seated at the table with Carmela. "Hey," Carmela said, "look who's here."

Betty and Mary beamed up at Joy.

"Joy's friends came to see her, so I invited them for lunch," Angela said happily.

Joy hobbled to the one empty chair at the table and dropped into it. "How did you two get here? How did you find me?"

Betty said, "We took the bus, and that nice girl at the café told us where you were staying, so we walked here."

"When I asked if they'd had lunch and they said they hadn't, I invited them to stay and join us. I'm glad you two came right home. I was just going to call your cell phone." Angela checked the pasta. "This is ready."

"Pasta for lunch?" I asked.

"I thought we'd have our main meal now and a light supper later," she said, nodding towards the two women and winking at me. She wanted to make sure they had a good meal.

Carmela went to the fridge and pulled out a large bowl of salad. "Hope, would you get the extra chairs from the bedroom, please?" she asked.

"Sure."

Angela placed the pasta bowl on the table and extra sauce in a gravy boat. As I passed the salad bowl, Mary looked at me and grinned. "Grace?"

"Who?"

Joy laughed. "She wants to say grace."

"Oh, well, of course," I said, setting the salad bowl back on the table.

Mary stretched her hands out to Betty and Angela, nodding for the rest of us to join hands. We did so, and Mary said a simple, beautiful grace, then looked up and grinned. "Let's eat."

Food was passed around the table, and the women piled their plates with pasta and salad.

"So, what's it like, being a homeless person?" Carmela asked Betty.

Angela shot her a warning look and cleared her throat, but Carmela persisted. "I would think it's hard, especially in the winter. I don't like the cold, so I don't think I'd be a good homeless person."

Betty shook her head. "It's not so bad. The shelter opens earlier in the winter, and there're places to go to stay warm and dry. I like the library, but Mary gets bored because she can't read."

At hearing her name, Mary raised her head, her mouth covered with sauce. Betty motioned to her, and she wiped her mouth with her napkin.

"I apologize for my mother. She shouldn't be bothering you with such questions," Angela said, once again fixing her eyes on Carmela. "Joy, how did your doctor's appointment go?"

"I have the walking cast, so it'll be easier on all of us. He told me I'll have this on for at least three weeks and, if all goes well, the cast will be removed altogether."

"Everyone at the shelter misses you," Betty said. "They'll be glad to see you again."

"Tell them I send my best, and I'll be back soon," Joy replied.

Angela looked at me, and I shook my head slightly, letting her know not to bring up the subject of Joy staying permanently.

"Hey, did I tell you all I've decided not to go to school? I'm just going to take a class or two," I announced. That shifted the conversation successfully.

After lunch, I offered Betty and Mary a ride back into the city. "Thanks, but it's a nice day. We'll take the bus," Betty said.

"Thanks for coming to see me," Joy said.

Betty said goodbye, but Mary bent and hugged Joy tightly. "I love you, Joy."

Joy wrapped her arms around the child-like woman. "I love you, too, sweetie. Be careful out there."

I escorted them to the door. The two women walked down the drive, waved and headed toward town. I helped Joy up from her chair, and she hobbled to the bedroom.

"I'm sorry they showed up like that. I hope Angela isn't upset," she said.

"Oh, yeah, you could see how upset she was about having two more people to feed. I think she enjoyed it. Angela should work for that charity. What's it called? Feed the World."

"Well, if all goes well, I should be out of here in a few weeks, and you all can get back to your normal lives."

I laughed. "There is no such thing as normal life here, believe me." I got the chair and pulled it up next to the bed. "Joy, I know for a fact that Angela would like to ask you to stay here permanently."

"Oh, um… I… I couldn't do that. I was afraid of that when I came here." She stuttered and I noticed her hands shook.

I put my hand on hers. "Hey, it's okay. You don't have to. I just wanted you to know she's going to offer, that's all."

She nodded. "Thank you. She's a wonderful person. So is Carmela. But I don't belong here."

"You have time to think about it. I've gotta run. I don't suppose you'd want to go to the shelter some evening to see your friends."

Her face brightened. "Really? We could do that? I'd love to."

"I'll call and see about it. Who do I talk with?"

"Ask for Catherine. She's the supervisor. Oh, thank you. That'll be something to look forward to."

~ * ~

I called the shelter that evening and made the arrangements to take Joy for a visit on Friday. "Catherine, how many women do you have there on any given night?"

"Our capacity is thirty, but now that it's warmer, we usually have twenty to twenty-five. A few of our ladies like sleeping under the stars in summer."

"Is there anything I can bring for them?"

"We have a group of volunteers who prepare dinner. What did you have in mind?"

"Well, it's a celebration, sort of. Would it be okay if I brought cake and ice cream and cold drinks?"

"That would be wonderful. I'll tell the volunteers not to worry about dessert. If you and Joy arrive by six, you can join us for dinner."

"We'll be there." I gave her my phone number in case she thought of anything else they needed.

When I called Joy, she was ecstatic. Then I ran to the mall to buy Joy a new pair of slacks that would fit over her cast, and a new blouse to wear for the occasion.

I told Angela about the cake and ice cream. She, of course, insisted upon baking a large sheet cake and decorating it. The cake she'd baked for Michael's graduation dinner had been an artistic masterpiece. I've eaten her cakes many times, so I didn't argue.

"Maybe I should go with you," she said.

"Do you want to?"

"I do. Of course, Mama will probably want to go, as well. Do you think that's okay?"

"I'll call Catherine and make sure. I think it would be fine."

Catherine was thrilled and assured me there would be plenty of food for dinner. I hung up the phone and felt a twinge as I thought we'd be taking food from the mouth of some homeless woman. I had to trust Catherine that it was fine.

On Friday, I arrived at Angela's at four o'clock and presented Joy with her new outfit. Her eyes sparkled. "Oh, that's lovely. Thank you so much. I'll change right away."

I went to the kitchen where Angela was carefully boxing and covering the cake. Joy had recommended yellow cake with chocolate icing. Angela had decorated the cake with festive balloons and a delicate flower border. "That's beautiful. You could make money at this, you know."

"I didn't know what to write on it, so I just filled it with color."

Joy emerged from the bedroom in her new outfit. "What do you think?"

Angela and I both turned and looked. "It's very nice. You can hardly tell you have a cast on," Angela said.

"That's the advantage of that wide-legged style. I don't like them, generally, but in this case, they're great," I said.

Joy's eyes filled as she looked at the cake. "You're all so good to me. I still don't know why."

I put an arm around her. "You're a nice person, Joy. I appreciate your friendship, and we're helping because we can."

Angela bit her lip and looked at Joy. "Now don't you get me started. This is not a day for tears."

"Fine, but once we get to the shelter, all bets are off," Joy said, wiping her eyes.

We settled the cake in the trunk and braced the box so it wouldn't move around. Angela got into the back seat and had Joy rest her outstretched leg across her lap.

Carmela settled in the front beside me. "This is great. I've never been to a homeless shelter. I'm sure experiencing a lot of new firsts for someone who's eighty."

"And it will be an experience. Brace yourselves," Joy said, laughing.

I pulled over the curb in front of the church that housed the shelter. The three women got out, and Angela supported Joy as she hopped down the steps to the shelter entrance. Carmela followed carrying the ice cream.

"Leave the soda, and I'll come back for it," Angela said. I set the case of canned soda by the top step, then parked across the street in a parking garage, removed the cake from the trunk and made my way back through rush hour traffic.

By the time I was inside, Joy was already surrounded by women, laughing and crying, hugging one another. Carmela stood next to Joy, right in the middle of the fray. Angela stood to the side, talking with a woman I assumed to be Catherine.

The women waved for me to join them. "I'm Catherine Akers. I can't tell you what this means to these women. They all love Joy and have missed her terribly. Here, let me take that cake back to the kitchen. It's beautiful."

"Thanks. Angela made it. She's a magician in the kitchen."

Angela beamed at the compliment. Joy released herself from the embrace of a large woman wearing a knit toboggan cap, even though it was June. She called us over.

"Listen, everyone. This is my friend, Hope, and her mother-in-law, Angela. And this," she said, putting an arm around Carmela, "is Sofialoren, just like the actress."

Most of the women smiled, shook our hands or hugged us, and gave their names. A few stood to the back of the group, eyeing us warily.

Joy got their attention again. "Angela took me into her home when I had nowhere to go, and I can't tell you how wonderful she has been. They've all been so welcoming. I still have this cast," she said, lifting her pant leg, "but I should be out of it in a few weeks and back here with all of you."

Mary, her almond-shaped eyes glistening, grinned and said, "Angela makes good sketti."

Angela, who was standing next to her, hugged her and said, "Thank you. I'll come and make you all spaghetti one day."

My eyes filled as I took in the change I'd seen in Angela. She'd moved past widowhood, taken on new color much like the trees in autumn. Her smile was wider, and her eyes sparkling. I liked thinking I had a little to do with that change.

Catherine rang a bell that hung on the wall above a window between the main room and the kitchen. Everyone stopped talking and turned.

"Our volunteers tonight are from Saint Mary's Church, and they've just told me that dinner is ready. Who wants to say grace?"

"I'd like to say grace," Joy said. She reached for the hands of the women on either side of her, and soon the circle was complete. "Dear God, Thank you for all of these women, my friends and family. Thank you for this shelter, and the kindness of those who support it. Thank you for all of our volunteers, and the many ways they feed us." She raised her head and her eyes met mine. "And thank you for bringing Hope into my life, and for Angela and Carmela. Bless them and bless our meal."

Everyone said a loud, "Amen." Catherine insisted we fill our plates first because we were guests. The meal was simple and delicious: baked ham, potato salad, a tossed salad, and rolls.

I sat next to Catherine and listened to her talk about the shelter and how she'd gotten involved in this work. I was surprised to learn she didn't have a social work degree, or any degree for that matter.

"The director of our board is a Social Worker. She gives us all the training and support we need. I was a stay-at-home mom most of my life. When my kids grew up and moved out, I found myself at loose ends. My husband went to work every day, and there I was with nothing to do. I started volunteering here a few nights a week and, the next thing I knew, I had a full-time job. My husband's not too happy that I spend five nights a week here."

"I can imagine. Anthony would probably have a fit if I took a job working nights."

She smiled. "Are you looking for a job?"

"Uh, I sort of have one, but I'll probably be quitting. Turns out I like the atmosphere of the book store better as a customer."

She laughed, and our attention turned to Carmela, who was telling the women the story behind her hair color. As we stood and some of the women cleared the tables, Catherine asked to talk with me privately for a minute. I followed her into her office.

"I just wanted to say that it's wonderful what you're doing for Joy. Your family is very generous. Not many people would take a homeless woman off the streets and into their home."

"I kind of got to know Joy a little. She told me her story. You know, she and I aren't all that different. We just have different addresses, you might say."

"Joy is unusual. Many of the women have histories of substance abuse, prostitution or serious mental health issues. Most have low self-esteem and very little education."

"My mother-in-law wants to offer Joy a permanent place in her home, but Joy won't take it."

"Homelessness is a conundrum for a lot of people. Most people just can't believe anyone would choose to live a hard life on the streets. The reality for most of those women out there is that they're acclimated to life on the streets. It's more frightening for them to think of a home and all that goes with it."

"I'm trying to understand that and to respect Joy's wishes. Well, I pretty much have to. She's a grown woman. Carmela wanted to try and reunite her with her children, but Joy doesn't want that, either."

"It's too hard for them to look back. Most of them walked away from something and have to keep on walking. And, for many, it was something awful. That's not always the case, though. Sometimes it's just too much to cope with life."

I nodded. "I consider Joy a friend. It'll be hard to see her back on the street. You have my number, if anything ever happens."

"Joy's fortunate to have found a friend like you. If you ever feel like working a couple of nights a week, let me know."

"I'll keep that in mind."

I went into the restroom and, as I walked back to the table, a woman approached. She looked to be in her late sixties, but it was hard to be certain. She put a hand on my arm and asked, "Can I talk with you?"

"Sure. Why don't we step over here where we can have some privacy?"

We walked to the corner away from the crowd. "What can I do for you?"

Her eyes were swimming in tears when she looked at me. "Nothing for me. I just wanted to say how kind it was, what you did for Joy, you and your family there. Not a lot of people would've done that. We're invisible to most people. They don't really seem to care, but you did." She smiled at me. "You've restored my faith in people."

I was taken aback. "What's your name?" I asked, working past the lump in my throat.

"Evelyn"

"Evelyn, I just did what I think any decent human being should do, what I would do for any friend."

"Well, everyone isn't decent. It was important for you to ask my name, wasn't it? And what you did for Joy, you did for all of us here. You gave us all hope, reminded each of us that we're people, too."

I bit my lip, then sucked in a breath. "Thank you, Evelyn, for telling me that. It means more than you know."

She squeezed my arm. "Well, we better get back to the party." With that, she turned and rejoined the group.

I stood for moment to regain composure, then followed.

Angela looked at me and asked, "Are you all right?"

"I'm fine. Looks like your cake was a big hit," I said, motioning to the pan bearing nothing more than a few crumbs.

Angela smiled. "Wait until they taste my sauce. You know, I've been thinking."

"Uh-oh. Is this going to get me into trouble with Anthony?"

"If it does, you let me know. He's not too big for me to handle. I realize that Joy isn't the only woman here who gets sick or has an accident from time to time. I'd like to offer my home and spare room as a place for a woman to come and recuperate, if need be."

"Angela, that's a wonderful offer. But, keep in mind, not all of these women are like Joy. Some of them do have serious mental health issues, and you have to consider that."

"I thought of that, too. But, if you were to work here, you'd get to know the women, and you could help decide who would be safe to bring in to the house."

"*If* I worked here. Anthony's not going to like this idea at all."

"I have faith that you can convince him," she said with a wink.

"I need to think about it first. But, you're right; I usually get Anthony to see things my way."

"That's because I raised a son who respects women. You could do a lot of good here. Think about it."

Seventeen

Walt, the manager of the book store, didn't seem all that surprised when I told him I was quitting. Ashley, her hair now streaked bright blue, nodded sympathetically and said, "This can be a hard job for older people. All that bending and lifting."

I resisted the urge to slap the stud out of her nose. Instead, I smiled, thanked her and said, "Goodbye, Ashley. Thank you for everything."

"You're welcome. 'Bye, Janet."

"Hope."

"Huh?"

"Never mind."

I left the store and went to Starbucks for a latte. Ricki was all smiles when I walked up to the counter. "Hope! I haven't seen you for a while."

"Yeah, I've gotten to be the busiest unemployed person I know."

She grabbed a cup and began to make my usual drink.

"How's Hannah?"

"She's getting so big. She's pulling herself up, and I swear she'll be walking any day now. My mom says it's too soon, but she looks like she's just about ready." She presented her left hand to me, and the light glinted off a small diamond.

"Oh, wow. Congratulations. When did this happen?" I asked, taking her hand to inspect the ring.

"Last Saturday. Tim's already gone to Virginia to start his new job, and he's looking for a house. We're getting married in September, and then Hannah and I will move in with him."

"That's great news. I'm happy for all three of you. You'll have to come to dinner and bring Hannah some evening before you leave."

"That'd be fun. You'll be getting an invitation to the wedding, too. If you hadn't told me to give Tim a chance to be Hannah's father, we might not have worked things out."

Another customer came into the café. I told Ricki I'd see her again and left. I crossed the street to the park and sat on my bench where I made a mental list of things I needed to get for Michael before he left for college in six weeks. My first child, my son, was leaving and striking out on his own. My throat tightened at the thought. Everyone seemed to be getting their lives together. What about me?

My husband and each of my children filled a specific role in my life. Anthony was my best friend, my lover, my other half who made me feel special and whole. Gabby was my baby girl, who brought drama and humor and spontaneity to my life. From the time Michael was an infant, he'd had a stabilizing effect on me. I was anxious as a new mother, so afraid I'd do the wrong thing and ruin him for life. Then he'd look at me with those huge, dark eyes and flash a smile that stretched from ear to ear, and I'd know everything was fine. He'd grown into a sensitive young man with impeccable timing, always knowing just what to say. He was still my stabilizer. I was going to miss him so much.

I removed my sunglasses, wiped my eyes and finished the latte. Suddenly I needed to be at home.

Anthony was shirtless and cutting the grass when I pulled into the drive. He turned off the mower. "I thought you were working today."

"I quit. Where's Michael? I thought he was going to cut the grass."

"Teddy called him in to work, so I took over. Gabby's gone to the mall with Megan and her mother."

Anthony's thick black hair was damp and his muscular chest beaded with perspiration. He was tanned and looked darned sexy in denim cutoffs. "So, it's just you and me?"

"Yup," he grinned. "Uh-oh. Something tells me this grass isn't getting cut today."

"Whatever do you mean?"

He stepped away from the mower and ran a finger down my cheek and along my jaw. "You've got the look."

I smiled. "What look?"

"The look you always accuse me of having." He brushed his lips against mine lightly. "I can finish the grass in half an hour."

"Or there's always tomorrow."

"For the grass or…?"

I stood on my toes and whispered into his ear, "You, me, the shower… ten minutes. Don't be late."

We moved from the shower to the bedroom. It had been a long time since we'd had a day alone like this. *Maybe Michael's leaving won't be so bad. Now, how can we get Gabby out of the house?*

~ * ~

"God, Jan, I think I'm having a heart attack, but at least I'll die happy," Anthony said as he struggled to control his breathing.

I rested my head on his shoulder. "Now, how would I explain that to your mother?"

"Well, you could drag me out to the back yard and tell her I died while cutting the grass."

"She'd never buy it. You don't smile like that when you cut the grass." I paused, then said, "You didn't say anything about my quitting at the book store."

"The last time you quit a job and I said something, all hell broke loose."

"We have a good life, don't we?"

He squeezed my bare shoulder. "We have a great life. Couldn't ask for anything more. Especially not since Hope appeared."

"What does that mean?"

He traced his fingers down my back, causing a shiver. "Well, you have to admit, since Hope came on the scene, we've spent a lot more time getting overheated."

"You think so? I always thought we had a healthy sex life."

"Honey, there's healthy then there's downright exciting."

"So, you like Hope better than Janet? Hope's exciting, and Janet's just so-so?"

He released me and sat up, shaking his head. "Oh, no. There's no safe answer for that one. I love my wife, that would be you. Jeez, you make it sound like I'm having an affair with Hope."

"No, you made it sound like that. Hope and Janet are the same person."

"That's what I just said," he shouted.

I paused, choosing to let this go. His confusion was, after all, my fault. "If I ever left you and the kids, would you come after me?"

Anthony looked down at me. "What? Where'd that come from?"

"Would you?"

"I'd hunt you down, hog-tie you, throw you over my shoulder and carry you right back here... literally right here," he said, patting the narrow space between us.

"Promise?"

He tousled my hair. "Are you planning on going somewhere?"

"I was just thinking about how fragile life is, how we can make one decision in a split second that changes our lives forever. Joy just got up one day and walked away from her life and her family. I'm not judging her for it, but as hard as I try, I can't understand it." I sat up and leaned back against the pillows. "I've spent the last few months looking for something I didn't think I had and believed I needed in order to survive. And I found it."

"Want to tell me about it?"

I scooted over and leaned my head on his chest. "When my mother died, I was scared witless. I was eighteen, but not ready to be on my own completely. I didn't know what was going to happen, where I'd go. Thank God for my aunt and uncle and their generosity. But, still, I was thrown into being an adult and taking charge of my life. I didn't have time to dream or to think about what I wanted to do. I just had to do it."

He rubbed his hand along my arm. "When I met you, you seemed to have it all together."

"I thought I did. Then these questions started coming up, and I didn't know what to do with them." I raised my eyes and looked at him. "Not about our marriage. You have to know that. Just questions about what I was doing, and if there was anything I'd missed along the way. I guess listening to Michael plan his future set something off in me. I'd never done that, really thought about it or had a dream to chase."

The tenderness in his eyes as he spoke brought tears to mine. "You scared me with the quitting and the name changing.

At first, I felt like I was losing you. I tried to make a joke out of it because I was too afraid to take it seriously. I just want you to be happy, but I want you to be happy here, with me and the kids."

I lowered my head again, feeling the rhythmic beating of his heart against my cheek. "I've always been happy with you and the kids. I just wasn't all that happy with myself. I think I've found something I want to do, and I don't think you're going to approve."

"Oh, jeez. Don't tell me you've heard the call, and you're going to the convent."

I laughed. "Now, that would be something. I want to work at the homeless shelter a few nights a week. But it means working overnight and sleeping there."

"You're right, I don't like it. You need to be sleeping here with me, where I know you're safe."

"I'll be safe there. They lock the doors once the women are inside."

"Oh, that's reassuring. Do you know how crazy some of those people are? And you'll be locked in with them."

"They're not crazy. Some of them do have emotional problems. Anthony, I finally figured out what I want to be. I want to be a person who makes a difference. I'm good at that, at changing things for the better, and I can do that just by caring and letting people know I care. I want to give people hope. Look at your mother. You know, she and I aren't that different."

"Please don't point that out right now," he said, pulling up the sheet to cover me. "I have to admit, she's happier than I've seen her in a long time. Isn't there a daytime shelter you can work at?"

"No. They just have the one. It opens at six in the evening, and the women leave at eight in the morning, after breakfast.

Anthony, when I took Joy there and spent a few hours, I felt like I'd stepped into a world where I could do some good just by being there."

He sighed. "How many nights are we talking about?"

"Two, three at the most. And," I said, running my hand through the thick hair on his chest, "we can send Gabby off for a Saturday with Megan now and then."

I looked at his face, eyelids drooped, grin twisted to one side. I'd struck a deal.

"By the way, who's taking this job, Hope or Janet?"

I snuggled against him. "I think maybe Janet's back. I needed to find Hope, and that's exactly what I found. It's time to come home."

"Can I ask a question?"

I waited.

"Can Janet stay blonde?" he asked, ruffling my hair.

I laughed as he eased me down on the bed and leaned over me, smiling. "Welcome home." At this rate, we'd each need another shower.

~ * ~

I woke to the sound of the doorbell, blinked and heard the shower running. I grabbed my robe and looked out the window. Angela's car sat in the drive. I called in to Anthony, "Your mother's here."

Angela and Carmela stood on the front porch, Carmela peering into the living room window.

I ran my hands through my hair, pulled the robe tighter and opened the door. "Hi. This is a nice surprise."

Angela looked confused. "Surprise? Didn't Anthony tell you we were coming and bringing dinner?"

Then I noticed the casserole dish she held with pot holders. "No, he didn't. Come in. Anthony's in the shower."

Angela walked through to the kitchen with the casserole. "I'll pop this into the oven."

Carmela grinned at me and winked. "I think it's great that you young people don't have hang-ups about doing it in the daylight."

"Oh, we weren't... Anthony was cutting the grass and I... um, I'm going upstairs to shower. He'll be right down."

"Take your time," Carmela said with another wink. I felt heat rush up my neck, and my ears spontaneously combusted.

Anthony was standing with a towel wrapped around his waist. "I'm sorry. I forgot to tell you. Mom and Grandma are coming over and bringing dinner."

I smacked his arm. "Do you have any idea how embarrassed I am? Your grandmother knew exactly what we'd been doing. She thinks it's great that we don't have hang-ups about *doing it* in the daylight."

He chuckled. "I'm glad for that, too. Must run in the family."

"I'm going to shower. You go down and entertain them. And don't encourage Carmela."

"Since when does my grandma need encouragement?" he asked, pulling on a pair of jeans. He walked over and slid my robe off one shoulder, then kissed the base of my neck. "Don't let Janet go anywhere. She and I need to get reacquainted later."

"Will you stop that? This isn't funny. How am I going to go back down there and face your mother?"

"Tell her you were out in the sun. That'll explain your shade of red." He pulled on a tee shirt and headed downstairs.

I showered and dressed quickly, then hurried down the stairs. As I reached the bottom, I heard laughter coming from the kitchen. Angela's voice was light and her laugh musical, bringing a smile to my face.

"Sounds like you're all having fun in here," I said as I entered the kitchen.

"Yeah. Anthony told us a joke. Now we all have something to smile about," Carmela quipped.

I rolled my eyes and turned to open the refrigerator. "Who wants something to drink? Beer? Soda? Iced tea?"

As each one called out a request, I removed the drinks and handed them to Anthony.

Angela looked out the back window. "I thought you were cutting the grass? It looks like you stopped halfway through the yard."

Anthony grinned and looked at me. "Yeah, it got too hot. I'll finish up later." He emphasized the 'later' and I returned to the refrigerator, this time examining the contents of the freezer and welcoming the cold blast on my face.

"Where's Joy? I thought she'd come with you," I said over my shoulder.

"I invited her, but she said she had something she needed to take care of, and a phone call she wanted to make. I think she's getting antsy and is about ready to move back to the shelter as soon as the cast comes off her leg," Angela said.

"By the way, I have an announcement," I said.

Carmela's eyes widened and she smiled. "You're gonna have a baby?"

"No. Will you stop asking that? I'm going to see about working at the shelter a couple of nights a week."

"That's wonderful. Maybe I could come and cook now and then," Angela said.

"Yeah, and I'll come and play cards or checkers with the ladies," Carmela added.

"Oh, good grief!" Anthony groaned and chugged his beer.

I made a salad while Angela's casserole heated in the oven. "I wonder what business Joy had to take care of?"

"I don't know. She asked me for note paper and envelopes yesterday, and spent most of the day in her room with the door closed," Angela said.

"I'll see her tomorrow. Maybe she'll tell me what's going on. Would you remind her of the doctor's appointment next Wednesday?" I asked.

Angela nodded. "I suppose she'll be leaving after that. I'll hate to see her go. I'll worry about her."

"She'll be fine. Besides, I'll be there a few times a week to check on her. Now, I want to plan a dinner for Michael before he leaves for college. I'm thinking a barbecue so he can invite his friends. Would you make another cake, Angela?"

"You know I will. I'll make a big pan of lasagna, too. When do you want to have this dinner?"

"He leaves on August twenty-eighth for freshman orientation, so I'm thinking the Saturday before that." My eyes filled. "I'm sorry. I've been doing this all day, every time I think about him leaving."

"He's going to be less than an hour away. He could still live here and go to college," Anthony said. "I don't see why he can't commute."

"He wants to live on campus and be on his own. Don't worry, you'll see him every weekend when he comes home with his laundry and to have a home cooked meal," Angela said. "Still, it's hard to imagine little Mikey going off to college."

"Yeah, I know. Wait till he goes to graduate school at Harvard," I said, forcing a smile.

Angela removed the casserole from the oven and set it on a trivet in the center of the table. We all sat, and Anthony passed the salad bowl to me and then dished up ziti for everyone.

After dinner and ice cream, Carmela and Angela prepared to leave. "Were you planning to come for dinner tomorrow?" Angela asked.

"Uh, yeah. It's Sunday," Anthony responded.

"Oh, well... I'm not going to be there tomorrow. I'm, uh, going out for the afternoon."

"She has a date," Carmela announced.

Both Anthony and I stared at Angela, mouths agape.

Angela blushed. "I don't have a date. I'm having dinner with a friend, that's all."

"A friend?" I asked, smiling. "Do we know this friend?"

Before she could respond, Carmela offered, "She's going out with Joe Bruschetti, the guy at the tire and battery place."

"I'm not going out with him. I stopped there the other day because my front tire was a little low. He was kind enough to check the tires and add some air. He wouldn't let me pay him and asked me if I would have dinner with him. I figured it was the least I could do," Angela explained.

"Uh-huh," Anthony said. "Are you buying dinner, or is he?"

"I assume he is," she said.

Anthony and I exchanged a look and said simultaneously, "It's a date."

"In any case, I won't be at home for dinner. I've already called Dante and told him not to come."

"Why don't I pick you and Joy up and bring you here for dinner?" I asked Carmela.

"That would be nice. I think Joy would like that, too, if she's not still busy with whatever she's been doing. I'll ask her and call you after we get home."

I walked with them to the car, taking Angela's arm and whispering, "Have a nice time tomorrow. You deserve it."

She smiled as she opened the car door. "Thank you."

I went back into the house to find Anthony rinsing the dishes and stacking the dishwasher. "Can you believe it? Your mother has a date."

"It's not a date. She's just thanking Joe for his kindness," he said, grinning. He dried his hands and pulled me against him. "I think it's great that she's getting out. See what you started?"

I leaned back and looked up at him. "I didn't start anything. Hope did."

"Oh, well, I'll have to thank her later."

He was nuzzling my neck when the back door opened and Gabby walked in. "Eeww, that is gross. I'm gonna be scarred for life if you two keep that up."

Anthony grinned at her, then bent and covered my face and neck with kisses, until we were both laughing.

"I'm going to finish cutting the grass," Anthony said as he headed out the door.

Gabby opened the refrigerator and asked, "What'd you have for dinner?"

"Grandma's baked ziti. There's some in that casserole dish. She and Grandma Carmela just left," I said. "Oh, Grandma Carmela and my friend, Joy, may come here for dinner tomorrow. I'd like for you and Michael to be here."

"Aw, Mom. I was going to go to a movie."

"We'll eat early, and you can go to a movie after. Joy will be leaving your grandmother's house soon, and I'd like to have a nice dinner here before that happens."

"Where's she going?"

"Back to the shelter, I suppose."

"Why would she do that?"

"I honestly don't know, Gabby. It's her choice, and I'd appreciate it if you didn't question her on it while she's here."

"If I wasn't here for dinner, you wouldn't even have to worry about that."

"You're going to be here for dinner, and I still won't have to worry, right?"

"Right." The microwave dinged, and she removed her plate and sat at the table.

I poured a glass of iced tea and sat with her. "Gabby, I'm going to take a new part-time job working at the shelter. It'll mean that I stay there all night a couple of nights a week. Your dad will be here, but I need to know that I can count on you to help out. I'll have to be there before six, and won't get home until nine the next morning."

"Why would you do that? What's wrong with working at the book store and having decent hours?"

"Nothing's wrong with it. It's just not for me. I need to do something that makes the world a better place for other people."

Her eyes lit up and I could see wheels turning. "You make a difference for other people here when you cook dinner and do laundry."

I narrowed my eyes at her. "You know what I mean. Can I count on you?"

"Sure, Mom. To be perfectly honest, I kind of like cooking. Laundry's not my favorite thing, but it's better than cleaning the bathroom."

"I appreciate your cooperation. Tell you what, let's you and me schedule a spa day for just the two of us."

"Can I get the works... massage, pedicure, manicure, and facial?"

"Why not?"

~ * ~

Joy sat in the kitchen and helped me shuck corn while Carmela surfed the net, assuring me she would not visit any porn sites.

"The doctor's probably going to remove your cast on Wednesday. I guess you're looking forward to that," I said to Joy.

"I am. I can't wait to have both my legs fully functioning again." She paused. "I'll be going back to the shelter after the cast is off. I don't want to seem unappreciative, but the longer I stay at Angela's, the harder it is for everyone. Angela asked me last night if I would stay with her and Carmela. I think she's trying to understand why I can't do that."

"She and Carmela brought dinner here yesterday. She said you had business to take care of and couldn't come."

"That's right."

She didn't offer to explain, and I wasn't sure if I should ask. "Is everything okay?"

"You mean, what was I up to?" she asked with a smile.

"Yeah, I guess that's what I mean." I sat down across from her. "What's going on?"

She set the corn aside and leaned back in the chair. "I thought about some of the things we've discussed, about family. I decided to write a letter to each of my kids and try to help them understand what happened. I want them to know I loved them, and my leaving wasn't their fault." Her voice cracked and she paused, then cleared her throat. "I called Harold first to see what the kids already understood. I didn't want them to get letters from a dead woman."

"What did he say?"

"He said he'd told them the truth; that I loved them, but I couldn't live with them anymore. As they got older, he was better able to explain about the depression. He said they never showed any anger or resentment towards me, and they get along well with their stepmother."

"Was he angry?"

"No. Not now. I know he was angry and hurt and confused back then, but he's moved on. He's happy, and I'm grateful for that. He gave me David's address at school, and said he'd tell both of the kids to expect a letter." She clasped her hands to control their shaking and met my gaze. "I was wondering if… do you think I could give them this address, if they want to write back to me? I don't want their letters to come to the shelter."

I reached over and took hold of her hands. "Of course. When the letters arrive, I'll make certain you get them."

"If," she said. "*If* the letters come. I won't expect anything."

"They'll come," I said. "I think they'll want to know more about you. They were old enough when you left to remember you."

"I don't know if I hope for that, or if I don't. I'm not sure the memories are good ones. I haven't been afraid in a long time, not even on the streets. But the thought of connecting again with my kids terrifies me."

"Oh, Joy. If they give you a chance, they'll see what a loving woman you are, and they'll understand the sacrifice you made for their sake. Did you bring the letters with you?"

She pulled the sealed envelopes from her pocket. "I just need to add the return address and stamp them."

I grabbed a pen, handed it to her, and recited the address for her to add to the envelopes. I called for Gabby. When she appeared, I handed her the envelopes. "Would you get stamps from the desk in the den, put one on each of these envelopes, then run them to the post office, please? It'll only take you a few minutes."

"Sure."

"Thank you." I looked at Joy. "Let it go and trust."

Anthony came through the back door. "The grill's almost ready. When should I put on the steaks?"

222

I tossed the ears of corn into the boiling water. "Five minutes."

Michael bounced down the stairs and into the kitchen. "Hi, Mom." He kissed my cheek. "Hi, Joy." He bent and kissed her cheek, as well.

The look on Joy's face brought tears to my eyes, and I swallowed hard to hold them back. "Michael, would you take this plate out to your father for the steaks?"

He took the serving plate from my hand and went out the back door.

"He's a wonderful boy," Joy said.

"Thank you. I like to think I had something to do with it, but I can't honestly figure out what that would be. Excuse me, I'm going to see what Carmela's up to, and let her know dinner's almost ready."

I walked into the den to find Carmela typing away with two fingers. "Who're you talking to?"

"I don't know. But this guy wants to know my name, where I live, and how old I am. I'm telling him my name is Sofialoren and I'm forty-five. I don't think I should tell him where I live, do you?"

I reached in front of her, hit the 'delete' button, then the 'off' button. "Come on, Sofialoren. It's time for dinner. You shouldn't give out personal information to strangers on the Internet."

"He wasn't a stranger. He introduced himself. His name was Big Dick. I never did find out his last name, though."

I rolled my eyes. *Oh, good Lord, give me strength.*

I lifted the corn from the boiling water, and Anthony, Michael and Gabby all came through the back door together, the steaks steaming on the platter.

We took our seats around the table, and Anthony began to pass the food. I put my hand on his arm. "Wait. I want to say grace." I reached for Anthony's hand and for Joy's, and waited for everyone else to join hands. Gabby and Michael clinked their forks on their plates. This wasn't something we'd typically done in the past. I guess, along with finding hope, I'd discovered the gratitude I felt for my life.

I looked at the faces of those gathered around my table, then bowed my head and closed my eyes. "I, um, I'm so grateful for my family," I began, squeezing Anthony's hand, "and for good friends." I felt Joy's grip tighten on mine. "I'm grateful for having people in my life who love me enough to let me get crazy, and who give me room to change." I opened my eyes and smiled. "Amen. Oh, and I'm grateful for this food. Now, let's eat."

Eighteen

Before I let Hope go completely, I needed to know what I'd learned from her. I drove to the State Park five miles from our house. I tucked a bottle of water into my hip pack, a granola bar in my pocket, and set off on the path circling the lake.

I made a mental list of what I'd learned about Hope, my alter-ego. She has self-confidence, she's carefree, sexy, loves her family and values her friends, and she has a sense of purpose in her life. And what about Janet? She'd become robotic, going through the motions and not knowing why.

Pulling the water bottle from my pack, I walked to a bench overlooking the lake. Bright summer sun hit the surface and broke into hundreds of sparkling reflections. I closed my eyes and let my head drop back, my face turned up to the sun. Bathed in warmth, I let my mind drift. A memory, ghostly and fleeting, emerged and skittered behind my closed eyes. I'd just turned sixteen. My mother and I had one of our rare moments together, sitting on the porch one summer evening, she with a glass of beer and me with a cold Coke.

I could hear her voice as clearly as if she now occupied the bench with me. "Janet, it's time to think about what you want to do with your life. Have you given it some thought?"

I'd sipped my drink and turned to face her. "I think I want to be a psychologist," I'd said.

She hadn't looked at me; her eyes were fixed at the hillside across from our row house. She'd finally nodded, then said, "That's a lot of work, honey. You have to get through college and then graduate school. It takes a lot of money to do that, too."

"I can get loans, and I can work," I'd said.

I remembered the look on her face then, her eyes filling with tears. "If your father had lived, we could help you. But, I can't. I wish I could…"

A lump formed in my throat as I recalled the sadness and defeat in her voice. "It's okay, Mom," I'd said. "It may take me a while longer, but I can do it."

"Why don't you think about something more practical, until you get on your feet financially?" she'd asked. She'd then suggested community college and secretarial skills that would serve me well. "That way you know you'll always be able to get a job."

Since I'd been good at math and liked working with numbers, I'd settled on accounting. Then she died just as I'd begun my first year. I'd finished the second year of the program and, with an associate degree in hand, went to work.

I lowered my head and opened my eyes, only then aware of my tears. The blur of light reflecting off the lake forced me to close them again. The tears were, I knew, for my mother. She hadn't gotten the life she'd bargained for, either. She'd had to settle for what she got; I'd learned to settle, too, to be safe. She'd never wanted me to have to work as hard as she had to take care of both of us. I understood that now.

I wiped my face and took a long drink of water, then looked out over the lake. I thought about picking up that sixteen-year-old's dream and getting a degree in psychology. Then I thought about my recent transformation and how I'd brought about change for Joy, Angela and even for Ricki. And I remembered what Fran had said to me about caring, and how it had been echoed by Evelyn.

Resuming my walk around the lake, I realized I felt lighter. I reached the boat house and noticed a bin with a sign: *Lost and Found*. It made me laugh out loud at myself, not a chiding laugh, but a relieved, contented laugh. I was afraid to look into the bin for fear I'd find Janet looking back at me.

I used the restroom and, when I emerged, glanced at my watch. If I left now, I could stop by the grocery and pick up things I'd need to make a really special dinner for Anthony and the kids. And right now, that was what I wanted most to do. A thoughtful meal was one way of saying, "I love you." *Maybe I'm Italian, after all.*

~ * ~

My first nights at the shelter had me disoriented and exhausted. Some of the women were wary and kept their distance; others wanted to know all about me and chatted until the lights were turned off. Catherine spent the first two weeks working with me, until I got the hang of things. Occasionally, we had a volunteer from the School of Social Work or from one of the sponsoring churches. By the second week, I'd adjusted to the hours and to being able to sleep on a cot with one ear attuned to the women sleeping all around me, much the way I had when the kids were small. I'd successfully averted two minor crises by remaining calm and listening to what the women were upset about, then helping them to resolve the argument. I felt useful and confident. Most of the women easily accepted and seemed to like me.

Anthony held me to my promise and found creative ways to get Gabby out of the house for a Saturday afternoon. She was so easily bribed and more than happy to spend time at the movies or the mall with friends, an extra twenty dollars in her pocket. Michael was working all the hours he could get until it was time to start his college courses. I found comfort in knowing I'd see him most weekends when he'd come home to do laundry and see what his Grandma Angela had cooked lately.

Carmela had finally settled on a hair color, a toned-down version of her original blue that had more of a silver touch and looked less clown-like. She insisted on buying herself a computer. I insisted on setting the parental controls.

Angela had a second 'dinner,' …she emphasized it was not a 'date'… with Joe Bruschetti. When I teased her about getting her 'tires rotated,' she actually laughed and blushed. I think she got the joke, and I think she'd already been thinking about that.

One afternoon when I collected the mail, there was an invitation to Ricki's wedding and an envelope addressed to Joy. The return address said T. Richardson, and I assumed it was her daughter.

I took the letter to the park and delivered it to Joy. She invited me to sit while she opened the envelope with trembling hands and read.

Joy's eyes were swimming when she looked at me with a wobbly smile. "It's from Tina, my daughter. She says she's not angry with me, and that she's often thought about me. She wants to meet me sometime. Can you believe it?"

"You're her mother, Joy. Of course she wants to know you. I'm happy for you."

"I was so afraid she'd be hurt and angry because I left, and she wouldn't understand why. She says she knows I did what I had to do, and that I must have believed it was the best thing for her and her brother. She says her stepmother is a good woman and took good care of them."

I took hold of Joy's hand. "Your daughter sounds like a very nice young woman. When are you going to meet with her?"

"I don't know. She told me to call and gave me her cell phone number. I guess we could meet for coffee one day."

"I have a better idea. Anthony and I are taking the kids to the beach for a long weekend before school starts again. Why don't you stay at the house and have Tina come there? You can have dinner."

"Oh, I… are you sure that would be okay?"

"Very sure," I said, reaching into my pocket and producing my cell phone. "Here. Call her now before you talk yourself out of it. We're leaving next Thursday afternoon and won't be back until Tuesday. The house is all yours." I handed her the phone, then stood. "I'll go and get coffee while you talk with her."

I walked into the café, and Ricki smiled from behind the counter. "Hey, Hope. It's good to see you. Did you get my invitation?" She'd not yet gotten the memo that Janet was back, alive and well.

"I did, and I can't wait to come to your wedding. By the way, I'm back to my original name, Janet. Do you need a babysitter while you and Tim go on your honeymoon?"

"What honeymoon? He's just started his new job. Our honeymoon is going to consist of setting up the house in

Virginia. Then I'm going to look into enrolling in college classes and finding daycare for Hannah."

She handed me a latte and a black coffee, and I gave her a ten. "I'm going to miss you here. You already know what I want when I come through the door."

"I'll be sure to train my replacement. So, your name's really Janet? Then, why…?"

"Why Hope? I knew who Janet was, but I needed to figure out who *I* was. Turns out, I'm Janet, but the new and improved model." I picked up the drinks. "Thanks, Ricki. I'll see you."

I returned to the park and handed Joy her coffee. "Well?"

Joy smiled broadly. "She's coming to dinner next Saturday, and she's going to see if her brother can come home and join us. He's in Philadelphia."

"That's wonderful." I pulled a slip of paper and a pen from my hip pack. "Tell me what you want to cook, and I'll make sure everything's there for you."

Joy protested, but I was insistent. "Look, I'd throw you all a party, but I think you and your kids need that time alone. So, please, let me do this much."

"It's been so long since I've cooked a meal, I'm not sure I'll remember how."

"Here's a suggestion… Angela's lasagna. I know she'll be thrilled to prepare a pan for you, and I'll have it in the fridge. All you'll have to do is make a salad and garlic bread. I'll even have her bake a cake. She'll be in her glory."

Joy looked at me through moist eyes. "You are such a good person. How'd I get so lucky to have you for a friend?"

"You must've needed a little hope," I teased. "And I guess I needed more joy."

~ * ~

As I'd predicted, Angela was thrilled at being asked to help Joy with the meal for her children. I turned a set of keys over to Joy, then hurried to the car where Anthony and the kids waited. "We'll see you on Tuesday. Have a great time," I called to Joy.

We drove along in silence until we reached the turnpike. Michael was engrossed in a book, and Gabby bounced and nodded to her MP3 player, earphones snugly in place.

After we'd passed through the gate and onto the Pennsylvania turnpike, Anthony reached for my hand. "So, did you pack enough for both Janet and Hope?"

I grinned. "I think so. Hope doesn't need much," I whispered.

"Hope springs eternal," he whispered back, grinning broadly.

Nineteen

The condo we'd rented on the Jersey shore sat a half-block back from the beach, facing the water. The seven-and-a-half-hour drive stretched to almost nine hours as we encountered a clog of vacationers all headed in the same direction. We'd made this trip every summer for the past ten years. I glanced back at the kids, Michael asleep, and Gabby, head bobbing to music as she read a magazine. I shuddered, remembering earlier trips when they weren't so easily amused.

"What are you thinking?" Anthony asked, glancing at me.

I put my hand on his thigh and squeezed. "Just remembering the days when the kids asked every ten minutes, 'Are we there yet?'"

"Feeling old?" He dropped one hand from the steering wheel and placed it over mine.

"No. Feeling content. I'm grateful we have teenagers who are willing to travel with us. We didn't have to threaten them or tie them to the roof of the car."

"It helps that Michael can drive. They can go off on their own for a while. I'm sure we'll find something to do."

I pinched his leg. "You just can't wait to see what Hope brought to wear, can you?"

He looked into the rear view mirror to make sure he wouldn't be heard, then whispered, "She brought things to wear? Now that's disappointing."

A few beats when by, then I said, "We have a good marriage. And we're raising two great kids."

"Were you doubting that?"

"No. I just wanted to say it out loud."

We reached the outskirts of Sea Isle City, and Anthony turned onto our exit. We opted for this quieter ocean town rather than Wildwood with its crowds and amusements. When the kids were younger, we'd take them to ride the amusement rides for an afternoon or evening, then return to the peaceful calm of Sea Isle. Now that Michael had his license, he and his sister could go on their own.

As we neared the dead-end, I saw the sign... The Seaview. "We need to look for parking spaces number forty-six and forty-seven. We have both, so park in either."

"Aye, aye, captain. We do this every year," Anthony said with a mock salute.

I turned and waved to get Gabby's attention. "We're here. Wake your brother."

My knees and hips complained about the hours in the car as I stood and stretched. A warm breeze carried the scent of the ocean and lashed at my ponytail. I closed my eyes and lifted my face to the sun, rolling my head to loosen a few knots.

Anthony popped the rear door of the Explorer open and began to unload. "Everybody grab a suitcase. Michael and I will come back for the rest after we get this stuff upstairs."

We were warmly greeted at the front desk as Anthony and I registered. The concierge handed us a welcome packet and four key cards. "It's nice to see you again, Mr. and Mrs. DeMarco. I hope you enjoy your stay. Please call us if there's anything you need."

Anthony thanked him and led us to the elevator. "Let's get unpacked and then go out to dinner tonight. We can hit the grocery store on the way back and stock up for the week."

"Can't Michael and I go to Wildwood or someplace fun for the evening? We can get something to eat there," Gabby whined.

"No. You'll have all week for that. It's been a long day, and we're having dinner together." Anthony's authoritative tone left no room for argument.

We entered the condo, and I walked to the balcony and slid open the glass doors, letting in the sounds and smells of the beach. "It feels so good to be here."

Anthony stepped behind me and put his arms around me, resting his chin on my shoulder. "Want me to let the kids go off on their own this evening?"

"No. We'll have all week for that," I repeated his words, teasing. "I'm exhausted. Let's have a nice dinner, get the shopping out of the way, and then sit out here and watch the sunset. I'm going to give Joy a call and make sure everything's okay at the house."

He kissed my neck, then my cheek. "I'll take our bags to the bedroom and unpack."

The kids were squabbling over who got which of the other two bedrooms. I heard Anthony's voice boom, then silence… argument resolved. I dialed our phone number at home and listened to four rings.

Joy answered tentatively, "Hello, DeMarco residence."

"Joy, you sound so professional. We just arrived, and I thought I'd call and let you know."

"Thanks. Did you have a good trip?"

"Longer than we expected because of traffic, but it was good. I'm glad finally to be here. Is everything okay there?"

"Everything's fine. I, um... I can't tell you how much I appreciate this. I still can't believe you just turned your house over to me."

"Look at it this way. We don't have to worry about anyone breaking in as long as you're there. So, you're really doing us a favor. I hope things go well for you on Saturday with your kids."

"I'm a little nervous about that. Angela's excited about preparing dinner. She wanted to serve a seven course meal, but I talked her out of it."

I laughed. "You mention cooking to Angela, and she's in her glory. Good luck. Oh, and feel free to use the computer in the den or anything else. Make yourself at home."

Joy laughed. "If I did that, I'd end up sleeping on your patio. I appreciate your call, but I'll be fine. You folks just have a wonderful week, and enjoy the sun and the ocean."

"Thanks, Joy. I'm planning to call again after your dinner with your kids. I'll be dying to know how things go. You have my cell number if anything comes up in the meantime. Have a good night."

Anthony and Michael went back to the car. They returned laden with extra pillows, the cooler and bag of snacks, and other miscellaneous items we'd each brought and probably would never use.

We drove the four blocks to a seafood restaurant in town and, after feasting on crab and lobster, headed to the grocery store. Anthony and I took the list and one shopping cart. "Michael, you and Gabby take another cart and get whatever additional snacks and drinks you want. Be reasonable. Meet us back here at the checkout in twenty minutes."

We'd have dinner out most evenings, but the fully-equipped kitchen allowed for keeping breakfast and lunch foods on hand. Angela had given me two large jars of sauce and a package of frozen meatballs. I dropped a box of spaghetti into the cart. Perhaps I'd cook Anthony a romantic dinner one evening while the kids were out.

Anthony must have read my mind. As we loaded groceries into the car, he said, "I'll be right back." He crossed the street to a liquor store and returned with four bottles of wine. "These should tide us over."

As soon as we'd returned to the condo and put the groceries away, Michael announced he wasn't tired and was going to walk back to an arcade he'd seen near the restaurant. "You coming, Gabs?"

"You bet. Give me a minute to fix my hair. And don't call me Gabs."

"Be back by eleven," Anthony ordered.

"Aw, Dad! It's vacation," Michael complained.

"Okay, midnight. Not one minute after. I'm sure the arcade closes by then, anyway. And don't leave your sister alone with anybody."

"How am I gonna meet girls with my sister in tow?"

Anthony grinned. "It's not easy, I'm sure. I always had your Uncle Dante tagging along with me."

"So, it could be worse?" Michael asked with a smile. "I won't leave Gabby out of my sight, and we'll be back by midnight."

Anthony dug into his pocket and produced a twenty. "Here, in case you want ice cream or something."

The door closed behind the kids and silence whispered through the room. I stepped out onto the balcony, arranging the chairs to take in the view. Anthony appeared with two glasses of wine and handed one to me, then sat down.

He took in a deep breath and let it out slowly. "I've been looking forward to this for weeks."

I reached for his hand, interlacing my fingers with his. "We're very fortunate."

He sipped his wine, then turned and looked at me. "I'm the luckiest guy I know, that's for sure."

We held hands and watched evening fall across the ocean until the waves could be heard, but were no longer visible as they rolled onto the shore. I lit a citronella candle to ward off insects and placed it on the table between us. When the mosquitoes developed an immunity to the candle, I stood and announced I was going inside to take a shower.

I came out of the bathroom to find Anthony flipping channels on the TV, searching for the late news. "You going to bed already?" he asked.

"I thought I'd read for a bit, but I'll probably fall asleep before I finish a page." I picked up my book from the coffee table and kissed him goodnight. "Just in case I'm asleep before you come to bed."

"I'm going to wait until the kids are in. I'll try not to wake you."

I laughed. "You'd need a marching band to do that, I think. Goodnight."

~ * ~

Anthony's side of the bed was empty when I woke to bright sunlight filling the room. My body felt as if my bones had been removed. I hadn't been this relaxed in a long time. I got up and used the bathroom, then pulled on my robe, noting it was past nine o'clock. When I entered the living room, the smell of coffee and bacon triggered a drool reflex.

"Good morning, sleeping beauty," Anthony said from his perch on one of the stools at the bar. "You ready for breakfast?"

"Are you cooking?" I asked, accepting the mug of coffee he offered.

"The kids are fed and on the beach already. Have a seat and tell me your pleasure, m'lady."

I raised my eyes over the rim of the coffee mug to meet his. "My pleasure?"

"That… or breakfast."

"I'll have scrambled eggs, bacon, toast, and melon."

"Coming right up. You just sit there and relax."

"Okay, am I still dreaming? I did have this dream once, where you waited on me hand and foot."

He walked over, pinched me lightly on the hip and nuzzled my neck. "Nope. You're wide awake. Don't worry. Tomorrow's your turn. Gabby's on for Saturday and Michael has breakfast on Sunday."

"Oh, I see. Nothing special, just our schedule."

He placed a bowl of melon slices in front of me then returned to the stove. He cracked eggs into a bowl and beat them with a fork before dropping the liquid into the skillet. Anthony was efficient in the kitchen. He was also darned cute in his cut-offs, with that apron on and a towel tossed over his shoulder.

"What are you staring at?"

I grinned. "Oh, nothing."

"Yes, you were. You were staring at my backside. Well, here, get a better look." He stuck his butt out and wiggled. "Turning you on?"

I laughed. "Not especially, honey. So, what do you want to do today?"

"I thought we'd hit the beach, get some sun and work on a tan. The kids want to go to the boardwalk in Wildwood tonight for some concert."

"Oh, really?"

"Aha, you're thinking what I'm thinking, Mrs. DeMarco. Just you, me, a bottle of wine and a romantic view."

"Who would you rather spend the evening with, Janet or Hope?"

He slid the eggs onto a plate next to the slices of bacon and removed the toast from the toaster oven, then set the plate in front of me. "Okay, so that's a trick question. I can't win, no matter what answer I give."

"It's a simple question. I won't hold the answer against you."

"Yeah, well. I'm afraid if I give the wrong answer, you won't hold anything against me, and I'm not taking that chance. Not tonight. How are your eggs?"

I swallowed and nodded. "Delicious."

"Okay, enjoy your breakfast. I'm going to change and get ready for the beach."

I cleared my plate and downed a second cup of coffee, cleaned up the kitchen and removed a package of meatballs from the freezer for dinner. I felt the irresistible urge to giggle. Even after nineteen years, anticipating a romantic evening with Anthony made me feel like a teenager.

~ * ~

Clouds began to roll in late in the afternoon. I kept an eye to the sky, wishing them away. I returned to the condo at four to take a shower. When I emerged, I was greeted by two soaking wet teenagers. One look outside told me there'd be no outdoor concert that evening, and my romantic dinner would be for four. Anthony stood at the balcony doors and scowled as lightning streaked and thunder boomed.

Gabby dried her arms and face with a paper towel and slumped dramatically onto the sofa. "Now what are we going to do? There's probably nothing on TV, and we're stuck here. If we were home, I could at least…"

"Stop whining. Now. You'd think you were in prison. Read a book or something. Plug that contraption into your ears and listen to music," Anthony grumbled.

"I'll call downstairs and see if we can rent a couple of movies. How's that?" I asked.

"Can I pick one?" Gabby asked, brightening up a little.

"Sure. Why don't you and I go down to the desk and see what's available. They have a whole selection there. Michael, any requests?"

"No, Mom. I'm probably going to read for a while. We just have to hope the power doesn't…"

Before he finished the sentence, the TV screen went black and the kitchen lights turned off.

"Great. Now how am I supposed to cook dinner?" I muttered.

"I'm going to my room," Gabby announced, trouncing off in a huff.

"Guess I'll take a nap," Michael said, following her down the hall to his room.

"I suppose we can have sandwiches and chips for dinner tonight. Honey, is that okay, or do you want to see if we can order pizza? It looks like every place around is out of power."

"Sandwiches will be fine. I guess I'll take a nap, too. I sure hope it doesn't rain all week," he mumbled before going into the bedroom. I understood his disappointment.

Hallway emergency lights told me there had to be a generator. I took the dimly-lit stairs to the courtesy desk in the lobby and picked up several pillar candles and a book of matches. "You know, Mrs. DeMarco, you can use the elevator. We have a backup generator for those," the concierge said.

I looked at the gleaming copper door, the color of a coffin, and imagined getting in there and having the generator fail.

"That's okay. It's only four flights, and I can use the exercise. Thanks. Oh, give me a deck of cards, too, please."

I was out of breath when I reached the fourth floor. I placed the candles around the living room and kitchen and lit them, creating a warm glow against the harsh flashes visible from the balcony doors. One by one, unhappy campers emerged from the bedrooms and joined me as I set out a spread of cold cuts, cheese and condiments.

It was the first time in a long time no one had to jump up from a meal and run off to some extra-curricular activity. And the evening Anthony and I had in mind had been effectively curtailed. As Michael started on his third sandwich and Anthony his second, I suggested we play cards.

"Mom, that's so lame," Gabby snorted.

"Got a better idea?" I asked.

Anthony shoved his plate aside and picked up the deck of cards. "Come on. Your mom and I will teach you how to play gin."

Gabby's mood brightened considerably when she beat us all. Just as I was sure I'd had enough, the lights flickered a few times, then stayed on.

"What time is it?" I looked at my watch. "Almost ten. Let's see what's on TV."

We moved to the living room, and I flipped channels, finding a rerun of *Law and Order*. Michael grabbed the corn chips, nacho cheese and salsa and set them on the coffee table, then stretched out on the floor. We stuffed ourselves with snacks and watched TV. Before long, Gabby was asleep, curled in a chair. Anthony's head rested against mine, and he snored softly.

I nudged him awake. "The storm's over and so is the program. I'm going to bed." I touched Gabby's arm. "Honey, wake up so you can go to sleep."

I was reading when Anthony came into the room. He stepped into the bathroom, then returned, clad in his boxers, and slid into bed beside me. "We should do that more often," he said.

"Do what?"

"Spend time like that with the kids."

"You gonna glue them to a chair at home, or shall I get the staple gun?"

He chuckled. "I sure hope it doesn't rain tomorrow. The kids really want to go to Wildwood."

I smacked him lightly with my book. "You could care less about the kids wanting to go to Wildwood. You just want to get me alone."

He took the book from my hand and dropped it onto the floor. "I've got you alone right now."

He had a good point.

Twenty

The storm brought cooler temperatures the following day, with a high only in the upper seventies. By the time Gabby stumbled into the kitchen, eyes half closed, I'd already started breakfast.

"I thought it was my turn," she mumbled.

"You're on vacation. I'll take care of breakfast this morning."

She turned back toward the bedroom. "Okay. Call me when it's ready."

I pulled out all the stops: French toast, sausage, fresh fruit, scrambled eggs and toasted English muffins.

"It smells great out here," Anthony said as he came through the living room.

"Honey, would you tell the kids this is almost ready?"

"Sure. Where's Gabby? I thought she was doing breakfast?"

"I was already up. She's getting her beauty sleep. Wouldn't want her to be too tired to go to the concert later."

A smiled cracked across his face. "No, we certainly wouldn't want that."

Everyone gathered and sat yawning while I set plates of food on the table. "Thanks, Mom," Michael said, stabbing a stack of French toast. I turned back to the stove and made another six slices.

As I sat down and watched my family come to life, enjoy the meal I'd prepared, talk about their plans for the day, I thought of Joy. I considered calling her again for moral support, but knew I had to let it be. She and her kids would work things out in their own way. I'd call later to see how it had gone.

Anthony cleared the dishes and loaded them into the dishwasher. The kids changed, grabbed their towels and headed for the beach. I poured a second cup of coffee and moved out to the balcony, breathing in the ocean air.

I had closed my eyes, but was aware of Anthony dropping into the chair next to me. "Want to go for a drive and check out the antique shops?"

I opened one eye and squinted, certain another man had stepped into Anthony's place. "I'd love to. What time do the kids want to leave?"

"I told Michael he could have the car at six."

"That's perfect because I have a very special evening planned for us. Remind me to stop on the way home for whipped cream."

Anthony's face twisted into a goofy grin. I rolled my eyes. "It's for the dessert."

"Oh."

It was a perfect day for driving along the shore with the top down. Unfortunately, we were in a Ford Explorer. Anthony intensely disliked shopping, especially the 'browsing' kind of shopping. I knew this day was a gift to me as he patiently followed me from shop to shop and looked interested when I picked up a piece of glassware and told him what it was and its value. I found a few pieces I knew Fran would've loved, but the prices were way beyond my budget.

At our final stop before heading back to the condo, I discovered a beautiful cameo brooch. It was small and delicately framed with silver. The price wasn't bad. I held it up to my neck. "What do you think, honey?"

"It's nice."

I set it down again, disappointed by his lack of enthusiasm. We exited the shop and Anthony said, "Wait here. I think I left the keys on the counter. I'll be right back."

I moved next door and browsed the window. He soon returned, dangling the keys in his hand. "Got 'em."

~ * ~

I was making a chocolate mousse pie when Michael and Gabby appeared, ready to leave for the concert. Gabby wore a midriff top that exposed her flat abdomen and navel. "Don't let your father see you dressed like that."

She went to her room and returned with a gauze shirt buttoned over the middy. "Bye, Mom." She kissed my cheek. "'Night, Daddy." She gave Anthony a kiss and hug. I could see his eyes go soft. He was strict with Gabby, but she still had him wrapped around her finger.

Anthony handed Michael the car keys. "No speeding. Park in a well-lit area. Don't let…"

Michael nodded and finished, " …Gabby out of my sight. Don't pick up strangers. Be home by midnight. Got it. Thanks, Dad. C'mon, Gabs…riella."

The door closed. Anthony waited, went to the door and peeked out into the hallway. He stepped back inside and began to dance around the living room in his own version of 'sexy.' "The kids are gone and we're alone," he sang tunelessly. He waltzed into the kitchen, took the spatula from my hand and twirled around with me.

I giggled and smacked his chest. "Put me down. I need to get the mousse into the fridge so it will set."

He eased me to my feet and bent over the stove to check the pasta. "This is just about ready. I'll pour the wine."

We had a candlelit dinner and emptied one bottle of wine. I leaned back in my chair. "I think I have to wait a while for dessert. How about you? Maybe I should call Joy now."

"Joy is probably still talking with her kids. Call her in the morning. And I can wait for dessert. In the meantime, let me give you this." He reached into his pants pocket and produced a small gold box, placing it on the table in front of me.

"What's this?"

"Open it. You'll see."

I raised the lid from the box and looked inside. When I folded back the tissue paper, I saw the brooch. "You sneak. You didn't forget the car keys." I lifted the delicate jewelry from the box. "It's beautiful, isn't it? Thank you."

Anthony stepped behind me and fastened the chain. As I fingered the brooch, he lifted my hair and traced kisses along my neck and shoulder. I shivered. Anthony walked to the stereo and hit the 'play' button, then returned with extended hand. "May I have this dance?"

I stood and melted into his arms, moving slowly to the oldies music. "Just like your mom and dad, huh?"

He stopped and, when I looked up at him, he smiled. "Have I told you today how much I love you?"

"Not in so many words, but I got the idea." I took his hand and, after circling the room to blow out candles, led him to the bedroom.

A few hours later, Anthony shrugged into his robe and went to the kitchen, returning with two large pieces of chocolate mousse pie and a can of whipped cream topping. He set everything on the nightstand, left again and came back bearing two glasses of milk. "Time for fortification."

We sat in bed, side by side, feeding one another chocolate mousse. We managed to get creative and empty the can of whipped topping.

I heard the door open and close, followed by Gabby's chatter, then Michael's voice outside our door. "We're home. Is there any dessert left?"

I looked at the empty can and burst into laughter.

"Mom?"

Anthony called out, "There's pie in the fridge, but there's no more topping. Sorry." When he grinned down at me and whispered, "Actually, I'm not sorry at all," I rolled my face into my pillow and stuffed the sheet in my mouth to stifle my laughter.

~ * ~

In the morning, I heard a light tap, followed by a more insistent knock on our door. Michael asked, "Can I come in?"

I pulled the covers up to my neck. Anthony was in the bathroom. "Sure, honey. Come on in."

The door swung open, and Michael steadied the cookie sheet doubling as a service tray bearing two cups of coffee, two glasses of orange juice, and two cherry-cheese Danish. Gabby followed with cream, sugar and a folding TV tray. She set the TV tray beside the bed and Michael held the cookie sheet while she unloaded it.

"Well, this is a surprise," I said.

Michael shrugged. "Just thought you and Dad might want to take it easy this morning."

Anthony appeared and looked at the food, then narrowed his eyes at Michael. "What happened?"

"Nothing happened. Well, nothing to be worried about." Michael's face turned crimson.

I tugged at the blankets, wrapping them around me as I sat erect, wishing I could get to my robe. "What happened?"

"I kind of scraped the bumper of the Explorer."

Anthony sat on the edge of the bed. "Scraped?"

"Yeah, just a scratch, really."

"That's all?" Anthony asked.

Gabby rolled her eyes. "Ask him what he scraped it on."

Anthony looked from Michael to Gabby, then fixed his stare on his son. "Okay. What did you scrape it on?"

Michael gazed at his feet, his shoulders hunched, and mumbled, "A merz-deez."

"A…what?" Anthony asked.

"A Mercedes. I bumped a Mercedes." He pulled a slip of paper from his pocket. "Here. I got the lady's information and I gave her mine. She said to have you call her today."

Anthony took the paper and stared at it. "Great, just great!"

I put a hand on my husband's arm, but looked at Michael. "Can I talk to your father alone for a minute?"

"Sure, Mom," Michael said as he turned and ushered Gabby towards the door.

"Thank you for breakfast," I said to their backs.

"Don't go anywhere," Anthony barked, then turned and glared at me. "You're thanking him? This is going to cost a bundle, I'll bet, and you're thanking him?"

"Honey, maybe it wasn't his fault. The Explorer is huge, and those Mercedes are so small. He probably didn't even see it."

He grabbed one of the Danish and ripped into it like a lion going after a side of beef. He then mumbled something that had to be English but sounded an awful lot like his mother's mutterings in Italian.

I waited a moment, then asked, "May I have a Danish, please?"

He passed the plate and stood. "I'm going to shower, then I'll call…" he looked at the paper, "…Mrs. Lawrence and see what the damage is."

I seized the opportunity to call Joy. "Hi, Joy. It's me. Did I wake you?"

"No. I've been up for hours."

"Well, how'd everything go? Did your kids show up?"

"They did. It was…good, I guess. My daughter's lovely. My son, well, he's not as forgiving as his sister. I think he saw this as an opportunity to let me know how angry he was when I left."

"Oh, Joy. I'm so sorry."

"Don't be. I figure I owed him that. At least he didn't come in, speak his mind and then stomp out. We talked. It was a start."

"So, you feel okay with the way things went?"

"I'm fine. Angela has a dinner date tonight, so Carmela's coming here to spend the evening with me. She wants to show me how to use your computer."

Oh, God help us.

"Well, you two have a nice evening. Tell Carmela I send my love, and we'll see you all on Tuesday."

Anthony emerged from the shower, pulled on his clothes and stomped out to the living room. "Michael, come here. I want you here while I talk to this Mrs. Lawrence."

I went to shower, leaving Anthony to handle the situation. When I'd finished and joined them in the living room, Michael was giving Anthony his side of the story.

"I was trying to parallel park and she came out of nowhere and tried to slide into the space behind me. I never saw her coming. I just scraped her car with the bumper, but I guess the Explorer sits so much higher and, well, it got her headlight and part of the fender."

"Were there any witnesses?" I asked, walking towards them.

Michael shook his head. "Just Gabby. I mean, there were a hundred kids on the street but, of course, no one saw anything."

I looked at Anthony. "How bad is it?"

"She's getting an estimate, but it's going to be bad. Good thing we have insurance."

Michael looked pale. "I can help pay for it with the money I earn working for Teddy."

"No, you won't. It was an accident. I could've done the same thing and, like your father said, we have insurance. You and your sister go on to the beach and forget about this for now." I spoke to Michael, but kept my eyes fixed on Anthony. He didn't interrupt.

"Thanks, Mom." Michael stood and hugged me, harder than usual, more the way he did when he was a little boy and something scared him. He shoved his hands into his pockets and hung his head. "I'm sorry, Dad."

Anthony exhaled. "Your mom's right. It was an accident. Just be more careful next time, okay?"

Michael nodded and headed for his room.

I sat next to Anthony, my hand on his. "You know how careful he is. You taught him to drive."

"It's going to raise our insurance through the roof. And it may mean he can't drive for Teddy, unless Teddy's willing to pay a higher rate."

"We'll deal with it. Don't let it spoil the rest of our time here. We can still afford another can of whipped cream, I'll bet."

"Well, in that case…" He grinned and kissed me. "My grandma's right about you."

"Oh, yeah?"

"You are good for the DeMarco family. All of us hot-headed Italians, and then there's you, cool and calm, and reasonable."

"Thank you. Now, we need to go to the grocery store. Unless you want to send the kids?"

Anthony looked at the note, then at the car keys. I could see him thinking. "Hey, Michael. Come here, please."

Michael appeared in the doorway. "Yes?"

Anthony tossed the car keys to him. "Would you and your sister go to the grocery store and pick up a few things? Your mom'll give you a list."

"Uh, sure." He turned and called to Gabby.

"Just be careful. Okay?" Anthony added.

"Don't worry. I'll have Gabby stand behind the Explorer and direct me."

Gabby appeared in time to hear his comment. "I'm not standing behind you so you can run me over."

"Your sister has a point. Just watch where you're going," I said as I handed him the list.

The kids left and I turned to Anthony, holding his face between my hands the way his grandmother often did. "You're a good man, Anthony DeMarco. Your mother raised you well."

And I believed that. Anthony is a good man. I have two wonderful kids. I have a great life. So, why do I feel like something's missing? *What is wrong with me?*

~ * ~

That afternoon Anthony announced he was going to take a nap. I seized the opportunity for some alone time. "I'm going for a walk. I'll be back soon."

I'd gotten used to my walks alone and missed my time with Hope. *Janet, you're dangerously close to having an imaginary friend—or a split personality.*

The temperatures had risen into the eighties, and the afternoon sun beat mercilessly onto the pavement. I walked to the business district and sought my favorite oasis, Starbucks. There was at least one in every town. I opted for a chilled drink and sipped it as I made my way to the open beach. My sneakers tied together and my socks stuffed inside them, I sank my bare feet into the warm, dry sand. I let the sounds of the waves block out the chatter of gulls and the shrieks of children dancing and splashing at the water's edge.

Okay, Hope, let's have a little talk. I think it's almost time for you to leave and for Janet to reclaim her life.

To my surprise, a response echoed in my thoughts. *You reclaimed your life the minute you became Hope. It doesn't matter what you call yourself. Don't blame me for taking away Janet's dreams. She gave them up a long time ago.*

I stopped and looked around to see who was talking to me. No one. My hand shook as I dropped the empty plastic cup into a trash receptacle. I continued along the beach.

I didn't give up anything. It was ripped from my hands before I had a chance to take hold of it—whatever 'it' was. That 'it'—that certainty we're supposed to have about what we want from life.

I was beginning to feel frightened by the conversation taking place in my head as Hope volleyed back. *Well, I didn't take it away from you. Things happen that are beyond our control. When your mother died, you stopped listening to me and went on your merry way. You never once asked me what I wanted to do.*

Again, I stopped and looked around. Had I said that out loud? No one seemed to be looking at me as though they needed to grab their children and run for safety. Still, my hands trembled as I sat on the steps leading to the boardwalk and put on my socks and sneakers. I walked hurriedly in the direction of the condo. I was obviously losing my mind. I wondered if this was how it started for Joy.

I trailed sand into the living room, grabbed a bottle of water from the fridge and went to the bedroom. Anthony was sprawled shirtless on the bed, sleeping soundly. The chilled water bottle dripped, and a cold splat hit his stomach.

"Jesus, what was that? Jan, what's wrong?"

"I'm going crazy. It's happening, and I can't stop it."

He sat up and looked at me. "What are you talking about?"

"Voices. I'm hearing voices. I think I'm losing my mind." My hands shook. He took the water bottle from me, set it on the nightstand and then pulled me down to sit beside him.

"Calm down. What are you talking about? Maybe you have heat stroke."

I jumped up and paced. "I don't have heat stroke. I have Hope and Janet talking to one another in my head, and Hope said that Janet... Hope said I gave up a long time ago, and that I gave up talking to her, too. And... Anthony, I'm scared. Hope isn't real. She was never real, but now she's talking to me and..."

Anthony stood and pulled me against him. "Honey, calm down. Of course Hope's real."

I jerked my head back and looked at him. "What do you mean, she's real? I made her up."

"Honey, listen to me. You couldn't have made up Hope if you'd tried. She's real because she's you. Well, she's a part of you. Come here, sit down."

We sat on the bed and he hugged me; I rested my head on his shoulder. "I thought about what you said, about never knowing what you wanted to be when you grew up. You didn't have time to think about it when your mother died. You had to tuck those thoughts, those *hopes*, away somewhere. Now it's time to let them out and look at them."

I cocked my head and considered what he was saying.

"Hopes, dreams, whatever you want to call it; it's the stuff that got shoved aside. It's like that old Teddy Bear I gave Gabby when she was four. Remember how excited she was when she found it in her closet last year?"

I nodded, shocked by Anthony's insight.

"I'll admit I've enjoyed Hope as a playmate. Maybe it was unfair of me to seem to take her so lightly." He titled my chin up and looked into my eyes. "But I've never taken *you* lightly, Jan. You know that, right?"

"So, I'm not going crazy?"

He laughed and squeezed me. "If anything, you're going sane."

I wrapped my arms around him and held on tight. "I was so scared. I thought about Joy and how she just walked away from everything, and I was hearing these different voices…"

"Different voices or the same voice with different names?"

"Oh, now that you mention it." I pulled back and looked at him. "How'd you get so smart?"

"I consulted a friend of mine, Tony. He knows more about women than I do."

We fell back onto the bed, laughing.

"Hey, maybe we should introduce Hope to Tony some time," he said.

"I think they'd make a great couple, Anthony."

"I agree, Janet."

~ * ~

It was our last night at the shore. The kids had gone to Wildwood after Anthony gave Michael lengthy instructions on how and where to park the Explorer. Anthony and I walked, hand in hand, along the nearly-deserted beach as the sun sank low in the sky.

"It's been an interesting week, hasn't it?" I asked.

"Interesting? That's one word for it. I hate to see it end. I could use a few more days of this."

"Let's plan a trip for winter, just the two of us, to someplace warm."

He looked down at me and grinned. "Just the two of us?"

"Yes."

He stopped walking and took hold of both of my hands. "May I speak with Hope for a moment?"

"Anthony…"

"Just one last time. Please?"

"Okay."

He leaned close, his lips against my ear. "Hope? Are you in there?"

I rolled my eyes, feeling ridiculous. "Yes."

"I just want to thank you for hanging in there with Janet, and for being there when she needed you."

My eyes filled, and I looked away. Anthony put his finger under my chin and lifted my face to his. "I want to thank you for holding the hope for her all these years, and for letting her find it again."

I leaned against his chest and hugged him tightly. "Anthony, I know what I want when I grow up."

He rested his cheek against my temple. "What, Jan?"

"This."

"Does that mean no more nights at the shelter?"

"*That* is a part of *this*," I said, leaning back to look up at him. "You and the kids will always come first. But I have to put myself up there somewhere, too. The work at the shelter does that for me. You should see some of the women's faces when I open the door and greet them, or when one of them comes and asks if she can talk. I make sure they know they matter to me, each and every one of them."

"That is one thing you do well."

I smiled up at him. "One thing? What are the others?"

A grin slid across his face, and his eyelids fluttered.

~ * ~

I hustled the kids out of bed in the morning while Anthony prepared breakfast. We needed to get on the road by ten a.m. While Michael and Anthony loaded the car, Gabby and I checked the condo for any items left behind.

"I think we got everything, Mom," Gabby said as she stood and looked around the living room.

"Okay. Let's go."

We stepped into the elevator and I pressed 'L' for lobby. "Did you have fun this week?"

To my surprise, Gabby put an arm around my waist and hugged me. "I had a great time, Mom. I actually like being with you and Dad...and even with Michael. I'm going to miss him when he leaves for college."

I squeezed her close, feeling the lump in my throat. "Me, too, sweetie."

"Mom, I've been thinking of changing my name. I'd like to be called Brie—you know, the b-r-i-e in Ga-brie-lla. What do you think?"

I smiled. "I think it's a nice name. Want to start now?"

"Yeah."

We walked to the front desk, and I presented the key cards to the concierge. "Thank you. My daughter, Brie, and I had a wonderful stay."

Giggling, we strolled to the car. Inside, *Hope* pumped her fist in the air and shouted a resounding 'Yes'!

"What's so funny?" Anthony asked.

"Oh, nothing." I looked back at my daughter. "Don't forget to buckle up... Brie."

"Brie? Who's...?" Anthony furrowed his eyebrows and turned to me.

"Sure, Mom," our daughter replied.

"Oh, brother." Anthony backed from the parking space. He looked into the rearview mirror. "Michael, when you find a girl you think you want to spend the rest of your life with, make sure she knows her name and what she wants to be when she grows up."

I smacked my husband's arm playfully, then said, "Mikey, pay no attention to your father. The most important thing is that you find a girl who loves you more than anything, a girl who's willing to give all of herself to you, even if she has to search to find out who that is."

Anthony squeezed my hand tightly. "Listen to your mother."

Twenty-one

I returned from the vacation and promptly came down with the flu. Which was odd, I thought, because it was late August. I couldn't keep anything down and all I wanted to do was sleep. Catherine covered my night shifts at the shelter. It was weird, really, because I'd feel fine, then all of a sudden have to run for bathroom and throw up. I chalked it up to the stress of preparing for Michael to leave for college.

When I recognized the pattern to my sickness, I broke into a sweat. *No, no, no. It can't be.* I grabbed my car keys and made a covert trip to the pharmacy. Back at home again, I locked myself in the bathroom and stared at the three boxes on the counter as if each one held a bomb. And they well may.

Fifteen minutes later, my fears were confirmed. I didn't know whether to laugh or cry. And I didn't know how to break this news to my husband who, unlike myself, happily prepared for his son's departure from home and eagerly awaited his daughter's graduation.

I busied myself gathering all the things Michael needed for his dorm room, and a lot of things he didn't exactly need, but I wanted him to have. I was sure that watching him drive away to start out on his own was going to be the single most difficult thing I'd ever face.

Michael caught me watching him, my eyes misty, and put his arm around me and smiled. "Jeez, Mom, you'd think I was going to Oxford or to UCLA. I'll be an hour away, in West Virginia. If it'll make you feel better, I promise to bring my laundry home every weekend."

"Thanks. That makes me feel so much better," I joked, but tightened my grip on his waist. "Some day you'll be in my shoes... watching your firstborn go out into the world for the first time and you'll understand how I feel."

Anthony had come into the room in the middle of this conversation. "Yeah, then you'll realize how much you're going to save on the food bill and you'll jump for joy."

I smacked Anthony's arm. "Don't tell him that. Michael, you come home for dinner any time you want. And bring a few friends." I grinned at my husband.

Michael grabbed a soda from the fridge and headed for the door. "I'm gonna meet the guys. See you later," he smiled at his father, "for dinner."

I watched him go, and let the tears spill.

Anthony's arm encircled me. "He's going to be fine, Jan. Now, we just need to figure out how to get Gabby, I mean, *Brie*, to jump a grade and graduate early. Then we have the house to ourselves."

My breath caught. I moved away from Anthony and stood against the kitchen counter, my fingers gripping the edge for support. "Yeah, um, about that. Uh... what if we didn't have the house to ourselves for a while yet?"

He narrowed his eyes at me. "What are you up to? Oh, for... you're not thinking of taking in the homeless again, are you? Isn't that what the shelter's for?"

"I'm not taking in anyone, Anthony. I just..." I shoved off from the counter and dropped into one of the kitchen chairs.

"Remember that day I came home, and you were cutting the grass and…"

His goofy grin answered my question. "Uh-huh." He bent and nuzzled my neck.

I pulled away and took a deep breath. "We, uh… weren't, um… careful."

"Careful? What do you mean?"

"Do you remember the month before when I went for my checkup, and the doctor took me off birth control because I was having problems with bleeding and cramps?"

He grimaced. "Yeah, do we have to talk about that *female* stuff. It creeps me out."

"Not as much the next topic is going to," I sighed.

"What? What's going on? Are you okay?" The concern in his eyes gave me the courage to go forward.

"I'm fine. I'm just …pregnant." In spite of myself, a smile tugged at my face.

Anthony blinked several times and his mouth hung open.

"Anthony? Can you say something?"

"Uh… I …yeah."

"Can you say something intelligible?"

"You're pregnant."

I laughed. "Yeah, I heard that. Do you need a glass of water or something? You look a little pale."

He shook his head and dropped into a chair. "You're pregnant. Again. Now."

"That's right. We're having another baby." I rubbed his back. "Just breathe, honey. It'll be okay, in another eighteen years and eight months. After all, you were the one who suggested having another baby when we had Hannah here."

"I wasn't serious." He looked into my eyes. "How did this happen?"

I burst into laughter. "You don't really need for me to answer that, do you? I was shocked myself. I even redid the pregnancy test twice to be sure. Three out of three were positive. Like it or not, we're having a baby."

My daughter's gasp pulled my head around. "Omigod, you and Dad are having another baby? Eewww. But that means you'd have to have… eewww! I don't even want to think about that."

"Just think, you'll have a little brother or sister to play with," I said.

"You mean someone to babysit, for free. What are my friends going to think? Oh, God, they're going to know that you two… eewww."

Anthony glared at her. "Would you stop that? Why is it unbelievable that your mother and I… your mother and I… uh… love each other. Besides how do you think you got here?"

She filled a glass with water and headed across the kitchen. "This is so embarrassing. How am I going to explain this?" She stomped up the stairs.

I glanced at Anthony and laughed. "This could be the best lesson in abstinence she could get."

"It's sure taught me a lesson."

A chill rolled through me. "Anthony, are you upset about this baby?"

"No, Jan. I'm just surprised. It wasn't something we'd planned, and it's going to be an adjustment, that's all."

A lump formed in my throat. "But you don't really want this baby."

It was as though he'd been shaken from a trance. "I don't not want the baby, Jan. I love you and our kids. And I'll love this baby, too. Give me a minute, and I'll probably be ecstatic."

I stroked his hair. "I know you were looking forward to time for the two of us, once the kids are on their own. I was, too. But the thought of a baby in the house again is exciting. Good thing we got that playpen from your mother when Hannah was staying here."

A broad smile stretched across his face. "If it's a girl, I think we should name her Hope."

"And if it's a boy?"

"Then we'll call him Hope-less. Because when he's older, if he meets a girl like his mother, that's exactly what he'll be."

I grabbed his face in my hands and kissed him thoroughly.

"Whoa. You keep that up, we'll be having twins."

I grinned at him. "You do remember what my raging pregnancy hormones did to my libido the last time?"

"I'm liking this idea more and more."

Just then, a wave of nausea hit me. I jumped to my feet and raced to the powder room.

When I returned, he had a packet of saltines and a glass of water on the table. He sighed. "I forgot about that part. That explains the flu you brought home from vacation." While I nibbled a cracker, he rubbed my back. "Jan, I know it doesn't seem like it, but I am happy. We make good kids. And this one will keep us young."

I leaned back and rested my head against him. "Thank you."

"For what? The baby?"

"For getting on board with me."

He wrapped his arms around me, resting his chin on the top of my head. "I got on board with you the day I asked you to marry me, and you said yes. And I'm not getting off until I have no say in the matter."

My voice thick, I looked up at him. "I love you."

He smiled. "Want to go for a drive, make my mother's day?"

"Carmela will have a chance to say 'I told you so.' She'll love it."

~ * ~

Despite Anthony protests, I insisted upon continuing my work at the shelter, at least for a while. The doctor assured us everything was normal, and I was healthy. I did acquiesce to Anthony's request that I not spend nights at the shelter. I'd go in and open up, stay until lights out, then Catherine took over.

Joy, along with most of the other women, was ecstatic when I announced the pregnancy. I'd waited until my fourth month. The promise of new life charged the air with laughter and chatter as the women shared how they'd each be an aunt, Godmother, or adopted grandmother, depending upon their age.

That's when I got my idea. "Joy, can I talk with you for minute, in the office?"

"Sure." She followed me into the cramped space. "What's up?"

"I wanted to ask a favor."

"Anything. Ask away."

I smiled, my hand resting lightly over my abdomen. "Will you be the baby's Godmother?"

"Oh, Jan. I... what about your family? Or Fran?"

"They'll be the baby's family. And Fran will still be my friend."

"But, me? Isn't a Godparent supposed to be able to step in and take over in place of the parent? I mean, what could I do for your baby?"

I took her hands in mine. "You'd love him or her. You understand something a lot of parents don't: how to make the hardest sacrifice for your children. I think you'll make a wonderful Godmother. And, honestly, if anything happened to me and Anthony, the DeMarco family is there to step in. Like it or not, you're considered part of that family. Besides, I want someone to be able to tell him or her about Hope... without laughing."

Her eyes filled. "I don't know what to say."

"Say yes."

"I'd be honored."

I hugged her. "Thank you."

~ * ~

We'd survived another DeMarco Christmas with all its wonderful craziness. Angela invited Joe to dinner, and her open display of affection when she kissed his cheek drew an audible gasp from her sons. Then she announced that Joe had given her a cruise for Christmas and that she was going, for two weeks. I thought Anthony was going to pass out, but he recovered and smiled. The look he cast at Joe told me the two men would have a conversation before we left that house.

~ * ~

It was late February and I was approaching my seventh month and remembering the downside of pregnancy: swollen feet, exhaustion, and the pressure of someone sitting on my bladder. In two weeks, I'd be taking a leave of absence. I'd promised Anthony to stop working at seven and half months. We were still discussing when I'd return to work. I suggested two months and said I could take the baby with me. He was adamant that I was not taking his baby around, "those street people who could be carrying any and all disease." While I was offended for the women, I could see his point.

As my final week at the shelter drew to a close, I was turning off the lights one night when the doorbell rang. I went to the intercom, assuming it was Catherine and that she'd forgotten her key. "Forgot your keys again?"

"It's Sergeant Miller from the Fourth Precinct. I have a woman here who needs shelter."

I opened the door to admit them. "I'm sorry. I thought you were the worker coming to relieve me for the night. Please, come in."

The woman stepped inside, her eyes fixed on the floor in front of her.

I cocked my head to try and make eye contact. "I'm Janet."

"She was in the bus station. They called us, but she hadn't done anything, so I couldn't very well arrest her. Thanks for opening up for me," the officer said.

"No problem. I can take it from here."

I locked the door behind him and turned to the woman. She wore a thin jacket, Capri pants, worn sneakers and ragged socks that rolled down around her ankles. Her shoes were soaked from walking in the snow. "You look frozen. Come into the office, and I'll get you a cup of tea. Then we'll talk."

She glanced around the room at the sea of sleeping bodies as she followed me to the office. I ushered her to a chair in front of the small space heater. "I'll be right back."

Her hand shook when she accepted the steaming cup of tea. I sat behind the desk and met her eyes. "What's your name?"

"Sandra."

I jotted her first name on the intake form and glanced back at her. "Last name?"

"Dawson." She took a sip from the cup. "I don't have no identification. My purse was stolen."

"That's okay. How long have you been on the streets?"

"Since I got here two weeks ago. Someone was supposed to meet me, but he didn't show up. Then my duffle bag and my purse were stolen with what little money I had, and my identification."

"Where did you come here from?"

"New Jersey. I met a guy in the bar where I worked, a truck driver. He told me if I came to Pittsburgh, I could stay with him." Her eyes flicked over mine, then down to the floor. "Stupid, huh?"

"How old are you, Sandra?"

"Twenty-two."

I gasped. She looked much older, tired and worn. She could be my daughter. I heard the door open and close and knew Catherine had arrived for the night shift. "Okay, it's late. You're exhausted, and I'm leaving soon. Catherine will be here in a minute and will explain the shelter rules. We have a shower room in the back, if you want a hot shower to warm up. And there's clothing there, too. You could use something a little warmer, I'm sure. Have you eaten today?"

She shook her head.

"We have leftovers in the kitchen. How about a sandwich and some soup?"

When she looked up, tears spilled down her cheeks. "Th-thank you."

"You're welcome, honey."

"Stupid of me to take off in this weather, get on a bus with nothing but a few dollars, and expect some guy I met once to hold good on a promise. I knew what he wanted, but I convinced myself he was trying to be nice to me." She sniffled and reached for a tissue from the box on my desk.

"We all make mistakes. The important thing is, you're here now and we're going to help you."

Catherine appeared in the doorway, and I introduced Sandra and explained her circumstances. I pressed a hand to my aching back as I reached for my coat. "I'll see you tomorrow night."

Sandra nodded. "You're so kind, and so was that police officer. It gives me hope."

At that moment, the baby kicked so hard, I thought he or she was making an early exit through my abdomen, like in the *Alien* movie. I placed a protective hand over my belly and smiled. "Well, if there's one thing we all need, it's hope."

Epilogue

Hope Angelina DeMarco arrived two weeks early on Easter Sunday morning. She was fortunate I was alert after fourteen hours of labor. Otherwise, she may have been dubbed Bunny DeMarco, since Anthony keeps calling her his, "…little Easter Bunny." He's head over heels in love. I can barely get her out of his arms long enough to nurse her.

Michael is the proudest big brother. He took the hospital picture of her, all red and wrinkled, and emblazoned it on a tee-shirt with her name and birth date. Some day, she's going to get even for that one. Gabriella plays the role of the annoyed middle sibling, but I've caught her slipping into the nursery, stroking the baby's downy soft hair and cooing to her. She's going to be a wonderful babysitter, er…big sister.

Naming the baby Hope was a no-brainer. We chose Angelina for Anthony's mother, Angela, who now insists on being called Gina.

My eyes filled as I laid out the white frilly christening dress that's not much bigger than my two hands put together. Anthony carried Hope in and placed her in the middle of our bed. "I changed her diaper already. She's good to go."

I laughed. "And she no doubt will, as soon as I have her dressed. Then you can change her diaper again before we leave for the church."

He stepped up behind me and pulled me back against him, nuzzling my neck. "Have I told you today how much I love you?"

"Only two or three times, but I never get tired of hearing it." I turned to face him, snaking my arms around his waist. "And have I told you how happy I am?"

"Every time I look at you, I see it. We're blessed, huh?"

"We are. Now, let me dress the baby. We don't want to be late."

~ * ~

Father McClaren greeted us as we entered the church. "It's a beautiful day for the baptism of a beautiful little girl." He cupped the baby's cheek in his hand, and she stared up at him with huge brown eyes. "This one's going to be another heartbreaker, Anthony. You'll be beating the boys off with a club."

Anthony nodded toward Gabriella. "I'm getting my share of practice now."

Brie rolled her eyes. "Da-ad."

The organ began to play. Father McClaren straightened his alb. "You folks go ahead and take a seat. If I don't process in when Mrs. Sabatini begins the entrance hymn, I'll hear about it later."

Anthony and I led the way, with Hope in my arms. Michael and Gabriella followed. Our family and friends occupied the front pews. But mid-way up the aisle, women in various seasons of worn clothing, and with shopping bags stuffed between them, filled several pews. Mary reached out to the baby as I approached, but Betty drew her hand back.

268

My vision blurred as I reached the first pew and slid in beside Joy, who would be Hope's Godmother. I was overcome by the love gathered in this church. As if sensing it, Hope Angelina hiccupped then let out a soft sigh.

When it was time for the ritual, Father McClaren invited us forward. Anthony and I presented our daughter for baptism, and then I handed her over to Joy and Dante, an unlikely pair, but Godparents, all the same.

Father McClaren scooped water from the baptismal font and poured it on the baby's forehead, declaring the baptism of Hope Angelina DeMarco. Anthony whispered in my ear, "Sure, for now."

I smiled and said my own prayer for my daughter... that she would always have the courage and grace to know who she is and what she wants, and the support of a loving family when doubt clouds her certainty. Regardless of what name she may eventually choose for herself, I prayed that she would always know Hope.

Meet Linda Rettstatt

Linda Rettstatt grew up in the small town of Brownsville, Pennsylvania. When she's not doing social work or writing, she enjoys travel and nature photography and is an avid reader. Her work has garnered recognition from Pennwriters, Inc. and Writer's Digest. Linda's first book, And the Truth Will Set You Free, finaled for a 2008 EPPIE Award. Finding Hope is her fourth novel.

VISIT OUR WEBSITE
FOR THE FULL INVENTORY
OF QUALITY BOOKS:

http://www.wings-press.com

Quality trade paperbacks and downloads
in multiple formats,
in genres ranging from light romantic comedy to
general fiction and horror. Wings has something
for every reader's taste.
Visit the website, then bookmark it.
We add new titles each month!